ANN HAZE...

LILY GI...

CHRISTMAS QUILT

American Quilter's Society
www.AmericanQuilter.com

Second novel in the *Wine Country Quilts* Series

Located in Paducah, Kentucky, the American Quilter's Society (AQS) is dedicated to promoting the accomplishments of today's quilters. Through its publications and events, AQS strives to honor today's quiltmakers and their work and to inspire future creativity and innovation in quiltmaking.

EXECUTIVE BOOK EDITOR: ELAINE BRELSFORD
COPY EDITOR: HANNAH ALTON
GRAPHIC DESIGN: LYNDA SMITH
COVER DESIGN: MICHAEL BUCKINGHAM

This book is a work of fiction. The people, places, and events described in it are either imaginary or fictitiously presented. Any resemblance they bear to reality is entirely coincidental.

 American Quilter's Society

PO Box 3290
Paducah, KY 42002-3290
americanquilter.com

Additional copies of this book may be ordered from the American Quilter's Society, PO Box 3290, Paducah, KY 42002-3290, or online at shopAQS.com

Text © 2018, Author, Ann Hazelwood
Artwork © 2018, American Quilter's Society

Library of Congress Cataloging-in-Publication Data

DEDICATION & THANKS

Lily Girl's Christmas Quilt

Christmas has always been my favorite season, so writing a Christmas book always makes me happy. I dedicate this book to my husband, Keith, who also shares my love of Christmas. My two sons, Joel and Jason Watkins, continue to be supportive and have given me many great Christmas memories.

My thanks to all the hardworking residents and businesses in the wine country region who spend an incredible amount of volunteer hours to bring a merry Christmas to all their visitors each year. I encourage everyone to experience Christmas in Missouri's wine country.

From my family and AQS Publishing, we wish you a very merry Christmas!

Feathered Star block

CHAPTER 1

"Good morning, Snowshoes!" I said as I opened the front door.

"Well, Lily Girl, it's nice to see you up and about," Snowshoes said as he handed me a package. "How's that head of yours doing?"

"It's fine, thanks! Every day is better than the one before. I may open the shop tomorrow."

"That's good to hear. Everyone has been worried about you since that horrific accident you were in. How's Mr. Conrey doing?"

"It's hard to say. I'm afraid he wasn't as lucky as I was. I think he'll be on crutches for a while."

"I was sorry to hear about Mr. Benning losing his life that way. He had no business driving with that heart condition of his. He's always been heavy on the bottle, too. It's a wonder you weren't all killed."

I'd thought about the possibility of all three of us perishing in the accident myself. "There's plenty of blame to go around. I would like to think that it could have been

1

avoided."

"Well, take care. Tomorrow's Halloween, and just so you know, you'll get plenty of trick-or-treaters in this part of town."

"Really? Well, I'd better get to Johann's and stock up on candy! I lived in a second-floor apartment before moving here. I didn't have any trick-or-treaters there, so this will be fun!"

He nodded and smiled. "Happy Halloween," he said, tipping his hat.

It was easy to see why everyone loved Snowshoes. Carrie Mae said he got his name by delivering mail wearing snowshoes to get around on one particularly snowy day.

I sat down to open my package. It was from Laurie, my sister in Wisconsin. I tore open the small package, and the note inside read, "Lily, use the lavender and frankincense in an Epsom salt bath and you'll feel as good as new."

I smiled at her thoughtfulness. Laurie, my middle sister, owns a touristy gift shop in Fish Creek, Wisconsin. She sells unique gifts and essential oils. She believes in special cures, astrology, and an entire world of imagination! Her shop is called Trinkets, and it pops with color and happiness inside and out. I'd had many aches and pains since the accident, so I hoped these products would help. Being in nearly constant physical pain caused me to remember the accident again and again throughout the day.

I was still frustrated with myself for allowing Nick to drive that evening. He had consumed a lot of wine and I'd known it. My protests about him getting into the driver's seat had fallen on deaf ears when we'd left Sugar Creek Winery in his convertible. As we'd approached a sharp curve, a vehicle had suddenly appeared in our lane! Everything went black, and that's all I'd remembered about the evening. I suffered a concussion and was released from the hospital a day later. I was still quite black and blue, but it could have been so much worse.

I'd had no updates or communication with Nick about his condition. Personally, I felt he at least owed me an apology or a note of concern, given his reckless drinking and driving. The accident had been blamed on poor Mr. Benning. He'd lost his life that evening. I couldn't help but wonder if Nick could have avoided Mr. Benning if he had not been drinking. I guess I will never know.

I'd met Nick during my move to Augusta, Missouri, this past summer. I'd been having lunch at a place on the Katy Trail when he came up and introduced himself. I'd learned that he was a popular artist, known for his paintings. He seemed to want to get to know me better, so when I ran into him again, I told him about my new business. When he'd learned that I had not yet acquired a sign, he'd offered to create one for me. I couldn't refuse, and it turned out to be just what I'd wanted! The catch was that I had to agree to go to dinner with him as payment for the sign. Carrie Mae had warned me about him being a womanizer and had told me that I needed to be cautious. I wasn't attracted to him, but I felt I owed him something since he'd refused monetary payment. I finally agreed to go out with him after some time had passed. I learned very quickly that evening that he was quite possibly an alcoholic. I'd made an unwise decision. The evening ended tragically with the accident when we'd hit Mr. Benning head on.

CHAPTER 2

An hour later, workmen arrived to continue their work on the porches. There was a lot to be done to the house that I had purchased from Carrie Mae. Improving the porches on each of the floors was my priority. Each day, I was impressed with the progress of the workmen.

"Would any of you like some coffee?" I asked as they went and up and down the stairs.

"No thanks, Lily," one of them said. "We have a lot to do today to prepare for the windows arriving tomorrow. I know we're making a mess, but after we're done, we'll clean it all up for you."

"Not to worry. You're doing an excellent job."

"Come spring, you'll have the finest breeze blowing through here," the smaller of the two men responded.

"I agree, and I think my view is pretty nice," I added. "I hope no one buys the land behind me."

"That's not your property?" the taller man asked.

"No, the owner was nice enough to split the property because there's quite a bit of land behind the house that I wouldn't have been able to afford. I do own the land next to the house where the old barn is falling down. I also own the little brick house. The one-room house is historic, but the barn and shed will be taken down next spring." I left them to their work and got on my way to Johann's little store in town to get some Halloween candy.

"Nice to see you, Lily," Johann greeted me.

"Thanks. I'm going to need some candy for tomorrow. I see you still have plenty."

"I sure do. I just marked it down. I figure most people probably have their candy by now, so your timing is good."

"Great! Do you stay open during trick-or-treating?"

"Absolutely! They count on me for a generous handout."

"Thanks for the bargain," I said as I left. "Happy Halloween!" I had what felt like enough candy to last for years! I decided to stop by Carrie Mae's shop to see if she could use some of what I'd bought.

"Good morning!" she called cheerfully from behind the counter. "It's good to see you out and about. What do you have there?"

"Halloween candy. Do you need any?"

She chuckled. "Heavens, no. I close early and pray for no mischief during the night. The way they come down the street sometimes, I have to worry about all of my things outdoors on the sidewalk."

"Do you need me to help you bring things inside? You have a lot out there that could get broken."

She shook her head. "Thanks, honey, I'm fine. Plus, I'll bet you're still a tad sore here and there, aren't you?"

"Yes, it probably shows, but I feel a little better every day."

"I hope you behave yourself and stay away from Nick. What about that nice man who helped you move out here? What was his name?"

"Marc. You're right. I felt terrible when I knew Marc had learned of my accident, and that I had been with Nick."

"Well, I guess so!" Carrie Mae shook her head in disbelief.

"I didn't want to go, but Nick kept pestering me, and I felt guilty since he'd made my sign for free."

"Nothing's free these days."

I chuckled.

"You are such an independent woman, and you should have known better. I'd warned you about him."

"I know, I know. I tried to explain all of that to Marc, but he's been very cool since that happened."

"How's Alex?"

"He's great! He and Lynn have really helped me out. Hey, enough about the accident. You need to see the progress on the porches. The windows go in tomorrow. I'm going to give Korine a call to see if she'll help me do some cleaning after they're done."

"I don't know if I'd count on her, Lily. She thinks you have a ghost in that house, and I think she's right."

"Oh, it's just Rosie. Nothing bad happens. She likes moving things around occasionally and rocking her chair back and forth, but she's harmless. I'll tell Korine I'll be there with her, if that makes her feel any better." Rosie was my friend at the antique shop back on The Hill who had been shot and killed. It was because of her that I was able to purchase her inventory and set up shop in Augusta selling quilts and antiques.

"Is the light still going on and off in Doc's house?"

"Sometimes. I'm just ignoring it for now. I can't figure it out. Maybe once I get it all cleaned out, it'll stop. I would like to use it for storage right now."

"It's a cute little building. I can't imagine it being big enough for him to see patients."

"I agree. I sure would like to find out more about him. Hey, thanks again for sending folks over to my store."

"The town is thrilled to have you. Are you still planning to go to your sister's house for Christmas?"

"Yes, and Lynn has invited me for Thanksgiving, which I'm looking forward to. What about you?"

"I go to Betty's every year. Every family brings a dish and it's quite a feast! I haven't decided about Christmas yet. I usually close the day after and do inventory. Korine has helped me with that in the past."

"That's right. According to Rosie's notebook, I'll need to do the same."

"Do you feel like you're just running Rosie's store?"

"Not really. I feel like it's mine, but I know she's around, which is a good feeling. Without her giving me first right of refusal to purchase her inventory, I wouldn't be here. When she got shot, I thought our relationship was over, but somehow, she thought I'd eventually come around and would buy the business. I guess it was because I was unemployed and needed to pursue a new direction."

"Strange things happen for a reason, they say. Did you ever get around to raising some of her prices? They were way too reasonable."

I shook my head. "No, I just can't. I feel I should just pass it on to the customer as she intended. When it's my merchandise, I'll use my own judgement. I don't want to be known for unaffordable prices."

"Don't worry. Word has gotten out about there being some pretty good bargains at your shop, so Rosie would likely approve."

I smiled.

CHAPTER 3

It wasn't quite dark when the trick-or-treaters showed up at my door. My antique basket was full of goodies. Everyone could reach in and get a good handful. One of the first groups to knock at my door were older teenagers, which surprised me. I reminded myself that they were just out having fun and weren't getting into other mischief.

"Cool haunted house," one of the teenagers said as he looked at Doc's house.

"Oh," I said as I noticed the light in the house flashing as it sometimes did. "I'm glad you like it." When I closed the door, I figured I could have really rattled them by putting Rosie's rocking chair on the front porch. She would have had great fun spooking them by making that rocker seemingly move by itself! By nine, I decided to turn my porch light off and call it a night. However, my neighbor in the brick house wasn't calling it quits. Feeling a bit uneasy about this being my first Halloween night in Augusta, I stayed downstairs for a while and checked my emails.

Loretta, Laurie, Lynn, and I have a sisters-only group

email that keeps us connected. Loretta, the oldest, lives in Green Bay and is the only one of us who had a child. She'd wished me a happy Halloween and reported that her daughter, Sarah, had recently been to the doctor and had received a good report. Sarah was pregnant and not married. Her affair with a married man had caused quite a stir within the family.

Loretta wrote, "Sarah is not due until around Christmas, but the doctor said she could deliver much earlier. I hope you are healing well. All of us here in Green Bay are certainly looking forward to everyone visiting us at Christmas. Love from all the family. Enjoy your Thanksgiving! That holiday will be here before we know it!"

It always made me happy to hear from one of my siblings. Since I was the youngest, they seemed to be a little more concerned about me. When I'd quit my job at a publishing company, I'd remained unemployed for months. My sisters became very concerned about my lack of a job. I then had an opportunity to buy Rosie's antiques after she was killed. My connection with Carrie Mae led me to Augusta in the wine country, which is where I settled and now operate Lily Girl's Quilts and Antiques.

The wine country had always been a refuge for me, especially when I was unhappy at my job. I did enjoy living in the Italian neighborhood called The Hill, but when I lost my friend Rosie to murder, I felt it was time for a change. That was especially true when Bertie, my landlord, died and the house I was living in was put up for sale.

Opportunities increased for me when Carrie Mae, who owned the Uptown Store here in Augusta, offered me an empty house in which to store my newly-acquired antiques.

I had known Carrie Mae for years, since I had purchased many antique quilts from her for my quilt collection. When I had to move out of Bertie's house, I asked Carrie Mae if I could buy her house. It was a bright, garish yellow color with green and white trim. Preservationists probably cringed, but I loved it. There was much work to be done, and I had a plan that I thought I could afford. Carrie Mae offered to sell me only the land on which the house was situated, making the price something affordable. The spacious yard and wooded acres behind me could be put up for sale if Carrie Mae decided to do that in the future. I hoped that would not happen anytime soon.

I named my shop on the first floor of the house "Lily Girl's Quilts and Antiques" because Rosie always called me Lily Girl. I felt I wanted to honor her in some way after her tragic death.

I ended my first Halloween night in Augusta by soaking in a clawfoot tub with Epsom salts, frankincense, and lavender, thanks to Laurie. It felt delightful and gave me some relief.

CHAPTER 4

When I awoke the next morning, my soreness had improved from the soaking. I was feeling anxious about opening the shop again. I got dressed earlier than usual because the workman would be arriving with the new windows. I couldn't wait to take my coffee to one of the porches, like I frequently did on the second-floor porch at my flat on The Hill when I lived there. When I opened the shop, I placed Rosie's rocking chair on the front porch as I had done since the day I opened. It was the perfect prop to display a quilt. My phone rang, taking me away from my job of arranging the quilt artistically across the arm of the rocker. It was Holly.

"How are you, girlfriend?" she asked cheerfully.

"I'm well. I had a good soak last night with some oils that Laurie sent, and I think it helped."

"Wonderful! I'm calling to ask if I could borrow a couple of quilts from you again."

"Sure, what do you need?"

"I'm doing a talk on hexagons, or hexies as they say now.

Do you still have that Grandmother's Flower Garden quilt?"

"Yes, I think so. It's on the rack for sale."

"I think you also had a wool Flower Garden quilt that was tied. It might have been from Rosie's inventory. I'll borrow that as well if you still have it."

I had to think for a moment. "Okay, but are you going to come out and get them? I have no plans to come to The Hill until Thanksgiving when I go to Lynn's house."

"Bummer. Well, I'll try to get out there tomorrow. I'll think of something to tell the monster."

The monster was Holly's abusive husband, Maurice. Why she continued to put up with him was a mystery to me.

"How is he feeling?"

"Not well. You should see how thin he's getting."

"Has he told you what's wrong?"

"No, and I've given up. He gets so angry when I ask."

"Well, you need to go on and live your life if he doesn't want help."

"Oh, he wants my help, but it's all the domestic duties that he wouldn't touch with a ten-foot pole."

"Whatever," I replied, hoping to not sound callous. I had given up on giving Holly advice quite some time ago. "Should I make lunch for us?"

"Why don't I just pick up lunch from a deli like I've done in the past?"

"Oh, that would be wonderful! Thanks!"

I hung up feeling frustrated. Hearing about her difficult life circumstances always made me feel ill at ease. I wondered what kind of ending her situation could possibly have. Holly had so much to offer, but her restricted life left her unable to enjoy the wealth that she and Maurice had acquired. We were friends forever, but sometimes the relationship was difficult to navigate. How would I feel if something bad happened to her? How much should a friend interfere with their friend's bad choices?

I had my first customers around noon. The two elderly ladies were both in good moods and seemed to be delighted when they saw my cute little shop.

"You have a lot of commotion going on here," the lady wearing a red hat said.

"I'm sorry for the hammering noise, but I'm having some new windows put in today."

"Are you Ms. Rosenthal?" the other lady asked as she removed her coat.

"Yes, I am," I answered as I tried to keep my eye on red hat lady.

"I have some things to sell, and I heard you may be interested in buying them," she said as her eyes took in the contents of the room.

"What are you selling?"

"Well, I live in a farmhouse near the Boone home and I'm moving in with my son. I need to sell almost everything. I have mostly antiques."

"Have you considered having an estate sale?"

"I may have to, but right now, I'm trying to sell some things myself," she explained.

"If she can sell something sooner, then she gets the money," red hat lady interrupted. "If she sells it at a sale, her son will take it all."

"Oh, I see. Well then, write down your contact information and I'll see what I can do."

"Oh, that would be wonderful!" she responded. "I want

to look around at some of your prices on the quilts and things, if you don't mind. I have no idea what some of my things are worth."

"Thanks for your honesty, but I hope you realize that these prices wouldn't be what you'd receive," I explained. "I have to purchase them low enough to mark them up."

"Oh, I understand." She nodded. "I see you have a lot of quilts."

"Do you have quilts?"

"I sure do! Nice ones, too, if I do say so myself. I sure hate to let them go."

"Well, surely you will keep some for yourself."

"If my son will let me," she responded as she shook her head.

"He won't let her if he thinks he can get a few bucks for them," her friend added bitterly. "Agnes has a few red-and-white quilts, don't you? I see you have a lot of them here."

"Yes, I have one called Broken Dishes and a really nice Turkey Tracks pattern," Agnes recalled.

"They sound very appealing. I don't have either one of those patterns," I said, becoming interested.

CHAPTER 5

Thirty minutes after the ladies left, there was still no money going into the cash drawer. I'd experienced a good opportunity to buy merchandise, but it was sad in a way to reap the profits of someone who must give up her treasures. I was eating a bite of lunch when a young woman came into the shop. She was very attractive and appeared friendly.

"Hi, Lily. I'm Susan from the library. I understand that you came in and asked for me and I wasn't there that day."

"Oh! It's nice to meet you, Susan. When I came to see you initially, I was looking for a place to live. Now, I could use some help learning about the doctor who once owned this house. I've been busy getting this shop open, so I haven't had time to continue my research."

"I keep up with your progress through Betty Bade. She comes to the library a lot."

"I see! Betty was my very first customer. I met her through Carrie Mae."

"Yes, they are longtime friends. I was curious about your quilts that I keep hearing about. I love quilts, and you may have heard that I teach quilting to a small group of ladies at the library."

"You do? I'm not a quilter but have great appreciation for those who are. I am partial to antique quilts."

"I love them, too!" she said as we gravitated toward the quilt room. "My goodness, you have a lot of them. I love the scrappy quilts. I grew up with them, and I love seeing how the quilters used what they had. Some aren't that pretty, but they all tell a story."

"You are so right. I personally like simpler patterns constructed with two colors. My friend knows a lot about quilts, and she says to always date a quilt by the newest fabric that was used in it. She loves to research patterns and then do lectures."

"I'm curious about the price on the blue-and-red Nine-Patch quilt," she mentioned as she looked at the tag. "I like that the quiltmaker threw in some black, which actually works surprisingly well. She was a creative person, I think."

"Let's open it up. That way, you really get the whole effect of the design. I love some black in a quilt as well."

"Oh, I have to take it home. The price is so reasonable."

"I'll give you the professional courtesy discount that I give to other business folks."

She beamed. "Thanks so much! I understand that you live upstairs."

"Yes, it's pretty handy," I said as I wrote up her sale.

"Oh, add this little child's tin cup as well."

"I'll be back to visit the library as soon as I get past the holidays. I'm going out of town for Christmas and I also have a lot going on here with workmen."

"I see. I would like to invite you to our little quilting

17

group so you can meet everyone. They would love to talk to you about quilts as a retailer. Who knows? You may decide to quilt a stitch or two! We meet every Monday at ten, just for an hour or so. You can just show up whenever you like."

"You are so nice to invite me, Susan. I can't promise anything right now. I have a shop to open at ten."

"Most shops don't open on Mondays, especially through the winter, so that's an opportunity for you."

"I'll consider that."

"It's a fun group, and you'll learn something too. I can't wait to get this quilt home. Thanks for the discount."

Off she went, and I felt I had made an acquaintance as well as a happy customer.

CHAPTER 6

By the end of the day, I marveled at my new windows, even though they needed a good washing. I decided to call Korine tomorrow to see if I could convince her to come back and help me. She had done such a fantastic job on the windows in the house when I moved in. I then crawled into bed with a book that I never opened before I fell asleep. I smiled at the thought of Holly coming to visit the next day.

In the morning, I really expected to get a call from Holly saying she needed to cancel, but it seemed that all was well. After I'd had my coffee, I made the call to Korine. She listened intently before she gave me an answer.

"Well, I do need some Christmas money, and if you promise not to leave me alone in the house, I'll come."

"It's a deal. How soon can you be here?"

"Tomorrow, I suppose," she said with hesitation.

"That's great! How about nine in the morning?"

"I'll be there."

I hung up the phone feeling very relieved and excited. I had been pleased when Carrie Mae recommended Korine, as she had helped Carrie Mae for many years. I got a text from Holly saying that she was leaving her house and that she would see me soon. I had so much to share with her. I could only hope that one day she'd leave her husband and move to wine country, but knew I was dreaming.

Alex called as I was carrying the rocking chair to the porch to start my business day.

"How are your aching bones?" he asked in a teasing voice.

"I still feel like I'm ninety years old, but I'm slowly getting better. Holly is coming out for lunch today."

"How did she manage that?"

"Good question. She needs to borrow a couple of quilts, and I told her to come and get them."

"Why does she keep borrowing quilts from you when she can afford to buy any quilts she needs?"

"What? Well, I'll mention that. Speaking of work, are you keeping busy?"

"Heavens to Betsy!" he exclaimed. "I'll never catch up! Once a magazine likes something you've done, they book you with assignments like crazy."

"That's great!"

"The steady money is good. You really should put your education and talent to beneficial use, Lily Girl."

"I would love that, but as you know, my life has taken another turn."

"Maybe you could open only on the weekends and write during the week."

"You're dreaming, but I suppose if I find that I can't pay the bills, I may have to consider some kind of freelancing."

"Hey, Lynn invited me over for Thanksgiving, which I

thought was sweet of her."

"Good! I was hoping she would."

"How was Halloween?"

I chuckled. "It was quite an experience. I guess you must be a mom to know all the characters, because I sure didn't. What happened to just being a ghost or a witch?"

He laughed. "I keep my porch lights off on Halloween. I worry a bit in this neighborhood about any tricks going on. Hey, I have to run, so you have a wonderful day!"

It was an abrupt ending to our conversation, but Alex was my very best friend. We used to work together at the same publishing house. He quit to pursue freelance writing and I continued to work there until I was burned out. I ended my job there without finding another, and now I'm a shop owner in the small town of Augusta. Who could have seen that coming?

A man came in holding several quilts in his arms. It certainly got my attention.

"Good morning," I said.

"Boy, I'm glad you're open," he said as he smiled. "I have these quilts I want to sell, and I heard you know a lot about them and might resell them."

"Yes, I do like quilts. What's the story here? Are you a dealer?"

"Oh, no," he chuckled as he shook his head. "I'm getting divorced and I want to get rid of these."

"It appears that these are quite new. I'm in the antique business, so I only sell old quilts."

He looked perplexed. "Well, we've had these quilts for a long time."

"Who made these? They are quite beautiful."

"Look, I'll take whatever you offer me," he said, ignoring my question.

"I'm sorry, but I'd bet that other family members would love to have some of this work from the quiltmaker. You can also donate them to worthy charities who could auction them off. I must decline. I'm sorry. They are lovely, but they are not what I sell."

He looked angry as he gathered them up and prepared to leave. "I don't know how you can call yourself a quilt shop when you don't carry all kinds of quilts," he said angrily.

I shrugged my shoulders and tried to smile.

After he left, I had to snicker a bit to myself. Who and what do folks think I'm supposed to be? I had to assume that the quilts were probably made by his wife, and he wanted cash for them as a way of getting back at her. I wondered if she knew what he was up to.

Holly arrived around noon. She was chatty and appeared nervous. "I forgot how long it takes to get out here," she said, putting down the lunch bag.

"The monster was asleep, I presume?"

"Yes, and when he gets up, he'll call me, so I have my phone turned off," she explained. "Let's eat. I'm starving."

"Let's go in here and sit down. Try to relax, Holly. He is far away."

"You don't look like you were in an accident," she said, looking me over.

I smiled. "My injuries were all internal. I'm still moving slowly. Hey, check out the porch, will you?"

"What a change! It will be lovely out here. You'll need some plants."

"Yes, I know. I have some furniture coming for both

porches. The upstairs porch will be private, so I chose a couch I can sleep on if I choose to. This one will likely have garden merchandise for sale on it. I can't wait to fill it up, but I want a table and chairs, so I can sit and be able to socialize as well."

"Oh, I envy you! I can't wait to look around and shop. I need to start my Christmas shopping."

"Great idea, but let's eat first."

We dove into our soup and sandwiches as we chatted away. She always had such funny stories, despite her stressful life with Maurice. I think her sense of humor helped her deal with her life's circumstances. We were interrupted when someone came in looking for antique canes. Since I had none, that customer didn't stay very long. After lunch, we pulled out the quilts Holly had inquired about. She was excited when she saw some quilts she hadn't seen before.

"If you plan on doing this lecture more than once, you really ought to consider purchasing them. I'd give you a fair price."

"You're right. If I get this blue-and-white Drunkard's Path, will you give me a decent price on that as well?"

I laughed and nodded. Holly was known as the "Queen of Free" among those who knew her well. "By the way, I was invited to visit a small quilting group at the library here in town."

Holly looked at me, surprised. "Are you seriously thinking of learning to quilt?"

"I don't know, but they could be potential customers, and I need to meet more people here."

"You visiting a quilting group is something I would like to see," she teased.

23

I noticed that Holly was glancing at her watch. "It's early," I reminded her.

At three, she brought a glass pitcher to the counter to buy with her quilts and said she needed to leave. I thanked her for lunch and her many purchases.

"This was so fun, Lily. I miss you. I hate it that we are so far away from each other."

I helped carry her purchases to the car, and we hugged. I was still unused to saying goodbye to those I loved.

CHAPTER 7

The next morning, I was pleasantly surprised that Korine showed up to clean, just as she said she would. She brought old newspapers to wipe the windows dry, which worked out amazingly well. I showed her the two new porches with their new windows and slate floors.

"Oh, Lily, I never thought these rooms could be so beautiful," she exclaimed. "I remember the first time I saw them. There was a big wasps' nest in the corner of the ceiling over there. I'm glad to see that's gone."

"I think the whole house has potential, but I've always liked spending time in a room that brings a little nature inside. I guess I miss my porch at The Hill. I spent a lot of mornings and sleepless nights on that porch."

Korine nodded as she listened intently. Then she said, "Well, I don't have all day, so I'd better start upstairs. You aren't going anywhere, are you?"

I chuckled as I shook my head. "I'll be here all day, so don't worry. I have some tuna salad made up if you get hungry and want lunch. I'll leave you to your work. I need to get the shop open."

"I hate to ask, Lily, but are you feeling okay? I hate to bring up your accident, but you look a little peaked."

"I know there are some reminders of it all, but I think I'm healing pretty well. I'm just still sore."

"You're just lucky to be alive!" Korine said as she started up the stairs.

When I took the rocker to the front porch, the wind was fierce. I wondered if the quilt would stay put, so I put a lantern on top of the bright green-and-white beauty just to make sure. Kitty pulled up just as I was about to go back in. "Good morning!" I said, shivering. "Come on in. I have hot coffee."

"No thanks, Lily. I just left a meeting at Kate's Coffee."

"You have to take a quick look at my porches before you go," I said, leading her to the porch.

"Not a very good day to enjoy it, but how lovely for you."

"It will be. Vic ordered some furniture through the gallery for me. He was able to get a nice discount."

"Great! Hey, the reason I stopped by is to ask whether you were going to do any kind of open house for Christmas. We're getting a list of events together to promote the holidays."

"How nice! I suppose I should since I didn't have a grand opening or anything."

"Yes, you should. It's no big deal. Just do a little Christmas decorating and have some hot cider or refreshments. It's helpful if there are a lot of us having something on the same night to make it worthwhile for folks. If you'd like to have a little drawing for a giveaway, that helps bring customers in, too."

"Sure, put me down, but I leave for Green Bay to have Christmas on the twenty-third."

"No problem. We were thinking of doing it on Saturday the twenty-first."

As soon as I signed on the dotted line, Kitty was on her way. I felt she did have my best interests at heart as a fellow shop owner. I was naive about so many things.

I went upstairs to check on Korine and noticed that she had made great progress. "Have you had any ghost sightings up here, Korine?" I teased.

"Lily, I know there's something in this house. I can feel it. Aren't you ever scared?"

"I guess not. My niece said she felt someone here, so you're not the only one. I really appreciate your help today. It's hard to wait on customers and get anything done around the house."

"I love seeing all the pretty things you and Carrie Mae have. My grandmother had some fancy things that we were never allowed to touch. They didn't end up in my house when she died, that's for sure."

"What do you like in particular?"

Korine paused, giving the matter some thought. Then she said, "Oh, most everything, but I'm partial to pretty dishes. I can't imagine eating off such things. We just bought plain white when I married Harold, and I still have them to this day. I love washing them up, but I'm always afraid I'll break something."

I left her to do her work, but her comments made me think back to the time when I was a little girl playing house with miniature dishes. I guess most little girls have those memories.

CHAPTER 8

It was five thirty when Korine finished her work. Suddenly, I heard her call my name. "Lily, you have got to come see this!"

"What?"

"Your rocking chair on the porch is rocking by itself!"

"Korine, the wind has been blowing all day out there."

"I'm going out the back door," she declared.

"Wait, here's your money," I said as I handed her cash for her wages.

She left without even saying goodbye. When I opened the front door, I saw with my own eyes that she was right. I knew that it would be a long time before Korine would step foot in my house again. I saw her drive away at a pretty good speed.

Nevertheless, I was happy with my very clean porches and windows. Maybe I was getting used to unusual circumstances regarding Rosie. I poured a glass of wine to enjoy on the porch. My phone rang, and I saw that it was Marc.

"Hello, stranger," I answered, suddenly feeling awkward.

"Did you have a good day?"

"I sort of did. I just poured myself a glass of wine. How are you?"

"I'm doing well. I wasn't sure whether I should call, but I was curious to know how you are recovering."

"I'm doing better each day."

"What about your friend?"

"He's not my friend. I tried to explain that to you, but to answer your question, I don't know how he's doing."

"I didn't mean to bring up a sore topic. No pun intended."

"Funny, Marc." I suppressed a giggle.

"Look, the reason I'm calling is to inform you that Lynn has asked me to come to Thanksgiving dinner. She said she didn't confer with you, so are you okay with it?"

I didn't know how to answer. I began, "Why wouldn't I be? I miss you, Marc. I hope you don't mind me being so direct. I like having someone like you in my life that I am comfortable with."

"Even though baseball season is over?" he teased.

I burst into laughter. Marc knew that we'd always have the St. Louis Cardinals in common.

"Well, I have to go back out to Washington again, so maybe we could have dinner while I'm out that way."

"I'd like that."

We ended our conversation, and I was so relieved that we could remain friends. He must have had some feelings for me, or he wouldn't have been calling me again. I took my wine upstairs to the new porch. It was very chilly in there, but as I looked out the windows into the darkness, I saw a full moon that made me smile. It was Marc's call that made the difference in my mood. He was the first man I'd let have part of my heart. My sisters had tried relentlessly to fix me up and marry me off, but no one seemed worth the trouble. Lynn said it was because Alex, my best friend, was the man in my life, but that wasn't true. Seeing Lynn struggle with what I'd thought was a perfect marriage and wasn't, plus Holly putting up with an abusive husband, sure wasn't encouraging to me. Why do friends and relatives feel it's their responsibility to make sure you have someone in your life? Is it because they want you to be happy like them, or is it because misery loves company?

I met Marc so innocently one afternoon when I was on a walk in The Hill. I'd sat down to rest on a bench in front of St. Ambrose Church when he stopped and asked for directions to Yogi Berra's boyhood home. He was pleased when I could tell him exactly where to find it. As it turned out, I ran into him again at an art reception that Lynn had hosted. He knew Carl, Lynn's husband, from law school, and he adored Lynn's artwork. He then asked me to a couple of baseball games, and it was quite fun. As much as I was hesitant to admit it, I thought he might be my kind of guy.

CHAPTER 9

It was a nasty week of cold sleet, which made for a quiet week in the shop. Tomorrow, my porch furniture would arrive, and I would have dinner with Marc unless he cancelled due to the weather. I went ahead and moved some of my garden-themed merchandise onto the porch downstairs. I'd have to get some plants from nearby Frisella Nursery in Defiance. I didn't exactly have a green thumb, but I knew that some plants were easier to grow than others. While I was organizing the new space, I got a text from Sarah.

> I had a false alarm and went to the hospital last night. I sure would like this baby girl to come early! I hope you are healing well. I can't wait to see you at Christmas!

I responded:

> Oh, no! The longer that baby girl stays put, the better! Still no name?

No, I have to meet her first.

Just for fun, I told her:

I have a dinner date with Marc!

She replied,

Way to go! I liked him.

I texted,

No big deal. I'm just glad he isn't mad about me being in an accident with another man!

She replied,

Where are you going for dinner?

I said,

I don't know. Keep me posted on that baby girl's activities, ok? Love you!

I was so glad she didn't bring up moving to Augusta, like she did during her visit here. Loretta, her mother, said she'd give her blessing regarding Sarah moving here if she finished her degree online and stayed with her mom and dad until the baby was born. I knew the plans would change in time.

I kept doing chores because the day brought me no customers. It gave me time to make lists, which was important for keeping me on track. One list was for all the things I had to do for the upcoming Christmas open house. Another list was for my trip to Green Bay and the gifts I would need to pack. Should I do something special for Marc? I'd have to give that some thought before making a final decision.

After little sleep that night, I got up early to make sure I was ready for the furniture delivery. I looked forward to Marc contacting me about dinner. To my delight, as soon as I finished my morning toast, the furniture truck pulled up in front of my house. I opened the front door. They weren't the friendliest workers, but at this time of the morning, I understood. I showed them exactly where I wanted them to put everything. I was pleasantly surprised when I saw the green print on the cushions because I had only seen the product online. As soon as I signed the release and the workers had left, I ran back upstairs to see how comfortable everything would be. For the first time, the place smelled like a new house instead of the gigantic antique that it was. I couldn't wait for Marc to see it!

I opened the shop. The air was freezing cold, but the sun was shining. Thanksgiving and Christmas were at our doorstep, so the weather was typical for this time of year. My mind flashed back to the hot radiators at my flat in the city. They were adequate, but hard to regulate. I wondered if the space had been rented to someone else. This time of year was busy on The Hill. Restaurants were booming, and it was almost impossible to get reservations. I began to feel a little nostalgic about the place I liked so much.

When the phone rang, I jumped. It was Marc saying

he'd be by at five to pick me up, if that suited me.

"Sure! I close the shop at four, so it will be perfect. I'll call The Silly Goose to see if they can seat us tonight. I think you'll like that place."

"Sounds great, but I've got to run."

I called the restaurant immediately and got a reservation for six. That was perfect and left us time to have a drink before we left for the restaurant.

CHAPTER 10

When I closed, my sales for the day were pathetic. I'd sold an old spittoon to a young man, two little doilies to a young girl, and a simple candlestick to her girlfriend. I knew my heat cost for the day would be more than what I'd earned. I was learning that cold drafts were abundant in this older house. I had to be more creative in my advertising, like perhaps participating in local events to attract more customers. I knew little about selling online, but if anyone would know, it would be Alex.

I dressed in casual black for my date with Marc and put on winter boots for the first time this season. I knew Marc would be in a suit, so I didn't want to go too casual. I got a text close to five o'clock telling me that Marc was running late. Since I was ready to go, I helped myself to a glass of wine. I went out on the upper porch to try out my new cushions. It was chilly out there, but as I stared into the darkness, I felt I was somewhere else, and all was well.

Still lurking in the back of my mind were my finances. With winter ahead, I wondered what else I could do to improve my income. I had to make payments to Carrie Mae, and taxes would be coming due at the end of the year. It seemed that other shops were busier, which made me begin to realize that my location put me at a disadvantage. I'm sure there were those who would tell me, "I told you so."

Marc finally arrived at a quarter to six, and I rushed downstairs to answer the door.

"Sorry, Lily," he said apologetically. "Everything was running behind today."

I smiled as I gave him a slight hug and a quick kiss on his cold cheek. His look of surprise was priceless.

"Well, absence must make the heart grow fonder," he teased.

"I'm just happy to see you. I guess we'd better go. The restaurant is holding our reservation, but can you take a quick peek at my porches? They are complete and I'm so excited."

First, he looked at the porch downstairs and confirmed that my using it for garden merchandise was a clever idea.

"I'm putting in some outdoor lighting around the house, so I can see what's going on out there in the dark. My security guy said he could easily do that for me. When we have snow, the view out here will be awesome."

"It may be here sooner than you think, because there's snow in tonight's forecast."

"I hadn't heard that. Let me show you the second-story porch. It will just take a minute."

Marc followed me upstairs, where he exclaimed, "Now you're talking! This is awesome, Lily. You have great taste, and I can't believe the transition from what it was like before."

"Thanks. I decided there may be times when I could

sleep out here as well. Well, okay, we'd better go!" As we began to go down the stairs, I noticed Marc looking toward my bedroom. Before I moved in, Marc had briefly seen the upstairs.

The Silly Goose restaurant was crowded, as always. I saw a few familiar faces, and one of them was Lisa, who was a great customer of Carrie Mae's. She had also bought a quilt from me. I nodded and smiled at her. Marc was impressed with the atmosphere. We made small talk after the waitress described their specials, and I answered a couple of questions from Marc.

"So, you were pleased with the outcome of your meeting?" I asked, wanting to hear about his day.

"I'm not sure. Time will tell. Sometimes things take such a long time with some of these transactions. It's hard, but that's what the courts are for."

CHAPTER 11

"I'm changing the subject, but have you seen Carl? He's agreed to go to Green Bay with us, by the way."

"Good. I saw him at a luncheon recently, but we didn't discuss anything personal. I think he's got a lot on his mind with work right now."

I nodded. "Yes, Lynn has mentioned that there may be some problem with embezzlement."

"I'm sure that stress is not helping their marriage."

"I wonder if he's seeing anyone," I said, not expecting a response.

"You know, when a person is stressed, they may do things they wouldn't ordinarily do," Marc offered. "I know he was always crazy about Lynn, but things happen."

We were interrupted when the waiter brought the Greek salads we ordered. We ordered beef Wellington as our main course. I was beginning to realize that Marc was somewhat of a foodie.

"Sometimes I miss cooking," I admitted. "It's too much trouble for one person, and living on The Hill, everyone wants to go to one of the many eateries in the neighborhood."

"You can't blame them." Marc grinned. "They are romantic and intimate, for the most part. A beautiful woman, a good bottle of wine, and some pasta is pretty hard to beat."

I smiled. "I do make a pretty good red sauce. I thought it would be great to master the art of breadmaking, but not with such great bakeries on every street corner."

"I'll tell you what, I'll bring bread from one of those bakeries if you make your sauce and pasta."

"Really? My winters will be long and boring, but would you mind making the drive?"

"In a snowstorm, perhaps not, but otherwise, I have no problem with it."

"It's a deal," I said, patting his hand.

"More wine?" the waiter asked. "You may want to stay for a while. Our first snow of the year has arrived and it's coming down pretty heavily."

"Oh," I said, feeling concerned for Marc. I looked out a nearby window, and it was a beautiful sight.

"Would you like to take a walk when we leave? I see you are wearing boots, and I think it could be rather romantic."

His question surprised me. "You are a romantic, aren't you?" I teased. "I'm a softy and somewhat of a romantic myself, so I'm game."

"Here's the check," the waiter said as he handed it to Marc. "Will there be anything else?"

"Yes." He nodded. "How about getting us a couple of hot coffees to go?"

"Sure! Do you prefer regular or decaf?"

"Make it black and regular," Marc instructed. "We won't want to miss a thing."

We laughed.

"Do you have gloves?" Marc asked, squeezing my hand.

"Yes, plus a scarf and a warm coat."

I could tell that Marc was pleased to hear I was game. We got up to leave, and I couldn't help but notice the very generous tip that he left for the waiter. We took a deep breath as we wrapped our scarves tightly around our necks. It was like walking into a snow globe.

"This is exhilarating!" I said as I extended my hands to catch the snowflakes on my gloves. "I'm glad there isn't any wind. It's like someone is dropping a feather pillow on top of us."

Marc laughed. "Hold onto my arm," he suggested as we crossed the street. "I don't want you to fall after you agreed to be so brave."

"My first snow in wine country," I announced. "I never thought it would be so lovely."

"Too bad you don't have a fireplace in that house of yours. That would be perfect on a night like this."

"I know. Every house should have one, especially an old house like mine. I would love to buy a gas fireplace for my upper porch, but I have other financial demands right now."

"Hmmm," Marc said as he put one hand on his chin. "You know, Christmas is coming, and I have been wondering what to give you."

"You have?"

"Would you allow me to buy you one of those fireplaces for Christmas?"

I was shocked and stopped in my tracks.

"Marc, you must have had too much wine. I couldn't possibly let you do that."

"I'm serious. I know it's something useful that you would enjoy, and if I'm lucky, I'll get to enjoy it, too! You can pick it out, and once you do, I'll put it on my charge. It's that easy."

Suddenly, a car drove by at a fast pace and honked for us to get out of the way. We ran across the street and onto the curb.

"I can't let you do that."

"You can't or won't? There's a difference. I really like you. Can't you tell?"

I blushed. "You are so sweet, Marc," I said as we continued walking. "I don't deserve a friend like you." If it was cold outside, I sure didn't notice. He was warming my heart.

"Is that a yes?"

We stopped walking again.

"Look, I'm not asking you to marry me. I just want to get you a nice Christmas gift!"

"Okay, okay," I said, feeling weak and selfish. "I could pay you back one day."

"It's a gift, sweetheart," he said, taking my gloved hand and lifting it to his lips.

Despite the fabric between my skin and his lips, I felt a surge of electricity run through me, completely taking me by surprise. "Now that's romantic!"

CHAPTER 12

By the time we got back to the car, my toes were numb from the cold, but our hearts were warm with delight in each other. We shivered as Marc cleaned off the windshield without the benefit of a scraper. It was a short ride down the hill to my house. When we arrived, my car was completely covered in snow. We got out of the car and marveled at how the snow covered the bushes and trees like a blanket.

"Hey, I wonder if this snow is wet enough to make a snowball?" I teased, picking up a handful.

"Well, let's see," Marc said as he helped himself to a large handful as well.

I was the first to hit Marc with my packed snowball, which hit him on the shoulder.

"Whoo!" he said, trying to dodge and get out of the way. "You're good!"

I was the next target, and Marc took action. When one brushed my cheek, the snowball battle was officially on! Marc gathered quite a good-sized ball and began to chase me to the other end of the yard. We were laughing hysterically, and as he grabbed my arm, the snow went into my mouth. As I shrieked in laughter, I slipped in the snow and fell squarely on my backside.

"Lily, I'm sorry! Are you okay?" As he took my arm to help me up, I surprised both of us by pulling him down on top of me. We rolled over in the snow, knowing we were being completely childish and reckless. Marc seized the moment and gave me a wet, warm kiss on the mouth. It was in sharp contrast to the cold flakes that continued to fall on my face. As we paused to catch our breath, our eyes met.

"You started all of this, you know," Marc said with a mischievous smirk.

"Well, finish it by helping me up," I retorted, keeping my eyes leveled with his.

Standing up, we tried to dust ourselves off as best we could, but we were completely soaked.

"That was fun! I don't remember having that much fun in the snow when I was a kid!" Marc exclaimed.

We walked into the house and began shedding our coats, scarves, shoes, and boots.

"You know, a warm fireplace would feel pretty darn good right now," Marc joked.

"No question. Put your things over the banister to dry them off. There's a heating vent there. I'll put some hot water on for tea."

Marc joined me in the kitchen wearing just his shirt and pants. We looked at each other and had to laugh.

"Here, put this quilt around you," I said as I reached for one of my quilts that was folded over a chair. "You know you can't drive home tonight."

He smiled. "It's not totally impossible."

"I think we've had enough excitement for one night," I said, chuckling. "I have a pretty comfortable couch upstairs that I slept on when Sarah was visiting. It's all yours, if you like."

He looked as if he wasn't sure how to answer. He scratched his head, but replied, "I think I'd better take you up on your offer, and hope the roads are clear in the morning."

"Bring your quilt and tea. Let's go on up."

He followed me upstairs. It was an awkward moment for both of us.

"Oh, this will be great!" Marc finally said, sizing up the room with the couch.

"I'll get some sheets and a pillow for you."

"I really didn't intend to be this much trouble," he teased, giving me a flirtations wink.

"Look at it this way, then. I am thanking you for a wonderful dinner and a hearty snow fight, which I honestly think I won."

"You won, all right, but are you sure you didn't hurt yourself?" His voice sounded serious. "I hope I didn't make you feel worse."

"I feel fine. The cold snow and your warm kiss were the best part of the evening."

He blushed, but with that comment, Marc dropped the quilt that was around him and took me in his arms. We then sat on the couch with our tea and talked for another hour. At one in the morning, I kissed him on the cheek and went to my bedroom. After I put on my pajamas, I peeked into the living room. Marc was wrapped in the quilt again and was sound asleep. I took a few extra moments to watch him sleep before crawling into bed, feeling a contentment I had not experienced in quite some time. Not a muscle or bone ached. It was a great evening that I would long remember.

CHAPTER 13

The next morning, I awoke to the sound of someone walking down the stairs. It had to be Marc, but surely he wouldn't leave without saying goodbye. I slipped on a robe, made a quick ponytail, and checked the makeup that I still had on from the night before. "Where do you think you're going?" I said with mock seriousness as I came down the stairs.

"I'm just getting my things together, so I can be on my way," he said with a big grin. "I've got things going on at the office. I really do need to go."

"Coffee? Did you sleep okay?"

"Like a baby! I'll take that couch anytime. I'll get coffee on the way in."

"I'm glad you stayed," I said softly.

"I am, too. I'll call you, and if I don't see you before, I'll see you at Thanksgiving."

"Sure. I hope the roads will be okay."

"We'll find out!" he said, giving me a hug goodbye.

He left as I watched from the front door. I looked at the

messed-up snow in the front yard, and it brought a smile to my face. I closed the door to the frigid air and headed straight to the kitchen to make coffee. My phone rang. My first thought was that it could be Marc, but it was Alex.

"How much snow did you get?" Alex asked immediately.

"Maybe four inches. What about there?"

"Not as much, but traffic is a mess. I sure am glad I work from home! Are you going to open today?"

"I have to. One sale is better than none. I have nowhere to go." I wanted to tell Alex about last night. "Marc and I had dinner last night."

"How did that go? Did he drive home in the snowstorm?"

I laughed. "I never kiss and tell, you know that," I joked.

"Lordy, girl!" he shot back.

"He slept on my couch, if you really have to know. We did take a nice, long romantic walk in the snow, however."

"You are smitten, Lily Girl!" Alex teased. "Lynn thinks he's a good catch for you."

"He is pretty wonderful. Lynn invited him to have Thanksgiving with all of us."

"Great! Just don't get too kissy-faced around us."

I laughed. "He's not the type. Not to worry."

"I'm making my chocolate ecstasy cake at Lynn's request and bringing it on Thanksgiving. I can't say no to her."

"Yum! What should I bring?"

"With a winery on every street corner out there, I don't know why you're asking."

"Oh, I guess you're right. I may get champagne, too. It's kind of a family tradition on Thanksgiving."

"Sounds good. Look, I need to go. I hope you get a sale or two."

"Me too!"

Alex always put me in a good mood. He "got" me. That was the best way to describe what I thought and felt about him. I then thought of Marc and wondered if he made it to work. Feeling brave, I decided to text him.

> Did you arrive? How were the traffic and the roads?

He responded immediately.

> It went well. They did an excellent job of clearing the roads. Stay warm and order your fireplace!

I smiled. Could this guy really be that generous? I finally got dressed and opened the shop. Around eleven, I was surprised when the front door opened. It was Snowshoes.

"Sorry I'm running late today," he said. "I almost had to get out my snowshoes!"

We laughed.

"Do you want some hot coffee?"

"I'll pass. I had a cup of tea with Carrie Mae. She's a bit under the weather this morning, so I tried to cheer her up."

"Oh, I hate to hear that. I'll check on her later."

"Thanks for letting me warm up. Here are your bills, and have a good day!"

I made a face at him, and I saw him smile as he went on his way. Amid what looked like mostly bills, I noticed a personal note and opened it right away. It was a party invitation from Nick. He'd added a note that read, "I hope forgiveness is one of your virtues and that you'll attend. Fondly, Nick." I knew this was an invitation that I would not accept. I never should have agreed to spend any time with him. I thought he lived out on a farm, so he could live a secluded life. A party right now seemed out of character, especially since he was still healing from the accident.

CHAPTER 14

A young couple came in the shop as I was refilling my coffee cup. "Good morning," I greeted them.

"Good morning," the young girl returned. "You should have a fire going today!"

"I wish!" I responded, thinking of Marc's offer. "How can I help you?"

"My mother loves antiques. It's her birthday, so we were looking for something appropriate," the man explained.

"How nice!" I said with a big smile. "Does she collect or like anything in particular?"

They laughed.

"Everything!" the man answered.

"Rob, there's a bunch of quilts in this room."

"She loves quilts," the man assured me as he walked toward the other room.

"I have plenty!" I boasted. "Does she like any particular pattern or color?"

"She loves lavender," the girl reported with dismay in her voice. "Look, here's one with lavender that's only fifty dollars."

"Oh, that's because it has some damage. As a gift, you may not want to give her something in such poor condition."

"It looks great to me," the girl insisted as she unfolded it. "Where's the damage?"

I stood there dumbfounded as I examined the quilt in the places where I knew it was torn. Everything looked just fine! How could I have been so mistaken? Some of the places where it had been damaged had been severe.

"Yeah, it looks great to me," chimed in Rob. "Turn it over."

The backside had a clean, white, perfect appearance, and I couldn't believe it. It was one of Rosie's quilts, and I almost hadn't put it on the rack because of its poor condition.

"Is the price still fifty dollars?" Rob asked.

"Of course."

"She'll love all of the embroidery," the girl said. "I think we'll take it."

"Okay, I'll wrap it up for you," I said, taking the quilt from her so it could be refolded. Within a few minutes, the couple left as happy campers, and I was engulfed with uncertainty. What kind of mystery was taking place with that quilt?

"Rosie, this has to be your doing again," I said aloud to her. "You made sure I could make a sale, I suppose. Please feel welcome to repair any of the other quilts!"

I needed to get my mind on something else, so I got on the internet to search for gas fireplaces. As I scrolled, I saw that one local company in St. Louis carried an all-white one. That would be perfect for my upper porch. I carefully wrote down the description so I could pass it on to Marc. Without hesitation, I sent a text saying,

> You asked for it!

I followed up the text with another outlining the details of the gas fireplace.

He replied immediately with a text that read,

> Consider it done!

I responded,

> Wow! I wish I could get such quick results on other matters! Thanks so much!

I was interrupted by someone coming in the front door. "Good morning!" I said to the elderly woman. She was completely bundled up in a fancy fur coat.

"Hello."

"Good of you to be out in the cold today, but you look warm and cozy in that lovely coat."

"Thank you, but I'd just like to look, if you don't mind."

Her response was so curt that it took me by surprise. "Sure. My name is Lily if you need any help."

I busied myself in the kitchen and let her browse. I was not one to follow customers around. I never liked it when retailers followed me as I shopped.

"Lily, Lily," she called.

I entered the room, wondering what had caught her eye.

"Where did you happen to get this Wedgwood candlestick?" she asked with anger in her voice.

"Oh, that piece was purchased as part of a bulk inventory from a shop in St. Louis."

"I believe it's mine!" she accused. "I had a robbery years ago and this was taken. I recognize this mark underneath where I damaged it from dropping it one day." She pointed out the mark. "I know it's mine!"

"I don't know what to say, because I don't know where the dealer bought it. As a matter of fact, the dealer I bought it from was robbed and shot to death."

She looked astonished.

"It's hard to know where things come from when you buy them in good faith from other folks."

"Well, you have stolen property in your shop, and goodness knows what else might be here," the woman fumed.

CHAPTER 15

"I feel badly for your situation," I responded. "I would never knowingly sell anything that was stolen. If you are so certain, then please just take it home with you."

Her look softened.

"Well, you should be careful about these things," she warned, still posturing for an argument.

"I will. I'll wrap it up for you."

She didn't know what to say, and I suspected she would have been ready to continue the confrontation had I not diffused the situation.

"For what it's worth, I'm sorry that happened to you," I assured her.

"I appreciate that. Thank you."

Just like that, she exited with a beautiful candlestick that was worth more than a hundred dollars! I wondered if it was a recurring practice for some folks to do what she had just done. Could Rosie have purchased stolen property by mistake?

The day continued in a very bizarre way. I finally closed

for the day and decided to pay a visit to Carrie Mae. When I arrived, she was helping an older man by showing him some antique pipes she had for sale.

"Hello, Lily! I'll be with you in a minute."

"Do you have any pipes for sale at your place?" the man asked me.

"No, sorry, I don't," I answered as I admired her collection.

"Well then," the man replied. "I'll be on my way!"

"Is your day going as strangely as mine?" I asked Carrie Mae after her customer had left.

"Oh, Lordy! I should have never opened today," she answered, sounding quite stuffed up. "I'm a bit under the weather and am not in the mood for some of these folks."

"Why don't I help you close up so you can go up and rest?" I suggested. "Snowshoes told me you weren't feeling well and that he had a cup of tea with you."

She chuckled. "I hope he doesn't spread it all over town that I'm not well. The rumor mill will have me dead in no time."

I wanted to tell her about giving away the supposedly-stolen candlestick, but I could tell that she needed to rest. When I left, I went across the street to get coffee and cookies at the cookie shop. I wanted to take a nice platter of delicious cookies to Lynn's for Thanksgiving. It seemed that every time I went in the shop, they had a new face behind the counter. I was placing my order when Susan from the library entered.

"Hello, Lily! Are you doing okay?"

I smiled and nodded.

"I was going to call you. Monday is the first class for the Christmas quilt. You sounded rather interested in the idea, so I hope you can make it. If you just want to listen and watch, that's okay too. The classes are free."

I had to think. "I suppose I could attend," I agreed. "I just hate to commit to too many things."

"Oh, my friend goes to Susan's classes and raves about them all the time," the girl behind the counter interjected. "I wish I could go with Heidi, but I work here on Mondays."

"Heidi is a sweetheart," Susan replied. "She's such a quick learner. It was her idea to do a Christmas quilt."

Susan placed her order as I treated myself to one of the chocolate chip cookies from my bag.

"It's at ten, right?" I asked before leaving.

"Yes. If you have a thimble, bring it. I have kits for everyone, so you don't need to bring anything else."

"Oh, I have quite a few thimbles for sale. Surely one of those will fit me."

"Bring all of them so you can make sure you use the right finger. The other students may even buy some thimbles from you."

"Okay. See you then!" I said, going out the door. What did I just commit to? I had mixed reactions after I left. Part of me wanted to get more involved in the community, and another part said I should just concentrate on this new business of mine, which wasn't doing very well. I supposed the thought of making a sale while I was out of the shop was not all bad.

When I got back to the shop, I remained closed. There didn't seem to be many people out and about. I went to find my thimble inventory. I had never paid any attention to them before. I think it was Lynn who had checked them off of Rosie's inventory. There were some plastic thimbles with advertising on them. They seemed to be a standard size. Some were marked as sterling, which explained the higher prices. Others were brass, porcelain, and aluminum. As I looked at my thimble collection, I wondered who had worn them and when. As I tried some of them on, they felt awkward. Why did we have to wear them anyway?

CHAPTER 16

After an uneventful, cold, and bitter Sunday, I got up on Monday looking forward to seeing friendly faces at the library. I clicked on my emails as I ate a muffin and drank my coffee. A family email came from Loretta saying that Laurie would be joining them for Thanksgiving, despite her busy season at the shop. She said snow had arrived early in Green Bay and that she and Bill would be going to the Packers' game at Lambeau Field, which was always a highlight for them. She once commented about how lucky they were to inherit season tickets from Bill's dad; otherwise they would never have been able to get their hands on them. She said that if they were lucky enough for Carl to show up at Christmas, Bill would take him to the game instead of Loretta. She also said that one of the spare bedrooms was set up for the baby's nursery. She cautioned Lynn and I not to buy clothes for the baby since they already had plenty. I'd already set aside some money for the baby girl.

I responded by wishing them all a happy Thanksgiving and told them that I was looking forward to eating Loretta's

Christmas stollen, which was my mother's recipe that we only enjoyed at Christmas.

I dressed warmly, grabbed my bag of thimbles, and started on my way to the library. I was going to become a quilter—maybe.

I was the first to arrive and was greeted warmly by Susan. She showed me the way to one of the side rooms, where the class would be held. I put down my thimbles and helped myself to a cup of coffee as she had suggested. Two others joined me and introduced themselves as Marilyn and Edna. They were a cute mother-and-daughter duo who favored one another with their red hair. When I introduced myself, they seemed to already be familiar with me and my newly-opened shop.

"Mom doesn't drive much anymore, so we thought this was something we could do together," the daughter, Marilyn, explained. "We were just talking this morning about wanting to see inside your shop."

"Yes, you should."

The next person to arrive was the girl named Heidi. She looked about forty years of age, and her hair was blonde and exceptionally long. After we met, she immediately made herself at home and was clearly comfortable in this environment.

"Hello, Judy," I said, recognizing a woman from Kate's Coffee. "You're a quilter?"

"I try!" she exclaimed. "When I heard that Susan was going to do Christmas blocks, I was in."

Susan invited everyone to take a seat as another woman arrived. She sat down as if she had been there before and was familiar with what was expected.

"Welcome, everyone," Susan began. "I think most of you know each other, but since Lily Rosenthal is new, let's go around the room and have you introduce yourselves."

"My name is Candace, Lily. I hear that your shop is wonderful, and I look forward to seeing it."

I smiled as I looked at Candace. She had that natural look and wore her hair in braids.

"Mom and I met Lily earlier," Marilyn said when it came to her turn.

"Then we have Judy and Heidi, but it sounds like you all have gotten acquainted," Susan decided.

"I'm pleased to meet you," I responded. "I'm making no guarantees that I can do what I'm supposed to do, but I love quilts very much and have been a collector for as long as I can remember. I feel rather guilty being here instead of opening my shop, but I'm excited to be here, too."

"You have to take time for yourself, Lily," Susan reminded me. "Now, here are my thoughts about how each of you could create your own special Christmas quilt. Instead of doing the usual motifs of Christmas, I want you to choose what to make in each block. I want your quilt to have special meaning to you personally."

"What?" Heidi gasped.

"Don't worry," Susan chuckled. "I have a plan. Let me give you an example. The first block we make should be about your favorite Christmas gift. It can be from your childhood or from a special time in your life. Think of something simple that stands out in your memory."

"How do we go about making it? I can't do anything without directions!" Heidi cried.

Everyone laughed.

"I will help you," Susan assured us. "You will be given a kit for each block. You can just use what is included or add anything else you may like."

"All I have is a lot of thimbles," I joked. "I don't think I have a bit of fabric in my house."

"Oh!" replied Edna.

"Thimbles are good, but we won't need them for a while," Susan added. "You all may want to try on some of them after class, if you don't have one."

"Oh, that's nice," said Heidi. "I've never had one on my finger. I will need one."

"We have thimbles from Grannie," Marilyn bragged with a smile.

"This is the finger most quilters use, by the way." Susan demonstrated.

"I don't think I can possibly wear one of those things," Candace said, shaking her head.

Well, quilting can tear your finger up if it's not protected," Susan warned.

Candace's eyes widened in surprise.

CHAPTER 17

"Today's class is about learning an appliqué stitch, because you are going to need it," Susan announced. "You may also choose embroidery and piecing, but you will need to know how to apply one fabric on top of another. In the kit, you have a 12-inch square, which will be the size of each block before they are sewn together. Keep in mind, all the methods will be done by hand, which I think is the best way to learn the basics. If you are more experienced, like Edna, you may feel comfortable using your machine. Most folks use a machine for everything now. I still like to do most of my work by hand. You will find your own comfort zone as we progress."

Did I have a comfort zone?

"I can't wait to learn to piece," Judy commented. "I am determined to piece a star and make enough for a quilt someday. I love star quilts."

"I can't imagine doing it all by hand," Marilyn said, her frustration heightening. "Mom gave me her machine and I'm eager to use it."

"And I'm sure you will," Susan assured her. "Just be patient."

My stomach was churning. What had I gotten myself into? I liked the idea of having my own Christmas quilt, but Lily Girl was sure in the dark. I might truly embarrass myself.

Susan explained that she was a visual person, as I seemed to be. She said her approach was to show us how things should be done. We got started with Susan's scraps that she'd brought for us to practice on. I did very well with my stitches on straight lines, but on curves, they looked decidedly awkward. I had embroidered as a young person, but I wasn't sure I could remember it at all. I loved redwork embroidered quilts and always thought it would be neat to make one someday.

Susan said she worked three days a week at the library. She invited us to stop in and ask for help when she was working. That was reassuring. When time was up, Judy asked if I wanted to go to lunch with her at the coffee shop. I declined, thinking I should open my shop for a few hours.

"I'll come by after lunch and purchase one of those thimbles," Judy told me. "I also need a Christmas gift for my favorite aunt. She collects glass pitchers, and I think I saw a few at your shop."

"Sure, I'll be there." I nodded. Maybe my day would not be penniless. I took my kit and thanked Susan for encouraging me. I told her I thought my stitches were better than Heidi's, but not as good as Edna's. She laughed.

When I arrived back at home, I opened the shop and grabbed an apple for lunch. I looked at my quilt kit and began to think about my favorite Christmas gift. I hadn't been a doll person growing up, but I did like paper dolls. I then remembered getting a gift that was the most surprising that I could recall. When I was eleven years old, Mother gave me a red, leather-bound book with all blank pages inside. She knew how much I loved to write. Anytime that I could find a blank side to any paper, I would somehow confiscate it. Mother had said that would be my first book, and it excited me. What if I would have to erase something? Not surprisingly, it took me forever to start writing in that book!

Cutting out a red book-shaped piece of fabric shouldn't be too hard. I could appliqué it on the white block and it would be all straight lines. I could then write or embroider a title on the book. Maybe something like, *Lily's First Book*. The block would surely have meaning, because receiving the book made Christmas very memorable that year. I made a quick call to Holly to tell her I had signed up for a quilting class. My news certainly surprised her.

"I don't believe it!"

"Well, we'll see, but I've already started to learn how to appliqué. We are doing a Christmas quilt, so I'm excited about that. I'll never be as good as you, but I'm willing to try."

"Oh, I always wanted to make a Christmas quilt," Holly shared. "Email me a photo when you get your block done. If you need some help, just give me a call."

"I'm not sure I can promise anything, but I also wondered what you were doing on Thanksgiving, since the monster isn't eating these days."

"Oh, as usual, he refuses to go out anywhere. He wants me to make a turkey and all the trimmings, just in case he decides to eat something. I love to cook. I can only hope that he'll take a bite or two before he criticizes me."

"Well, let's hope for the best. You sure have your share of

drama coming into the holidays."

"Well, forget me. You have an enjoyable time at Lynn's."

"I will. I'm bringing wine, which tells you a lot about my cooking talents."

She laughed.

I hung up the phone just as Judy walked into the shop.

"Well, I sure had a better lunch than what you're eating," Judy teased when she saw my apple.

"I'm sure you did! The pitchers are in here, if you want to look them over."

"I remember one of them was shorter and in yellow glass," Judy described. "I know my aunt doesn't have anything like that in her collection."

"Great. I'll give you a discount once you see which thimble you want."

"The silver one that has an 'S' on it."

"Yes, it's beautiful, but did you see how expensive it was?"

Judy laughed and then warned, "Lily, that's not how you make a sale!"

CHAPTER 18

Judy not only left with a thimble, but with the glass pitcher and a rather worn velvet pincushion. With the help of a couple of other customers, my day ended with a decent amount of sales.

I retired for the day with many scenarios going on in my head. I was hoping for a simple call or text from Marc. Since I was going to see him on Thanksgiving, perhaps he felt no communication was needed until then. I tended to be a somewhat old-fashioned girl in that I was hesitant to be very aggressive about contacting men. I turned out the light, deciding to wait for him to contact me.

Waking up to darkness on winter mornings was depressing, but I had a lot to accomplish today. The thought of hot coffee always managed to get me going. I turned the light on at my bedside table and was shocked to see the red book from my past sitting there. Was I dreaming? Where did that come from? I didn't remember packing it when I moved. Was it Rosie at work? I sat up and quickly went through the pages that showed my awkward handwriting. I propped my pillow behind my head and read some of the silliness that had preyed on my mind back then. A poem on the last page read,

Give me a pencil, or pen.

A writer I'll be –

I just don't know when.

I smiled to myself. I wasn't much of a poet, but my heart had been in the right place! All these years later, I still didn't know when I would be an official writer. An editor was always rewriting other people's words. Would my thoughts and words matter to anyone else?

My thoughts moved to Alex and how he'd encouraged me to do some freelance writing for extra money. I'd thought that being a retailer like Rosie would give me enough income. That still remained to be seen. Alex had certainly made the right move when he'd quit his job in order to pursue a freelance writing career.

As I closed the book, I wondered which box I could have packed it in. Obviously, Rosie had taken it upon herself to put it in my sight, like she did with Marc's toolbox a while back. She was giving me a sign to proceed with my quilt block, I supposed. The book was four inches by six inches and would fit perfectly on the white piece of fabric, which was twelve inches. I held my treasured childhood gift close to my chest, pleased to be reunited with it. "Thank you, Rosie," I said aloud.

With renewed energy, I got up and started my day. I could see the sunrise from my upper porch windows. What a beautiful sight on a frosty winter day! Anxious to make some money for the day, I opened exactly at ten. I put Rosie's rocker on the front porch with a bold-colored Log Cabin quilt. Who could miss that as they drove by?

Two women came in, chatting away to one another. One had a question about almost everything. Her friend meandered through the shop and wasn't as talkative. Finally, the talkative one decided to purchase an inexpensive ring holder I had in a cabinet.

"Well, I'm ready. How about you?" she said to her friend, who was coming out of the quilt room. "I don't see anything else I'm interested in."

"Okay, I'm ready," the other said as she quickly joined her friend.

How frustrating to respond to so many questions when the customer was not particularly interested in the answers. I went into the quilt room to see if the quiet customer had messed up any linens or other merchandise. It was then that I noticed an empty spot on my quilt rack. One of my red-and-white quilts was missing! It had to have been taken by the woman who had just left when I was preoccupied by her friend.

I quickly ran to the front door and opened it to see which direction they may have gone. It occurred to me to alert Carrie Mae in case they visited her shop. To my horror, I discovered that the Log Cabin quilt on the rocker was gone as well! I began to shake. I was frustrated and felt violated. How could I have let this happen? I rushed to my phone and called Carrie Mae. I talked fast and felt short of breath as I shared my experience with her.

"Call this number, Lily," Carrie Mae instructed, giving me a local telephone number. "The county police will respond. They may not come right away, but it's the best you can do. These gals are likely long gone, especially since they were successful. I'm sorry, honey."

"Thanks. I hope I don't discover more things that are missing."

"It's the old trick of one keeping you busy while the other one does the dirty work."

"But how could they take such a large item like a quilt and keep me from noticing it?"

"With coats on, you can slide in a lot of merchandise," she warned. "Always pay attention to what folks bring in and are wearing when they come in the door. If she leans over, the quilt can slip right in her coat, and out the door they go!"

"That's disgusting! How bold of them to take the quilt off the rocker when I'm right there!"

"But you weren't right there, and they knew it. It's only stuff, and these things just happen, Lily Girl."

CHAPTER 19

As soon as I hung up, I called the number to make a report. As Carrie expected, they would not likely be out right away since it wasn't an emergency. I couldn't help but blame myself for not being more business-savvy. I should have learned from Rosie's murder that there are bad people out there with no conscience. I had always been a trusting person, but that would have to change.

Finally, an officer showed up. I hated the thought of his police car being parked in front of my shop, the way this town talked. After getting a description of the customers, he seemed to think a shop in Washington had had the same experience. He said coats are the biggest problem in the winter, as Carrie Mae had indicated.

"Also, don't be surprised to see some folks try to return something from your shop that they never purchased," the policeman cautioned.

"I'm going away for a few days around Christmas," I fretted. "Does anyone around here check on businesses?"

"Your own neighbors are the best watchdogs," he said.

"We're kept busy with road issues. Say, were you involved in the accident that killed Mr. Benning?"

I nodded.

"I thought so. You are lucky to be alive. We see way too many serious accidents around these parts."

I decided to close for the remainder of the day. I turned to paying bills and taking inventory of the Christmas decorations I had on hand. Most shops already had decorations for the Christmas season. I didn't have much. I had an old-fashioned Santa that stood on its own, some antique ornaments, and some clever vintage Christmas signs that were popular these days. I needed to get out and cut a small tree and find lots of pine branches. It was fun to think about something positive for a change. I then remembered one of Rosie's cookie jars that was shaped like a jolly snowman. She also had a delightful selection of vintage Christmas tablecloths, which would be useful for making displays. It certainly was an asset to have all the red-and-white quilts. They easily set the theme for Christmas. At my apartment, I had used a red-and-white patchwork quilt top as a tree skirt for my miniature tree. There were many nice memories of my apartment that popped into my mind. One year, I'd even had a decent-sized Christmas party. Alex was a huge help that year with decorating, and he also served as my bartender. The memory made me miss Alex, so I picked up the phone and called him.

"What's up?" he asked. "Are you okay?"

"Yeah, other than having two quilts shoplifted."

"Holy mackerel!"

I told him all the details, and without realizing it, revealed my concern about finances. "I really thought I'd have more customers than I'm getting," I complained.

"It's hard to say with a new business, but I've told you before that you could be making some extra income doing freelance writing like me. I know you want to write that book, but until an idea pours out of you, you could be making a little cash by writing smaller pieces."

"I wouldn't know where to start," I confessed.

"I'll tell a couple of my agents and see if they would give you a try," he offered.

"I guess it wouldn't hurt. I can't do anything until the first of the year, of course."

"Okay then, I'll keep it in mind."

CHAPTER 20

Before I got out of bed on Thanksgiving morning, I thanked the Almighty for all my blessings. The weather was cold and drizzly, but it wasn't going to ruin the day with my family. I checked my emails and phone messages. I already had holiday wishes from Laurie, Loretta, and Sarah. They were counting the days until our Christmas visit.

As I packed my tray of cookies and three bottles of wine, I worried a bit about driving on the slick roads. I really dreaded driving where our accident occurred. In fact, the whole experience had left me tentative about driving altogether. I sent Lynn a text telling her I was on my way, and she answered with a smiley face.

Sprinkles of rain splattered on my windshield as I drove out of Augusta. Most people were still asleep, and it was too early for any tourist activity. I took it very slowly around the deadly curve where the accident took place and tried hard not to think about it. Finally, the rain stopped. I was so grateful.

As I arrived near The Hill, I had that warm feeling of

coming back home. I thought about Harry and wondered what his plans were for the day. I parked in front of Lynn's house and decided to give him a call before my busy day began.

"Happy Thanksgiving, Harry!" I said as soon as he answered.

"Is this Lily?" he asked in a weak voice.

"Yes, how are you? I'm at Lynn's house today for Thanksgiving."

"I see," he said, and a long silence followed.

"Are you okay?"

"I guess not. My son wants to put me in one of those old folks' homes. Can you believe that?"

"Oh, Harry, I'm so sorry. Have you been ill?"

"He just wants to sell my house and pocket the money," he complained.

I was at a loss for words. "When are you going? I want to see you before you go. What is the name of the new place?"

"Oh, I can't remember," he grumbled. "I'll miss everyone around here."

"I know you will, but you'll make new friends, Harry, because that's how you are. Don't worry."

"It's nothing more than a landfill where they put old geezers like me."

I cringed.

"Say, Lily, will you watch over Bertie for me? You know how she gets when she doesn't see me for a while."

I blinked. I couldn't believe my ears. Now I was beginning to understand. Bertie had died some time ago. Harry must have gotten Alzheimer's disease.

"Sure, Harry. Don't worry, okay?" I said before hanging

up. I wanted to cry. At least he'd recognized my voice.

I gathered my thoughts and greeted everyone but Marc, who had not yet arrived. He'd told Lynn he would be a little late. I immediately told Alex and Lynn about Harry. They were as sad as I was. Alex knew it had been a difficult way to start my day, and he brought me a glass of wine. I left the kitchen to say hello to Carl.

"Good to see you, Carl," I greeted as he poured water into the goblets on the table.

"It's good to see you as well, Lily," he said, giving me a sincere smile. "It's so nice to hear that you and Marc are still hanging out."

"I guess we are," I responded with uncertainty. "I think a lot of him."

"And it's obvious that he thinks a lot of you as well," he replied. "I take it that you have recovered from your accident?"

"Pretty much. I still am reminded of it every now and then when I experience some aches and pains."

"Well, here comes Marc now," Carl noticed.

The two of them hugged, and then Marc's eyes began to center in on me as he removed his coat.

CHAPTER 21

The merriment began with everyone talking at once! There were a few other folks invited, like Carl's father and his sister, who were delightful conversationalists. At the table, we held hands and said grace. I sat with Marc on one side and Alex on the other. I was so lucky to have my two favorite men on either side of me. When the meal was finished and we began clearing the table, my phone rang. It was Holly, so I took the call in the den where I could be away from the others. I answered cheerfully, wishing her a happy Thanksgiving, but I got only sniffles in return.

"Holly, what has happened?"

"I don't know what set him off. I had everything perfectly timed and had prepared a very nice meal. He started complaining about the turkey being too cold. As he ranted on about this and that, he picked up the turkey and threw it in the trash!"

"He is deranged. What happened then?"

"He just left the house," she said between sniffles. "He said he could find a better dinner at the Salvation Army."

"It's good that he left before he became more violent. Were you able to save some turkey? You should at least enjoy some of your dinner."

"I really don't care. What did I do to deserve this?"

"You have never deserved any of his angry behaviors. He is mentally ill. It's all about making you feel bad. He doesn't want you to enjoy or feel good about anything you do. I think he's jealous of your talent and all the friends you have. He doesn't want you to be happy."

"I'm sorry I interrupted your day," she said apologetically. "I just had to talk to someone."

"It's okay. Calm down and have a glass of wine. Take some time to enjoy some of that delicious food you prepared. He is the loser today. But you are giving him the reaction he wants. Think how bothered he would be to return and see you enjoying your nice dinner. Why don't you go to a movie later to get your mind off what he might want?"

"Oh, I don't know. Thanks for just listening, Lily. I hope your day is going well."

"It is, but we'll talk tomorrow," I said before hanging up.

Marc heard part of my conversation as he entered the room to check on me. "Was that call from your friend that you told me about?"

I nodded. "I can't believe the lives some folks choose to live," I said, shaking my head. "Nothing will change for her, but at least she can vent to me."

"That's what friends have to do sometimes. They don't ask for advice and they wouldn't take it anyway. They need a sounding board and sympathy."

We joined the others. Some of them were playing dominos. Lynn and I had a chance to confirm some of the details of our trip to Green Bay. I observed Marc with everyone and was amazed at how well he fit in. By four, I decided I wanted to get on the road. I said goodbye to everyone. Lynn had prepared a wonderful box of leftovers that I was happy to accept. As Marc walked me to my car, it gave me another chance to thank him for the fireplace I'd ordered.

"I'll let you know the minute it arrives, so we can enjoy it," I promised.

"It will be my pleasure, Ms. Rosenthal. Be careful going home. It was great being with everyone today."

As we gazed into each other's eyes, he moved closer to give me a gentle kiss on the lips. I couldn't help but think that the others were watching us.

"Goodbye," I whispered.

CHAPTER 22

The rain had stopped, but cloudy skies brought darkness earlier than usual. All the way home, I recalled my Thanksgiving Day and decided that it was nearly perfect, except for Holly's phone call.

When I pulled in front of my house, the light was on in the brick house. Why tonight? Why sometimes and not at other times? Why was it happening at all? Feeling somewhat frustrated, I unlocked the door and placed my goodies from Lynn in the refrigerator downstairs. I went upstairs to change, but felt it was too early to crawl into bed. My phone indicated that I had gotten a text. It was from Marc.

Are you home safe and sound?

Yes. How about you?

Yes. Just made a few calls and am ready to turn in.

Me, too. Sweet dreams!

Only of you.

Now my day was complete. I was falling for that man. I didn't think I was ready to call it love, however. Could I live without him? Of course I could. Was I too old to really fall in love? Had Marc already fallen in love, or was he just nice and sweet? Marc was so secure that he wouldn't need anyone. I liked that about him. I did want to spend more time with him. I wanted to know more about him. What was his favorite food? How did he get hooked on baseball? What did his place look like? Did he have any regrets in life? He always had more questions for me than I could ask about him. My relationship was also physical with Marc, unlike my friendship with Alex.

It was getting late when I finally pulled back the covers. Tomorrow would be my shop's first Black Friday. Would I make any money? I needed to get up early and bring in fresh greenery to make my shop appear more festive.

It was hard to get to sleep, but once I did, morning arrived quickly. Crawling out from underneath heavy layers of quilts was dreadful. I put on jeans, a heavy sweater, and my everyday boots. I couldn't get to my coffeepot fast enough! When I got to the bottom of the stairs, I peeked out the window to see if the light was out in the brick house. It seemed to be. I drank a few swallows of hot coffee, then found a knife and a pair of scissors to take outdoors with me to gather the pine branches. The frigid air was brutal, and there was barely enough light to see.

I headed toward the backyard, where most of the trees were located. I spotted a small cedar tree that was perfectly shaped and smelled like Christmas. It reminded me of my childhood. My father had insisted that cedar trees were the only real Christmas trees. If I'd owned a saw, I would've tried to cut it and use it for my Christmas tree.

I spotted a pine tree with very low branches. I began to break them off with my hands. My body was freezing and I needed to get back inside. When my arms were full, I headed back to the house. I passed the cedar tree and told him I'd be back later to get him.

I poured myself another cup of coffee and turned on all the lights so I could begin to decorate. I didn't have twinkling lights, but I had many candles and lanterns. I began decorating one area at a time. In a small amount of time, the shop was turning into a vintage wonderland.

CHAPTER 23

As I embellished my display with greenery, I felt the Christmas spirit. I had to begin thinking seriously about presents to give, putting Marc at the top of the list. The fireplace was a generous gift. My quilt collection was my greatest resource, but I didn't sense that would be the best gift for him.

I placed some bells on the front door with a ribbon attached so I could hear customers come in the door. It wasn't five minutes later when I heard them jingle as the front door opened. A handsome man with salt-and-pepper hair came in with a large bag under his arm.

"Hi, are you Lily Rosenthal?" he asked, displaying perfectly white teeth when he smiled.

"Yes, I am. How can I help you?"

"My name is Butler Hayes. Carrie Mae suggested that I come see you."

"Really?"

"I deal with high-end antiques, mostly online. My business also includes great antique quilts when I can get them. I recently inherited some very nice quilts belonging to my family. I feel a personal responsibility to make sure I pass them on to capable hands. I chose to keep some, but I have a couple that I'd hoped to sell to Carrie Mae, as I have done many times before. When she saw them, she said quilts were your specialty, so I should have you look at them."

"Well, it's always nice to meet Carrie Mae's friends, and I appreciate you stopping by. Let's see what you have. I am in the process of decorating, but let's clear a space on this table."

"It smells like Christmas in here, and at first glance, I'd have to say that you have a very attractive shop."

"Thank you, but I'm a newbie to the antique business. I've been a quilt collector as long as I can remember, so I am anxious to see what you have."

"I have two amazing Feathered Star quilts," he stated as he pulled them out of a bag. "I know enough about quilts to know that these are in exceptional condition and that they have a lot of visual appeal."

I was stunned when I saw them. He had the correct pattern name, but the piecing had variations that I had not seen before. The pieces were extremely small, and there were little stars within the Feathered Star. The quilts were identical, except for one being red, white, and blue and the other being green, red, and white.

"Oh, my goodness, Mr. Hayes, these are amazing. I have never seen this pattern variation before. The red-and-green one must be from 1850 to 1870, and the red, white, and blue one would be closer to the turn of the century, I think. The condition and hand workmanship are too good to be true."

"I agree."

"How can you possibly give them up?"

He chuckled. "When you've been in the business as long as I have been, you learn that you can't keep everything. Since they are family quilts, I want them to go to folks who will give them proper care. I knew Carrie Mae would make sure they didn't get into the hands of just anyone. I've had them appraised in New York for fair market value, but I'm willing to adjust that value if I know they're going to the right owner."

"You realize the Midwest market may not honor or recognize the same value."

"Yes, I know. That seems to apply to other antiques as well. I've sold some pristine antique bears to Carrie Mae for her collection, and I take that into consideration."

"Oh, I've heard about the bears, but I've never seen them."

"It's wise of her not to show them to everyone. She has a fortune invested in them."

"Here is my room dedicated to mostly quilts," I said, inviting him into that area of my shop.

"I see that your passion is red and white."

I nodded. "Red and green also tug at my heart, and I'm afraid to ask the price on that Feathered Star. It has Christmas written all over it."

He smiled.

"Where do you live, Mr. Hayes?"

"Please call me Butler. I live in the Central West End, which you are probably familiar with. Carrie Mae said you came from The Hill."

"Yes, there are times that I miss it. My friend Alex lives in the Central West End in a wonderful apartment. I don't know if you recall a shop on The Hill called Rosie's Antique Shop, but when the owner passed, I bought her inventory and moved out here."

"Yes, I knew Rosie. I was shocked to hear about her death and robbery. I could go into her shop, buy at retail, and still have room for a markup. Now that you tell me that, I think I recognize some of her items. Her strategy was to move products at reasonable prices and have a quicker turnover."

"I know. I haven't changed her prices, and folks tell me all the time how cheap they are."

"That is amazing. What did you do before opening this shop?"

"I was an editor but chose to leave that profession. I was looking for a change. When Rosie put in her will that she wanted me to have the right of first refusal of her inventory, I knew she had felt sorry for me. I love antiques, but I would mostly talk quilts with her, not antiques. I was likely one of her better customers, and we became friends."

"How are the quilts selling for you?"

"Not that great. I need to build a clientele, and my location isn't the best. Do you mind if I open up this red-and-green quilt?"

"That's why I brought them here," he said as he helped me unfold it. "Pretty spectacular, isn't it?"

"The maker must have never have used this. Do you think it was just stored away through the years?"

"From what I know, that would be the case."

"I have never seen such precise piecing with such very small pieces! Was this from a wealthy family that didn't have to use their quilts?"

He nodded and chuckled. "Yes, you could say that. By

the way, the last family member to have it died at ninety-nine years of age. There was going to be a big party, but her heart failed too soon."

"Oh, how sad," I said as I picked up the red-and-green quilt to touch once again. It was hard not to run my fingers across the texture of the tiny stitches. "I feel the love."

Butler looked at me and smiled. "I'd like to look around a bit while you enjoy the quilts, if that's okay," he said as he walked into the kitchen area.

CHAPTER 24

"Good morning, Lily Girl," Snowshoes said as he entered the shop.

"Hey, good morning," I responded. "Is Carrie Mae any better today?"

"Yes, she appears fine." He nodded. "Did you have a nice Thanksgiving?"

"I did. How about you?"

He chuckled. "Well, the turkey took its good old time to thaw, so we didn't eat until ten at night!"

"That will be a night you won't forget anytime soon!"

He laughed and went on his way.

Butler came back into the room with a grin on his face. "I love this community out here," he remarked. "I suppose everyone knows everyone, which I find charming."

"You think so?" I joked. "They know your business too, and since I'm still a newcomer, I'm not sure what they think about me."

"They're lucky to have you. I do see some things of Rosie's I'd like to purchase, if you'll assist me."

"Sure. Do we need a cart?" I joked.

Following his instructions, I carried a luncheon set of Nippon china, a Tiffany vase, a set of silver grapefruit spoons, and a silver platter to the checkout counter. I was stunned, knowing it would easily add up to approximately two thousand dollars.

"These are very reasonable prices," he said as he looked under one of the teacups.

"I know, but as I learn, and as Rosie's inventory thins out, I will know my price ranges better."

"Well, with my purchases as a bribe, do you think I can entice you to buy one or both of the quilts I brought?"

"Oh, I'm sure I can't afford them, but I guess I have to know what you're asking, just in case."

"I brought the appraisals with me if you want to look them over."

I looked at the bottom line of each, and the value for each one was eighteen thousand dollars!

"Goodness," I gasped.

"Don't panic. I am willing to work with you on the prices."

"I have to decline. I'm not questioning the appraisals. They're just out of my league. I don't think I have paid over two thousand dollars for any of the quilts in my collection, much less one for resale. I'm not sure Carrie Mae could even afford these, but I may be wrong. It's a pleasure to just see them up close, especially the Christmas quilt."

"The Christmas quilt?" he asked with a grin.

"Oh, the red-and-green one. It has Christmas written all over it."

"I think you're right," he said as he helped me wrap his purchases. "The red, white, and blue one is so patriotic, I thought that would be your favorite. They are quite sought after now."

"Oh, I'm sure they are. I hope they get good homes. I can't thank you enough for purchasing all of these things."

"I think I'm the lucky one. I feel as if Rosie is right here. I think you'll be very successful. One day, hopefully sooner than later, you'll give me a call to see if I still have these quilts for you to purchase."

"Oh, that's so interesting of you to mention Rosie. Sometimes I touch her things and it's like she's in this room."

He nodded and smiled. "We have a spirit that came with my old house. As I had the place restored, I felt someone was giving me advice, like perhaps the guy that built the place."

"Who is 'we'?"

"My nephew, James, moved in some years ago. He's like a son to me. He goes to Washington University, which is close by. He helps me with my business, too. He's very sharp and takes an interest in antiques, which is great."

"Well, that's nice for both of you."

"I guess I need to get going. It looks like you're about to get some more customers. The next time I come out, perhaps we could have lunch or dinner."

"Absolutely. I'd love to hear more about this high-dollar quilt world you have access to! I'll help you take these packages to your car."

"Oh, no need. I wish you much success, Lily. Your love for quilts and your knowledge to learn will do you a good turn."

"Thanks so much."

What a nice compliment. He made a couple of trips as I turned my attention to the three ladies heading to my door. I waved goodbye as he drove away in a black Mercedes SUV.

CHAPTER 25

I hurried to assist the three ladies as they scattered. They admired my décor, antiques, and festive efforts, but no sales were made. I heard the frequent complaint that they needed to get rid of their own things rather than make more purchases. I stayed open later to take advantage of the Black Friday crowd, but I felt the day should be over. I finally closed at seven, feeling the results of a very long day. I surprised myself when I added up my sales because it was quite a successful day, thanks to Butler Hayes, of course.

I left the lanterns out and headed upstairs to pour myself a glass of wine. I changed into a gown and robe and headed towards my upper porch. It was so quiet and peaceful. I kept thinking about the Christmas quilt Mr. Hayes had dangled in front of me. Would I ever be able to afford such a beauty? After I put my feet up, I gave Alex a call to tell him about my successful day. He said he'd just gotten home after helping Lynn at her gallery during a show.

"How did that go for you?" I asked, interested.

"I basically just schmoozed the patrons and made sure they had some wine," he laughed. "Her place looked great. That girl has such talent. It was great to get away from my laptop for a while. She had a pretty good day, like her sister."

I told him more about Butler, and he was puzzled and amused when I told him how well he knew Rosie. "He said he could feel Rosie around the place when he looked at her things!"

"I believe it! Sounds like he'll be a great contact for you. Back to this Christmas quilt. Would he let you make payments on it?"

"You mean like a thousand dollars a month for eighteen months?" I joked. "I can't even imagine having that sort of discussion with him."

"Well, you weren't in any condition to buy a house either, and look at you now, baby."

We laughed.

"Seriously, though, it would be so sad for a collector to buy it, because those things end up in storage, never seeing the light of day unless they get resold," I said.

"If those quilts came down from family, it sounds like money, honey," Alex noted. "By the way, has Marc asked you out for New Year's Eve?"

"Heavens, no. It's too far away."

"No, it isn't. We've spent many New Year's Eves together, so I was thinking of having a party. I'll invite Marc, of course."

"That sounds great. I could be with my two favorite men! Could I do anything to be helpful?"

"With food?" he asked sarcastically. "Are you kidding

me? You bring the wine and I'll cook up a storm."

After an hour's conversation with Alex, I called Holly, hoping she would still be awake.

The monster answered, which caught me by surprise.

"May I speak to Holly?" I asked.

The phone went dead! Just like that, he'd hung up on me! It wasn't the first time it had happened. I hoped that she was okay. I decided to send her a text.

> Let me know if you're ok. He just hung up on me.

She immediately responded.

> Talk to you tomorrow.

I felt somewhat better just to hear from her but couldn't help but wonder what was really going on.

CHAPTER 26

The next day was Saturday, so I was hoping the retail surge would continue. I decided to go to the coffee shop, and Judy happened to be working.

"So, do you have your block done?" she joked.

"No, but I do have an idea," I reported. "How about you?"

She beamed. "A little secret you don't know about me is that I have always been a sock monkey fan," she admitted with a chuckle in her voice. "I'll never forget when I got my first one. I was around five years old. For my block, I've decided to use a real sock and appliqué a sock monkey on it."

"Wow, that's pretty cool, but can you accomplish such a thing?" I asked in disbelief.

"I don't know, but Susan can help me."

"That is so cool. Mine will be rather plain, I'm afraid."

"Sorry, Lily, but I'm needed in the kitchen," Judy said as she looked at her fellow employees.

I ordered a veggie quiche to go and headed toward the door after my food was heated and bagged. Kitty was about to enter, and we exchanged greetings.

"Did you have a good Friday?" she asked with excitement.

"The best day I've had so far," I bragged.

"I'm so glad. Are you going to Nick's party?"

"No way," I said defiantly.

She looked at me strangely.

"I can't believe he sent me an invitation."

"Well, I suppose he got some bad press after the accident and is trying to mend fences."

"Whatever, but he has issues that I don't want to be a part of."

She nodded. "Have a good day. Let's keep this business going through the holidays."

I agreed, smiled, and went on my way to Carrie Mae's shop. I wanted to thank her for sending Butler Hayes to me. Since she was alone in the shop, I told her about Butler's purchases and how thrilled I was. I teased her about the two quilts she should have purchased. She wasn't surprised when I told her that Butler knew Rosie.

"I want to know if you purchased any of the quilts," Carrie Mae asked. "Weren't they magnificent?"

I laughed and shook my head. "The red-and-green Christmas quilt stole my heart. When he showed me the appraisals, I was shocked! I once thought I could build up my quilt collection and own some of those pristine quilts, but when I started the shop, I knew that would never happen."

"You know you don't pay his asking price!" she said with her hands on her hips.

"I know. He told me to make him an offer, but I couldn't insult him with my limited budget. I haven't added to my inventory since I've been out here."

"He may have to sell to a collector who wants to keep

them. You and I both don't have the clientele to resell something like those quilts."

"I agree. I was surprised at how I gravitated to the red-and-green quilt. Christmas always tugs at my heart, and that quilt said it all."

"Well, we all can't have everything we want, but I'm glad he helped you out by buying some things. He bought a painting I'd had here for some time. I knew nothing about it, but my gut tells me he did some research on the artist and the darn thing is probably worth a lot of money. That's what a good dealer does, and he's done well!"

"I see you brought out some feather trees."

"Yes, but they aren't for sale. The big one has a collection of antique ornaments I bought from the Boxdorfer estate some twenty years ago."

"My goodness!"

"I had Korine decorate it for me, and I told her I'd skin her alive if she broke one of them," she teased.

"How is Korine?"

"She's fine. She'll be helping me out with my inventory this month."

"I just hate that I lost her," I complained.

"She was quite fond of you, Lily, but she's superstitious and convinced that your place is haunted."

I eventually said goodbye, needing to get back to the shop. Once there, I brought out my rocker and debated whether to put a quilt on it since one had been stolen recently. I looked at my selection and chose a very worn green-and-red star quilt that still looked somewhat festive and wasn't expensive. I took a small, empty bushel basket and filled it with some greenery to place beside the rocker.

I was ready for a second cup of coffee and decided to check my emails. To my delight, I got a notice that the fireplace was going to be delivered tomorrow. I immediately sent a text to Marc, letting him know and thanking him once again.

To my surprise, Vic from the gallery arrived.

"Good morning, Vic! What takes you out of the gallery?"

"I needed to start my personal shopping and wondered if you had any antique perfume bottles. My wife, Ruth Ann, collects them, and our bathroom is filled with them."

"I do. They are over here. These are part of the inventory I purchased. I know nothing about them."

Vic picked several up and examined them, like he knew what he was looking for. "I like the fancy stoppers, and I think this Victorian one will do nicely. I'll take it!"

CHAPTER 27

"I guess I'll see you at Nick's party in a few days," Vic said as I carefully wrapped his package.

"I won't be going," I said, offering no further explanation.

He looked at me strangely. "Oh, I just assumed the two of you were seeing each other. I'm sorry."

"I'm sure folks might tend to think that since we were in the accident. It was an unpleasant evening from the start. I shouldn't have agreed to go."

Vic didn't know what to say. He paused and then offered, "As you know, Nick's paintings are in our gallery. He's been feeling pretty confined since the accident, so I think that's why he planned this party."

Vic obviously didn't know that Nick had cancer. To their credit, Vic and Ruth Ann were kind people who probably wanted to think the best of everyone. I didn't feel the need to say negative things about Nick at this point. I did, however, want to let myself move past that unfortunate and tragic evening.

"Well, enjoy yourselves, and I hope Nick recovers soon,"

I said simply.

"Your shop is looking quite festive, by the way," Vic remarked as he was leaving. "We are having an open house the same night as you, so I hope we both do well."

"Yes, and thanks for the purchase, Vic," I said as a woman and young boy entered.

To be honest, I always felt uncomfortable when customers entered with their children. I never knew whether to ignore the children and concentrate on making a sale, or make sure the children didn't destroy the shop! The mother said she was just looking, so I pretended to be busy as I kept an eye on her little one.

"Mommy, Mommy, there's a mean Santa in this room."

"Oh, Sammy, Santa isn't mean," the mother replied in a soothing voice.

"Come, Mommy, come!" he insisted. "He wants to come after me." The mother secured her son's hand and tried to get him away from my antique Santa.

"He's a very old papier-mâché Santa that goes back to the turn of the century," I explained. "His painted eyes do seem to follow you everywhere."

The boy started crying and repeated how mean the Santa looked. He tugged frantically on his mother's coat.

"It's okay, Sammy. Look, touch his little hat. I think he likes you."

Sammy refused to touch the hat. Suddenly, the hat flew across the room, shocking all of us!

"What just happened?" the mother questioned as she pulled her son closer.

"Oh, it was barely on his head," I replied, knowing Rosie was playing games again. I picked up the Santa, carefully standing him on the counter. I put his hat back on his papier-mâché head.

"I don't like him, Mommy! Let's go home!" The boy's cries had escalated into near shrieks.

"Okay, but Mommy hasn't had a chance to look," she said firmly.

With that, the poor child cried out much louder, leaving his mother no choice but to leave the shop.

I couldn't help checking throughout the day to see if my quilt was still on the rocker on the porch. Around four, I brought everything in, feeling the cold breezes make their way into the house each time I opened the door. A fireplace right now would be so appreciated. I poured myself some wine to collect my thoughts. I needed to get my quilt block done, so I went upstairs to attempt the challenge.

CHAPTER 28

I laid everything out on the upstairs kitchen table and began cutting out the shape of the red book. As I began appliquéing the book in the center of the block, I knew I had to jazz it up a bit with something other than an embroidered title. It was taking me forever, because I knew Susan and the others would be looking at my stitches. After a while, I took a break and looked out the backyard windows. Snow was starting to accumulate on the tree branches, making a beautiful outdoor scene.

When I finished the stitching on the book, I decided that my corners were too blank. Holly leaves and berries would make it look more like Christmas, so I took advantage of the green fabric in the kit and cut holly out for each corner. I was getting hungry and impatient. Oh, how slow my progress was!

I went downstairs to heat up some soup, and the Santa's eyes followed me. I had to chuckle as I remembered how frightened the little boy became, although I totally understood how that antique was so different than the

Santas of today. I took my soup upstairs, and after I finished, I got ready for bed. Looking outside once more, I gazed into the darkness as the snow glistened on the horizon. How my world had changed since I'd moved to wine country! I crawled into my cozy bed, feeling relaxed from my wine and hot soup. Then, my phone rang.

"Lily, it's Nick. I haven't gotten a response from you regarding my party, so I thought I'd give you a personal follow-up call."

I was shocked and had no idea what to say.

"I received your invitation," I stated, "and I'm not able to attend."

There was a long pause. I was determined to let the silence continue, which it did for quite some time.

Nick finally replied, "You are not able to attend, or you don't want to attend?"

His voice sounded so very angry. I was determined to hold my ground. "Perhaps both," I admitted. "I'm very busy, and there's no reason to continue our relationship."

"Wow, you are angry with me," he responded, sounding surprised. "I thought reaching out to you would help."

"Don't be concerned about me, Nick. I wish you well with your health and I hope the coming year is good for you."

"Thanks, Lily. So, with that, I'll wish you a merry Christmas."

"The same to you," I responded, hanging up. Now I was fully awake but pleased that I held my own with my feelings. I didn't want to think of Nick as I tried to go back to sleep, so I thought of all the pleasantries I could think of. The red-and-green Christmas quilt began to dance in my head. Oh, I wished there was a real Santa Claus!

The bright morning sunlight woke me, causing me to want some hot coffee. I wasn't in any hurry to open the shop since it looked like it could end up being a snow day. My sidewalk and porch were completely covered in snow. I didn't own a shovel, so any snow removal would have to be tackled with the power of a single broom. Forget going to church today, like I'd half-planned to do. I decided that just staying in my robe for the entire day wouldn't be all that bad, once I'd had my coffee!

I took another look at my quilt block. It desperately needed embroidery floss, which I would get from Susan tomorrow. Going through this small quiltmaking process made me appreciate finished quilts even more. As a collector, I took a lot of talent for granted. I was probably one of many who really aren't cut out to make quilts, but my passion for quilts could certainly be enhanced by getting all I could out of these classes.

CHAPTER 29

Around noon, I looked out the front window of the shop and saw there wasn't a tire track in sight on the street. I then looked out the back window from the kitchen and saw that snow was piled high around the little cedar tree I'd admired. If I just had a saw, I would put my boots on and go out and cut it down. I had the perfect antique ornaments for that little tree. I felt that I really needed a tree for my open house and the Christmas Walk.

I nibbled on peanut butter and apple slices for lunch as I thought about the gifts I would give this season. What could I give from my shop that would not cost me money? Of course, I was able to bring wine, but it sure wasn't a very personal gift. It was overly generous, but I had one more old radio left in the shop that I could give to Holly. She would love that for her collection. What a strange thing to collect, but Holly seemed to enjoy them immensely. Thinking of gifts for Alex, Lynn, Sarah, Loretta, and Laurie would be challenging. My phone rang, taking me from my thoughts of shopping.

"Lily?" a man's deep voice asked. "It's Butler Hayes."

It took me a while to recall the name.

"I'm the one who showed you the Feathered Star quilts."

"Of course. The owner of the Christmas quilt."

He chuckled. "I see you have Christmas on your mind these days," he teased.

"As a matter of fact, I do. I'm snowed in today, so I'm doing Christmas planning for my open house."

"It's a good day for that. I don't think we got as much snow here as you did."

"Well, who would have known how much I'd need a shovel out here? I don't think my broom will do the trick." He must have thought I was dimwitted.

"I wish I could help, but the reason I'm calling is that I'm coming your way to purchase some things from an estate in Marthasville on Wednesday. I wondered if you'd like to have an early dinner."

"Assuming my shop will be open by then, I'd certainly be free around five."

"Five thirty would be perfect. Carrie Mae keeps recommending The Silly Goose, so if you approve, I'll make a reservation."

"Wonderful. I'll see you then."

"I'm looking forward to it," he said as we hung up.

I was dumbfounded. Not only did this handsome man have a sexy voice, but he was asking me to dinner. Even if it was classified as business, I couldn't help feeling flattered. Maybe he thought he could sell me the Christmas quilt with his flattery. What would Carrie Mae think about this? I called her immediately. I sure didn't want to make another mistake like I did by going out with Nick.

"What are you doing on this snow day, Ms. Wilson?" I asked.

"Oh, honey, I slept until noon! I don't intend to go downstairs for even a minute. Korine had given me some soup that I put in the freezer last week, so I'm all set. How about you?"

"I'm not getting much done, I'm afraid. I can't believe we've gotten all this snow and I don't own a shovel."

She laughed. "The boys were clearing here a bit ago. I'll tell them to get on over to your place."

"That would be great! By the way, you'll never guess who called me today to ask me to dinner."

"There's no telling. Who?"

"Butler Hayes. He's coming this way to buy from an estate in Marthasville."

"That's wonderful!"

"It is?"

"Why wouldn't it be? If I were thirty years younger, I'd be all over him."

I laughed. "I don't know him at all. After my experience with Nick, I'm questioning my judgement on folks. I know it's just a business dinner, but he is very interesting."

"And, Lily Girl, he is a widower and mighty handsome."

"A widower?"

"Yes, his wife was killed in a car accident a good while ago. He was devastated. You couldn't ask for a nicer fellow."

I paused. "Well, I'm quite fond of Marc. They don't come any nicer than him."

"No harm done. I'm sure Marc has business associates who are women that he has business lunches with. You can trust Butler. He is not a womanizer like Nick. He wouldn't have to work a day in his life if he didn't want to. He comes from old money, but you'd never know it. He loves antiques and can afford the best of them. He's not a bad contact to have!"

CHAPTER 30

Less than half an hour later, the boys were shoveling in front of my shop. I put on boots and a coat and went out to say hello.

"Hi, Ms. Lily," Kip greeted me. "We should have thought to come by here."

"I don't own a shovel, so I really appreciate this," I admitted.

"It's no problem, but if you want to buy one, Johann's has them," he said, wiping his nose.

"Great!" I responded. "Now, do you think you could take care of another little job for me?"

They shrugged their shoulders, not certain what they might be getting into.

"I don't own a saw and I want to cut down a little cedar tree in my backyard," I explained. "It's just the kind of Christmas tree I want. Can I show you?"

They smiled and followed me to the backyard. "That little thing?" Kip asked with a grin.

"Yes. Our family always had a cedar tree for a Christmas

tree when I was growing up. This is the perfect size for my apartment upstairs. Do you have a saw with you?"

"Sure. It's in the truck," Kip said. "We'll have this down in no time. Do you have a stand for it?"

"Oh, no, I don't," I said.

"Well, get a bucket of water and we'll put it in there until we can come back tomorrow and make a stand."

"Thanks so much!" I said, rushing to do as he said. I quickly brought out a bucket of water, and the tree came down in a flash. I was so excited to know that tomorrow, I would have a Christmas tree.

That evening, I finally heard a snowplow come by. I hadn't been sure the county owned one. I was relieved, because I'd need to get to my quilting class tomorrow. As I watched the progress of the plow, I noticed that the boys had cleaned off my car as well. It was good day!

I stayed awake in bed that evening thinking about my dinner date with Butler. I then switched my thoughts to Marc. Marc wasn't a good match when it came to my quilts and antiques, unlike Butler. It could be good to have a contact like Butler. How awful it must have been for him to lose his wife like that. It must be hard to move forward after such a shock.

On Monday morning, the sun was shining. The snow glistened so brightly that one could hardly look at it. Hopefully, my fireplace would arrive today. I dressed and brought down my quilting bag for class. I poured a cup of coffee and heard voices in the backyard. It was the boys attaching a wooden stand to my Christmas tree.

"Here you go, Ms. Lily," Kip said when I came to the door. "Where do you want it?"

I took him upstairs to the upper porch and told him where to place it. The cold room would be good for it right now. "I'm getting a fireplace in here soon," I explained.

"Whatever, but why didn't you get a bigger tree? You certainly have the room for it."

"No, this five-foot tree is perfect. I'll be able to see it from afar through these windows."

I generously paid the boys and proceeded to clean up all the wet and dirty tracks the activity made. To my delight, the aroma of the cedar told me it was Christmastime. My phone rang, and it was the fireplace delivery folks.

"Sorry, Ms. Rosenthal, but we're behind in deliveries with this weather, so your fireplace won't be there until Wednesday."

"No problem," I responded. It was disappointing, but it couldn't be helped. Now I had to get to quilting class. After it was over, I would stop by Johann's to purchase a shovel and a saw.

When I arrived at the library, Susan was talking to Edna, the oldest and most talented in our quilting class. She was showing Susan her favorite doll, Milly, which was appliquéd onto her block. It had darling details and embellishments. It was amazing. I got a cup of coffee and joined the others as they began to show their blocks. After seeing a few of their results, I wanted to go out the door and run!

When it was my turn, I told them mine wasn't finished and that I needed floss to complete some details. I did tell them the story about me receiving the red book with the blank pages. They seemed to be touched by the sentiment, and everyone encouraged me to keep going.

"For the next block you make, I want you to think of your favorite Christmas carol," Susan announced.

Everyone began chatting at once. My mind was blank for now, but I never got tired of hearing Christmas carols. I had started playing them right after Thanksgiving in the shop. I peeked in our kit. This time, Susan had included more colors of fabric along with the 12-inch white block. She encouraged us to keep our scraps in case we needed them for future blocks.

Judy once again asked me to go to lunch, but I told her I had a stop I had to make.

CHAPTER 31

Johann's tiny store was crowded with many customers who needed attention. I found the stacked shovels right away but had to ask him where he kept the saws. When I couldn't answer what size or for what purpose, Johann decided I didn't need one. He was probably right, especially since I'd had the help of the boys. I was about to leave when I noticed a pick-up truck filled with lots of green pine wreaths for sale. I bought two, a large one and a smaller one. I loaded my car, and the fragrance was awesome! I didn't have bows, but I had lots of pine cones and other seasonal accessories.

When I arrived home, I didn't waste any time deciding what to do with the wreaths. The large wreath was going on my front door and the smaller one was going on Doc's house. After I hung them in place, I embellished them with berries and pine cones. I took photos on my phone to send to my sisters. I was entirely pleased with my efforts! I was about to go inside when Snowshoes came my way.

"Don't you need to use your snowshoes today?" I teased.

"No, I've been walking in the streets all morning," he

explained. "Your place is sure looking nice."

"Thanks. I just put up some wreaths."

"Yes, it looks like the Doc is in the office again," he teased back.

"Somebody's there," I admitted, smiling to myself.

Off he went, and I glanced at my mail. To my delight, there was a Christmas card from my Aunt Mary. It was the one time of year when we caught up with one another. She had been a seamstress all her life, and even at the age of eighty, she kept her fingers active. I remembered when she made Loretta's bridal veil. I made a mental note to respond to her quickly.

After I'd had a bite of lunch, I got out my quilt block to start the embroidery. As I stitched, I thought about my favorite Christmas song. I loved "Silent Night," but that would be too hard to create. The song that always affected me through the holidays was "I'll Be Home for Christmas." I could stitch a house with a fireplace that had stockings hung for everyone in my family. I'd have to embroider all their names, which I knew would be challenging. I remembered that Susan would help me.

Later in the day, I called Alex. I missed him, and I wanted him to know about my dinner date with Butler.

"Business date, huh?" he teased.

"He's a resource for me, Alex. When I want to buy or sell, it's good to know a man like him."

"Well, enjoy yourself, but you have to know that Marc has serious feelings for you."

"Do you really think so?"

"Is the Pope Catholic?" he teased. "I think you'd better think about what that relationship means to you before you meet up with Butler. I'm just sayin', Lily Girl."

"How did you become such an expert at relationships?"

He laughed. "Okay, that's a fair question. I'll have you know that I'm having lunch with Tracey tomorrow. Do you remember her from work?"

"Oh, Treacherous Tracey? How well I remember her! She always did have a thing for you. What brought her out of the woodwork?"

"Now, be nice," Alex teased. "She called to get a source on a story she's writing. She suggested that we go to lunch, and it sounded like fun. I like to catch up on the latest gossip back at the publishing company."

"It's my turn to lecture you, my friend. You'd better decide ahead of time what you want that relationship to be, because she is a manipulator and a tease."

"I understand. As I've gotten older, I'm not a pushover with women like I used to be. I'll be good."

"You'd better."

"The same goes for you, Lily," he reminded me.

CHAPTER 32

The next morning, I was completely surprised when my new fireplace arrived! I could hardly contain my excitement, but the two delivery men were much less excited when they learned that it was going upstairs to my porch. In no time, the installation was done, and I saw flames appear. They were glad to make me so happy, and they left to make more deliveries. I wanted to spend the day watching the flames, but I had so much to do, and I still didn't know what I should wear to dinner.

I eventually took the rocking chair and a red-and-white quilt to the front porch. I took some leftover greenery and draped it here and there. It added to my excitement about Christmas in my own shop and all the festivities to come. As I came inside, I saw a male customer coming my way. We said a simple hello before he headed straight to the quilt room.

"Is there anything special I can help you find?"

"I'm just looking, thanks," he answered as he got closer and closer to look at certain quilts.

"If you need help opening them up to see them better,

just let me know."

I busied myself while I kept an eye on him. I couldn't believe my eyes when I saw him sniffing the quilts, as if they smelled! He finally pulled a pink and green Ohio Rose quilt off the rack. He put the quilt to his nose, as if he detected an odor.

"Do you have any more pink quilts or quilts with a lot of pink in them?"

I had to think. "Well, let me see. I know there is a crib quilt over here that has pink in the background."

"May I see it?"

"Sure. I also have a Nine-Patch youth-size quilt that has a blue one to match it."

"I'm not interested in the blue one, but let me take a closer look at the pink one."

He held that quilt to his nose and gave it a good sniff! How strange, I thought.

"This one is perfect. Let me take another look at the rose quilt." He rubbed his hands across the appliquéd flower and then put the quilt in his hands, along with the Nine-Patch.

"If I take these two, can you give me a discount?"

I paused. "Let me see the price tags. You seem to only like pink."

"There's no question that pink quilts smell the best," he said.

He seemed quite serious. I nodded and tried not to smile. "I think I can take twenty-five dollars off the rose quilt, but not anything off the Nine-Patch."

He remained quiet for a while. "Okay, I guess that'll work. I have a tax number, by the way," he added.

I finished the sale as he glanced around the shop. "Thanks so much. Do you live around here?"

"No, but I always come out here to see what the Uptown Store has for sale. I've been buying from her for many years."

"Oh, good. I was about to tell you about the Uptown Store. Well, you have a merry Christmas, and please come back."

He left, quite pleased with his purchases. It was a good thing that no one else was in the shop. I couldn't wait to call Carrie Mae. This was one for the books!

"Hey, Lily Girl! What's up today?" Carrie Mae asked.

"Well, you didn't tell me to carry as many pink quilts as I could!"

She exploded into giggles. "Oh, Mr. Pink paid you a visit?"

"That's what you call him?"

"Girl, he's a trip, but his money's good. I'll bet he paid you in cash, didn't he?"

"Yes. He also wanted a discount."

"Yes, like always. Did he describe all the furniture in the house and tell you what he does with all the quilts?"

"Not really. I think he knew I was blown away by his behavior."

"I never have understood what the guy does for a living, but he always deals in cash."

After my chat with Carrie Mae, I told myself to be more diligent in adding entries to my journal. There were no two days alike in retail. I wondered if Mr. Pink had paid Rosie a visit when her shop was open. I'd have to ask him if he came back again.

The day was somewhat profitable, thanks to Mr. Pink, so I closed early to get ready for my dinner date with Butler. Part of me felt guilty that I had accepted his invitation. However, I felt that Butler would be amused by my story about Mr. Pink!

CHAPTER 33

Taking extra care as I dressed, I chose a black-and-white wool dress to go with my black dress boots. Socially, Butler was certainly out of my league, but I valued his intellect regarding quilts and antiques.

I answered the door to let Butler in, and he was right on time. His sharp black overcoat went quite well with his salt-and-pepper hair. He had an air of New York sophistication about him which differed from the upper crust of the Midwest.

"It's so nice of you to accompany me this evening, Ms. Rosenthal," he teased politely.

"My pleasure! I'm anxious to hear why you would want to take time for dinner out this direction."

"Are you serious?" he asked, smiling. "I think we both indicated that we wanted to pick each other's brains, but having dinner with an attractive woman is a bonus."

I blushed. "Okay, I'm flattered, but also starved, so should we be on our way?"

He nodded, and we were off. We made the short trip

up the hill to The Silly Goose and joined the packed room of happy customers. Butler immediately sized up the place and was fascinated with how it managed to fill a need in this region. Before we ordered, we shared a bottle of wine that had a name I couldn't pronounce. It was like a red favorite of mine called The Other, which I frequently purchased at the Wine Country Gardens. When I casually mentioned that Carrie Mae told me I had a wine cellar in the basement, his eyes lit up.

"That is awesome!" he replied. "You need to restore it someday, if you can. With the age of your house, it would be a real asset."

"I know you'll think I'm weird, but I've never been in my basement," I admitted.

He grinned. "I'll bet there is a big, bad bogeyman down there that you need to know about."

I nodded. "I know. That's why I'm staying above ground."

As our dinner progressed, I got in a few quilt-related questions when I could. He kept drawing the conversation back to me. To add a little humor, I did tell him about Mr. Pink. He laughed out loud but said nothing in retail would surprise him. I surprised myself when I told him about Rosie occupying the house. He thought it was charming and confirmed that I was very lucky to have purchased her inventory.

"I have to ask you if you still have the red-and-green Christmas quilt."

He grinned.

"I can't seem to get it off of my mind."

"I still have it, but the red, white, and blue one went to a dealer in New York who collects patriotic quilts."

"I worry that the really unique and rare quilts are disappearing," I said softly.

"Yes and no. I watch them travel from owner to owner. As a collector, you know that we like to 'buy up' in our collections. Trends sometimes impact their moving as well."

"I wish I could afford to improve my personal collection, but since I've bought the shop, that budget has become my priority."

"You are a new business, so that's understandable. The more successful you become, the more you'll be able to treat yourself occasionally."

"I hope so," I said, suddenly feeling a little sad for putting myself in that position.

"You remind me of the early days when my wife, Jenny, and I started collecting. There were times when we took a chance with some high-dollar quilts and it paid off."

It was the first time he'd mentioned his wife.

"That's wonderful."

"Well, it's Christmas!" he announced, ready to lighten the discussion. "Do you want to go anywhere else? The night is still young."

"This has been such a pleasant dinner with tasty food and wonderful conversation that I don't think we can improve upon it."

He smiled and nodded. "Considering the drive back, I should probably be on my way. When do you leave for Wisconsin? I'd like to see you again."

"I leave on the day before Christmas Eve. Before that happens, however, I have an open house coming up, and Augusta has a Christmas Walk that everyone talks about. You may want to experience what a small town does this time of year."

"Well, all of that sounds good, but I was referring to seeing you," he clarified. "I'd like to hear more about those sisters of yours. I'll bet you share wonderful memories with them."

"I suppose I do," I said with a chuckle. "Life is never dull when we get together. I have a niece from Green Bay that may be moving here. That will be fun, and somewhat challenging at the same time."

"So I should stay tuned, right?"

I smiled.

The restaurant was about to close when we finally got up to leave. Butler had been so nice and gracious. He said "Merry Christmas" to the staff as we left. When we pulled in front of my place, our attention went to the light in Doc's house. Butler made a few comments about it and just pretended it was supposed to be that way. He then walked me to the door and gave me a nice hug.

"Call me anytime if you have any questions."

"I will. Thanks for dinner, and if I don't see you again before the holiday, have a merry Christmas."

With that, he winked at me and gave me a quick peck on the cheek.

I went through the door and immediately went upstairs. I couldn't wait to turn on the fireplace after being out in the cold. Without a doubt, this would be my new nesting place. As I undressed, I thought of Marc and what he might be doing.

CHAPTER 34

The next morning, I was still going over all the useful information Butler had shared with me. Why he had taken time to have dinner with me was beyond me. I was still having my first cup of coffee when Alex called.

"I feel a bit like Scrooge lately with all this Christmas commotion, but enough about me," he started.

"I'm feeling a bit overwhelmed myself, but last night's dinner with Butler was very pleasant as well as educational. I hope I can continue to pick his brain."

"So, it was all business, huh?" he said, snickering.

"Pretty much. He did ask if he could see me again before Christmas."

"Ahhh! I wonder what Marc would have to say about that?"

"Am I wrong to think that we are talking about apples and oranges?"

We laughed.

"Some other folks from *Spirit* magazine joined Tracey and me for drinks last night. I found one of the ladies to be quite attractive and asked her out. She's just moved here from Minnesota. What an accent she has! She is a writer. I don't know about her baggage, but I'm willing to find out."

"Cool. What's her name?"

"Mindy. Mindy from Minnesota."

"I like her already," I teased. "She must be very lonely!"

"Hey!"

"Do you think you could come out for my Christmas open house? Better yet, bring Mindy. I need live bodies. I've never done this before."

He laughed.

Someone had knocked at the door, so I needed to hang up. It was Snowshoes.

"Hey, Lily! I just wanted to hand you the mail in person so I could ask you to check on Carrie Mae. She's usually open by now. I hope she's okay."

"Oh, I will. Thanks."

Off he went, and I didn't waste any time giving her a call. The phone rang and rang before she picked up.

"How are you?" I asked.

"Slow going today, I'm afraid. I have a bug. Betty and I were at her son's house a couple of days ago and one of her grandsons was sick, so I think that's the source. Betty is complaining that she doesn't feel good as well."

"Can I bring you some soup or something?"

"No, I'll be fine. By the way, who told you I wasn't feeling well?"

"Snowshoes was concerned when you weren't open at your usual time, so he thought I should check on you. That's sweet, don't you think?"

"Oh, for land's sake. I guess by now the whole town

knows about it."

"He just cares about you. I also want to tell you that Butler and I had a nice dinner last night at The Silly Goose."

"Nice. I knew you would."

"He still has the Christmas quilt, but he did sell the red, white, and blue one."

"Did he tell you what he got for it?"

"No; I wanted to ask, but I was already asking too many questions. He says he wants to see me again before I go away for Christmas. I'm really busy, and I don't want him to think I want a personal relationship."

"Oh, you are too modern, my friend," Carrie Mae said with a chuckle. "Be yourself and enjoy his friendship for what it is. He is a wonderful professional resource."

"I suppose you're right. Oh, and guess what? My fireplace from Marc arrived yesterday. You must come and see it. I have it on the upper porch, so I can sit out there all winter."

"Wonderful! I will do that. I suppose I should get this place open before the townspeople think I died."

We laughed.

When we hung up, I wondered what Carrie Mae had meant when she said I was too modern. I guessed it would be the opposite of old-fashioned. I opened the shop and looked out the window, so I could spot any live bodies that might be coming my way to make their purchases!

CHAPTER 35

Kitty dropped off the maps for the Christmas Walk so I could have them for my open house.

"So, are you ready?" Kitty asked as she browsed through the store. "Your place looks great!"

"I'm ready, except for the food. Cooking is not my thing, so the menu will be hot cider, chocolate chip cookies, and a few appetizers."

"Sounds perfect. I like that you're having a hot drink instead of wine, like everyone else."

"I thought so, too."

"By the way, I know you're friends with Nick Conrey. I wondered if you knew how he was doing?"

Her question threw me. "Why do you ask?"

"He didn't look good at his party, and someone told me he's been going to the hospital for tests. Do you know what's wrong with him?"

"No, and I'm sorry to hear that. We were never close, Kitty."

"What is it about the Christmas season that makes so many get sick and even die?"

I just shrugged my shoulders.

"Well, good luck tomorrow night," she said, opening the door. "I hope we all do well."

"Me, too!" I said as two women came in the door.

I barely acknowledged them as my mind went to poor Nick.

"I'm looking for an antique quilt in a king size," one of the women said as she pulled a quilt off the rack.

"I only carry antique quilts, and there wasn't such a thing as a king-size bed back then, so you'll find that most of these are for smaller beds." I felt like I was talking to a child that should know better.

"These are all small?" she asked, almost defiantly.

"The exact size is on each tag. Some are bigger than others. In fact, some quilts from the 1850s to the 1870s were rather large because of the high poster beds. That's when some people actually used bed steps." She looked at me strangely while her friend scoped out the other rooms. "You will want something to cover an area as big as a 108-inch square, because that's the standard size of a king bed."

"Well, that's crappy," her friend said in disgust. "I told you right away to get a new one. You can get them as cheap as a hundred dollars."

I wanted to avoid that comment. I knew where she did her shopping.

"Well, I can't use red and white anyway," she noted. "That seems to be all you have. My bedroom is blue and yellow."

"Some folks get really creative by using two complementary quilts to cover a larger bed," I suggested.

"My bed is an antique reproduction, so an antique quilt would have been perfect," she said, her disappointment apparent.

"We need to go," her friend said, moving towards the door.

"You didn't see anything you liked anyway, right?"

With that comment, I left them alone so I could say hello to someone who had just opened the door.

"Oh! This is just antiques!" the lady said, clearly disappointed.

I didn't have time to respond before she closed the door in my face! My mood was quickly turning sour, so I went into the kitchen to pour a cup of coffee.

"Hey," the quilt lady called.

"Did you find something?" I replied.

"I'll take this dresser scarf," she said, putting it on the counter. "It will do nicely on my dresser."

"Sorry we couldn't find you a quilt," I said.

She had no response.

I was glad to see the two of them leave. Do some people even realize how rude they sound? I was happy to get the thirteen dollars for the scarf, since it was a slow day.

My phone rang. To my surprise, it was Marc!

"How's it going, Lily?" he asked sweetly.

"Let's just say it's not been a gold-star day," I complained.

He laughed. "I'm sorry to hear that, but I hear there's a wonderful open house tomorrow night. I'd bet that everyone is waiting to come then."

"Yes, it's the talk of the town," I joked. "Are you thinking of coming out?"

"I know you'll be busy, so I thought I could bring us some dinner from The Hill, if that suits you."

"Awesome! I'm making chocolate chip cookies that you'll like."

"Great! I'll see you then, Lily Girl!"

CHAPTER 36

This was the first official event of Lily Girl's Quilts and Antiques. I was excited to debut my shop during this festive season. Before I got dressed, I turned on the fireplace to take the chill off the upstairs. I came downstairs and turned on the oven, getting ready for cookie baking. The aroma would be an added attraction and might encourage customers to hang around for a while. My first cup of coffee gave me confidence for the day. I was also looking forward to seeing Marc and hoped he would approve of the fireplace I had chosen for my Christmas present. I could only hope that Alex and Lynn would come. I knew better than to expect Holly to attend such an event out here.

I lit all the candles and turned on all the lamps to make everything look more festive. The aroma of cookies in the oven was filling up the entire house. I grabbed a piece of holly and stuck it in my ponytail to make myself look a bit more in tune with the season. I opened the shop and carried Rosie's chair out into the bitter cold.

The first person to arrive was Carrie Mae's friend, Betty.

"I baked you and Carrie Mae some cranberry bread. I make a bunch of loaves every Christmas. I'm sure you can use it throughout the evening. Boy, it sure smells delightful in here."

"Thank you so much!" I said, giving her a little hug. "I love anything with cranberries. Will you have a cup of cider and a cookie?"

"Thanks, but I need to get back to Carrie Mae's. I told her I'd help her a bit in the shop. She's still not feeling all that well from that flu she's had."

"I'm glad you can help her. I hope you and your family have a merry Christmas!"

As she went on her way, I had to admire the wonderful friendship that she and Carrie Mae had enjoyed through the years.

The morning activity was rather slow, but after lunch, things started to pick up. I recognized many local faces, many of whom I couldn't call by name, but their compliments were uplifting.

Heidi and Susan from the quilt group came by to say hello. The evening was turning into more of a social event than a sales promotion. I guessed I should have known that. The refreshments were a hit, and folks were just happy to be warm. To my surprise, around four, Alex and his friend Mindy from Minnesota arrived.

"Oh, Lily, it's so good to meet you," Mindy said. She had a soft, sweet voice. "Alex spent the entire ride out here telling me all about you!"

"Oh, you unfortunate thing," I replied.

"Mindy loves antiques, which happens to include quilts as well," Alex revealed. "I want her to see your quilt inventory."

I followed them into the quilt room. "Are you a quilter yourself?" I asked, curious.

"No. I prefer antique quilts. I like a more primitive look, but I admire those who have the talent to make quilts."

"Please help yourself to refreshments," I offered. "I made the cookies myself, and this variety happens to be a favorite of Alex's."

"They are the best, but we have dinner reservations at Chandler Hill, so we don't want to spoil our appetite," Alex warned as he took one of the cookies for himself.

"Sounds like a nice evening!"

I let them look as I noticed someone at the checkout counter.

Marc then walked in the door. "Merry Christmas!" he cheered.

"Merry Christmas to you as well! Good to see you!"

With that, we hugged.

"It looks like the party is going well," he observed. "Do you want me to put our dinner in the refrigerator down here?"

"Yes, and when you go past the quilt room, say hello to Alex and his new friend."

"Great!" he said as he walked away.

The place became merrier as the shop filled up with customers. I could have used some help with all the questions and distractions I was getting. Judging from the laughter in the quilt room, Alex and Marc were having an enjoyable time. They finally all came to the counter to join me.

"I fell in love with this Fan quilt, Lily," Mindy said as she handed it to me. "It's perfect for my sister. She loves pastel colors, and I was stumped as to what to get her for Christmas."

"I'm glad this will work," I said as I began to wrap it up. "It's in really good condition. Alex, thanks for bringing in this good customer."

We all chuckled.

"You've done an excellent job making this place look so festive," Alex said. "You could have never done all of this on The Hill. It looks like you've had some sales from the looks of that spindle. Marc just left to help a lady get a cookie jar from the top shelf in the kitchen. You might think about hiring him. We need to be on our way. Hope I can see you before you leave."

"Nice to meet you, Lily," Mindy said as she pulled her gloves on.

"Merry Christmas, and I hope I see you again if Alex will let me!" I teased.

CHAPTER 37

As the two left, I had a good feeling about their relationship. Mindy was cute, like the girl next door, and she seemed very sweet. Marc came to the counter with the cookie jar lady. He blushed when she bragged about how helpful he had been.

"I'm sorry I couldn't get back there," I said apologetically. "Did you find anything else?"

"No, but I did enjoy your cookies. Thank you so much!"

"Thanks for helping her, Marc."

While I packed her jar, Marc continued to ask customers if they needed any help. It was interesting to watch him work. The doorbell jingled and in came Butler, which totally surprised me. My mouth had to be open.

"Well, hello!" I greeted him.

"Merry Christmas!" he replied. "You've got quite a crowd here."

"Yes, it's been great!" I paused awkwardly. "Butler, meet my friend Marc Rennels. Butler is my antique dealer friend that I probably told you about."

Marc nodded but looked a bit puzzled.

"He deals in things I could never afford."

Butler chuckled. "Someday you will!" he responded. "Nice to meet you, Marc."

Marc smiled and shook his hand.

"I can't believe you drove out this way tonight," I said.

"Well, I had a purpose in mind and hoped I could talk to you for a moment in private, if you can spare it."

I looked at my shop. It was full of folks.

"This is really not a good time, Butler. Could I call you later tonight, or first thing in the morning?" I could tell he was disappointed. Marc was watching the two of us.

"Sure, I understand," he said.

"Won't you have a cup of cider before you leave?"

"Don't mind if I do," he answered, surprising me again. "I want to drop in on Carrie Mae when I leave here."

"That would be nice," I remarked. "Her friend is helping her tonight."

Butler went into the kitchen, and Marc looked to me for an explanation.

Thankfully, a woman wanting to purchase a child's tea set came to the counter to check out. Marc continued to assist me. Moments later, Butler came to the counter to tell me goodbye. As he wished me a merry Christmas, he kissed me on the cheek, which took me by surprise. I knew Marc was watching.

"I like that touch of holly in your hair," he said as he lightly touched it. I could feel my face turning red. "Nice to meet you, Marc," he said as an afterthought. "I'll talk to you tomorrow, Lily," he added, going out the door.

People were starting to thin out as I refilled the cookie

tray.

"It looks like the cookies were a big hit," Marc said.

Finally, the last person left. I was so tired of talking and entertaining! I wanted to drop. I looked at Marc and announced how hungry and tired I was.

"I'll get our dinner and you go on up," Marc instructed.

"I just need to blow out the candles and bring the rocker inside." Having finished that, I slowly went upstairs and turned on the fireplace. I poured two glasses of wine. Marc put deli sandwiches and pasta on plates and set them on the coffee table. He was full of compliments about the fireplace and was pleased that it made me so happy.

"This is such a treat, Marc. Thank you again for helping me tonight."

"It was my pleasure, and I'm happy your first open house was a success. So, tell me more about Butler."

"Well, Carrie Mae sent him to me. He had a couple of wonderful quilts for sale that I couldn't afford. He deals with folks all over the world and is quite successful at it. He had a red-and-green Christmas quilt I would have killed for, but it was way, way out of my price range."

"How much was he asking?"

"He didn't say, but the appraisal for it was for eighteen thousand dollars."

Marc looked stunned. "You don't mean eighteen hundred dollars?"

"No. Thousand."

"I didn't realize that quilts could be that expensive."

"Sure, and even more than that, but that's not the market I deal in," I explained. "As a collector, you can imagine how my mouth watered. I prefer just red-and-white quilts, but this was so striking and beautiful."

"He seemed to have a special attraction to you," Marc stated.

I didn't know how to answer. "Really?" I paused. "He's a great contact for me professionally, but there's nothing personal there."

CHAPTER 38

There were moments of silence as we watched the flames in the fireplace. Marc agreed that putting it on the porch added the element of bringing the outdoors inside.

"I may not see you again before Christmas, so I want to give you your gift," I said as I took an envelope off the side table. "I think this has your name on it."

"What? I don't see a bow or any paper to unwrap," he teased.

"You're going to love it!"

"Oh, will I now?" he said, giving me a wink.

When Marc saw the baseball tickets, his face lit up.

"Am I right? Did I do good?"

"Honey, you've got the touch. This is awesome! There's a lot of games here."

"Did you notice that they are for two?" I hinted.

"I did! Let's hope you have these dates already set aside on your calendar."

"I'm sorry. I'm a business owner in Augusta, so you'd better not count on me for all of them."

"Thank you so much!" he said, placing a lovely kiss on my lips.

I knew he shared season tickets at work, but this would be a bonus for him. It was hard to compete with the fireplace, but I also knew I couldn't go wrong with the tickets. We continued to chatter about baseball as we enjoyed our wine and sandwiches.

"Marc, I haven't talked to Lynn lately about Carl. Do you think he's really serious about going to Green Bay with us?"

"I do. I think he's trying to keep their marriage afloat, but don't ask me what else he may have going on. He seems distracted."

"Do you think he gave up someone else? Maybe that's what's bothering him."

"Let's not go that far. I think he loves Lynn and is trying to make it work. I haven't had a chance to tell you, but I'm going to make a quick trip to New York on Christmas Eve to see my sister, Meg."

"That's great!"

"For the record, she suggested that I bring you."

"Really? You told her about me?"

"My dear Lily. You are a story to be told, period. She knows I'm a bit smitten with you, but then she gets excited at the least hint of any woman in my life."

I smiled.

"She doesn't feel that a man should live alone, I guess."

"That sounds a lot like what my siblings say about me."

My phone rang, which was unusual at such a late hour. It showed Butler's name, so I let it go to voicemail. Why would he call this late? I acted like it was just a nusicance call of some kind.

"Important?"

"No, I'll call back tomorrow," I said, wanting desperately to change the subject. "You know they have a lot of snow in Green Bay."

"You'll have a white Christmas. That's always special."

"More wine?" I asked.

"No, I'd better not. My eyes are feeling heavy. I should be on my way."

"Are you okay to drive? Would you like to stay over?"

He grinned and paused before he said, "The right thing to do is to be on my way. I have a Christmas lunch with the staff that I don't want to miss. I'm glad I came out tonight. It was a fun evening seeing you in action here at the shop."

"You are quite a salesman!"

"I've had a few sales jobs in my life, by the way."

"Well, it showed."

"I'll say goodbye and wish you a safe trip and a merry Christmas. Give me a call and let me know how it goes."

"I will. I'm going to Lynn's the night before, so we can go to the airport early. Maybe we can have a quick drink if you're still in town."

"That would be really nice," he said as he pulled me close for a kiss goodnight.

I couldn't resist giving him an extra-tight hug as I looked into his eyes.

"I think I'm falling in love, Lily Girl," he whispered.

"I think the feeling is mutual, Mr. Rennels," I whispered back. "Getting this close to someone is frightful at times."

"You don't ever have to be afraid of me," he reassured me. "You know I don't want to leave tonight, but you have to let me know when you're ready to spend more time with me."

I knew what he was thinking. "You're giving me a lot of power," I said.

"Indeed. Now let me go before I change my mind."

I pulled back with a giggle. "Merry Christmas, my love," I said, surprising myself, as he went out into the evening.

CHAPTER 39

The next morning, I wore a smile on my face as I thought about Marc falling in love with me. My first open house had been successful, and tomorrow night was the Christmas Walk that everyone bragged about. If it were as successful as my open house, my taxes could be paid with enough money to spare to get through a couple of leaner winter months. My phone rang. It was Butler. I had forgotten to call him back.

"I'm sorry, Butler. I saw that you had called, but I had a very busy night," I explained.

"I'm happy for you! The reason I was so anxious to talk to you is that the red-and-green star quilt is missing."

I wasn't sure I had heard him correctly.

"The Christmas quilt is gone? What do you mean?"

"I couldn't believe it myself. I was careful to question James as well as my own memory to make sure I wasn't mistaken. My security system did not give me any clues, nor do I have any signs of a break-in."

"Is anything else missing?"

"Not that we've found so far."

"Are you sure you didn't show it to someone to purchase and forgot it? There must be an explanation. I'm sure many people would be attracted to it without their even knowing its worth."

"You and Carrie Mae need to be aware that someone may try to resell it. They would be happy to get far less money for it than I was asking. Check the web when you can, if you will."

"Of course I will. Have you ever had anything stolen before?"

"Never!" he said emphatically. "I am very careful. I'm sorry to make this a concern of yours, as I know how much you loved it. The police asked for a list of those I had shown it to, so they may be giving you a call or a visit. With it being red and green, it's an appropriate time of year to unload it."

"I understand. I'm so sorry, Butler. This is a terrible loss for you."

"I have insurance, of course, but that quilt was more than an investment."

Our conversation ended with a feeling of sadness. How could something like that happen? I knew how violated I felt when my inexpensive quilt was taken from the front porch. Now I knew why he had been so anxious to talk with me. I sure hoped he didn't think I stole it since I had envied it so. I reluctantly opened the shop with that weighing on my mind. I thought it would likely be a slow day since everyone would be coming out tomorrow for the festivities. However, I had just finished turning my lanterns on when someone came into the shop.

"Brrrrr," the attractive lady complained as she shivered.

"Good morning! Brrrrr indeed!"

"I'm Karen from The Cranberry Cottage. We're across from the gallery."

"Yes, I've been trying to get there when you're open."

"I know. We have odd hours because we have a second business that we must attend to. I wanted to get here last night for your party, but we were as busy as you were, I'm sure."

"I'm Lily. I'm glad to finally meet you. What is your other business?"

"We make barn quilts. Since you're in the quilt business, you've likely heard of them."

"Oh, indeed! I love them. The front of my house is so ornate that I couldn't possibly hang one, but I think they are neat. My tattered barn out there couldn't hold another nail before it would fall down!"

"As soon as we can get enough of them up in wine country, we'll have an organized tour for them. So, tell me about you. All I know is that Vic said you moved here from The Hill."

I nodded. "I've always loved coming out here. When I knew I had to make a substantial change in my life, I purchased my friend's antique shop inventory, consulted with Carrie Mae, a longtime friend, and here I am!"

She chuckled.

"Of course, there's more to it than that, but I feel it was meant to be. Everyone has been so supportive and friendly."

"I've found that to be true as well. Your shop is quite lovely. I haven't started shopping for my husband yet. Vic said you had a delightful selection of beer steins, which my husband happens to collect."

"Sure. They're over here. I know nothing about them.

They were in my original inventory, so they have the prices on them from the previous dealer."

When Karen saw them, her face lit up like she knew what she was looking at. "This one from Switzerland is quite rare. I'll take that one and this tall one here as well."

I guess she saw a good deal!

"Great!" I responded happily.

"Lily, I work with quilt patterns a lot. What is your favorite?"

"I like two-color patterns, but I'm very fond of the Feathered Star. Do you make that one?"

"Yes, and I see you like a lot of red and white."

"I focused on collecting them a long time ago."

"It's a popular combination. You need to come and see the ones we have in red."

Before she left, she suggested that we meet for coffee sometime soon.

CHAPTER 40

The next morning, I could already feel the excitement of the Christmas Walk. The temperatures were to get warmer, which would help folks wander around town more comfortably. At eight thirty, I had a call from Esther at the Red Brick Inn of Augusta Bed and Breakfast. She had guests who were wondering what time I was planning to open. I told her to send them on down when they were ready.

"I've heard such wonderful things about your place," I gushed. "I'd like to see it sometime."

"You are welcome anytime," Esther said in a friendly manner. "We should exchange cards. We have a full house this weekend, but we always do for this event."

"I'm looking forward to it, but I just wish I could get out and about to see it."

"My husband, Chuck, and I are volunteering at the carriage ride booth. By the way, the carriages come by your place."

"Really? How nice. I'm hoping to get some takeout

food at Ebenezer Church, if I can find someone to watch the shop."

"They have the best vegetable soup," Esther bragged. "Chuck loves their chili dogs."

"Well, hopefully I'll find out. Nice of you to call. I hope you'll come see my shop soon. Do you like quilts?"

"Yes, I do! I hear that you have a lot of them!"

"Merry Christmas!" I said before hanging up. There was no doubt that events like this brought folks together.

Traffic started picking up after I entertained my early customers from the bed and breakfast. They were from Chicago and were quite delightful. I sold a doll quilt for a granddaughter and sold one of my fancy walking sticks. My phone rang, and it was Carrie Mae.

"Oh, glad you called, Carrie Mae. Did you hear from Butler about the quilt?"

"Yes, I sure did. Isn't that terrible? Someone else besides him must have known the value of it."

"I loved that Christmas quilt," I confessed. "You don't think he suspects I had anything to do with it, do you?"

"Lands, no! Why would you ask such a thing? It will all be discovered in time. I must go. I just got a large group coming in all at once. Talk to you later."

To my delight, Susan, my quilt teacher, came in. She introduced me to her husband and then wanted to confirm that I would be at the next quilting class.

"It will be a crunch with my schedule, but I'll try," I responded.

"There's a flu bug going around, so we may have some who are absent."

"Can I help the two of you find anything?" To my

surprise, customers were filing in at an astounding rate!

"We have several folks in mind to buy for, so I'm sure we'll find a little something," Susan responded. "Let us browse for a bit."

Judy from the coffee shop came in with a friend. "I have to work tonight, so I'm getting to as many places as I can. The shop looks great, but if it's not too much trouble, could I look at the red-and-white quilt you have displayed on your rocker outside?"

"Not at all. Stay here. I'll bring it inside." I bought the frozen quilt in and realized what folks were feeling as they walked around the town all bundled up. "This pattern is called Churn Dash," I shared. "Some folks call it the Hole in the Barn Door as well."

The two friends looked at one another and smiled.

"Why on earth would it have a name like that?" Judy's friend asked.

"Quilts take different names from their makers and from different areas of the country," I explained. "If your mother always called a quilt a certain name, that name would usually stick from generation to generation."

"I really like it," Judy said as she looked at the back of it. "How old is this? Do you know?"

"I can't tell you for sure, but most red-and-white quilts like this were made between 1880 and 1920," I estimated. "That was their peak. The condition of this one is very good. I'd be happy to give you a shop owner's discount if you think you want it."

She smiled. "Sold! I'll call it Hole in the Barn Door. Susan! Look what I'm about to buy!"

"It's very cool," Susan answered. "You know, that is an

easy pattern to make. I admired it myself as I came in the door."

"Merry Christmas to me!" Judy cheered.

I wrapped it up and Susan placed some books on the counter.

"Can you hide these and wrap them up for me?" Susan whispered. "I don't want my husband to see that I'm getting these for him."

I smiled and nodded.

"Don't you have some help today?"

"No, I'm afraid not," I admitted. "I would at least like to get out long enough to get some food for this evening."

"Well, I can come and help you for a while, if you want me to do that," Susan offered. "I think I can handle this. I see you have a cash drawer, and I'm a pretty good salesperson."

I couldn't believe my ears!

CHAPTER 41

The afternoon continued to be very busy, but I was anxious to be relieved and see the festivities for myself. When I had a break, I checked my emails, knowing there would likely be some discussion regarding Christmas in Green Bay. My siblings didn't disappoint.

Loretta reminded us that it was now Sarah's due date, but her doctor wouldn't be surprised if she went as late as Christmas. Laurie said her sales were down due to the latest snowstorm they'd had. She was also feeling frustrated about her winter cold lasting so long. Lynn added that she hoped Carl would not change his mind about joining her on the trip. She thought the mention of a Green Bay Packers game sealed the deal. She was also delighted that Marc had recently bought a small painting from her to give to a good client for Christmas. Marc hadn't mentioned that to me, but I was pleased to hear it.

I quickly added that I was in the middle of the Christmas Walk in Augusta and had sold two quilts so far. I sent a separate message to Sarah to hold out for a Christmas baby. Touching base with my siblings was always comforting and a practice I hoped we'd continue. Mother and Dad would be pleased that we've kept our communication going.

"Merry Christmas, Lily!" Snowshoes greeted me cheerfully.

"You're late today. Have you been celebrating too much with all the shop refreshments?"

He chuckled as he handed me the mail.

"I have a little something to put under your tree. It's a gift card you can use all year long," I explained.

"Thank you, Ms. Lily," he said with gratitude. "Yeah, everyone wants to visit with me this time of year, which makes my route a bit longer. By the way, I don't want to spread unwelcome news, but did you hear that Nick is in the hospital?"

I paused to think about what he'd just said. "Is it serious?"

He nodded. "You did know he has cancer, didn't you?"

"I did, but he told me not to say anything."

"Well, it's a shame with all his talent and all. It seems like Christmas has a way of bringing some folks bad luck. Well, I'd better get on. Thanks for the gift."

I was glad no one else was in the shop, because the news about Nick had shaken me. I didn't even know if he had family nearby to help him now that he was really sick.

Suddenly, I was taken aback by Christmas music coming from outdoors. I looked out and saw a group of Christmas carolers standing in my yard. Six folks were dressed in old-fashioned costumes, singing their hearts out. I grabbed a shawl nearby and opened the door, eager to hear them sing "We Wish You a Merry Christmas." They were in perfect harmony, and I found myself singing along.

Other folks gathered around to join in as they sang "Oh Come All Ye Faithful." It brought tears to my eyes as I thought about going caroling to nursing homes when I was in high school. When I came inside, some of the people followed me to get out of the cold. I offered them a cup of hot cider, which was well received.

"Lily, my name is Beverly Sue Bade," a young girl said. "I think you know my Aunt Betty."

"Oh, Betty Bade?"

She nodded and smiled. "My mother recently passed away and Aunt Betty thought I may want to talk to you about something."

"Oh, I'm sorry. How can I help you?" Usually the next question was whether they could sell me quilts.

"She thinks you're pretty special, by the way," she added.

I smiled. "Let me check on the customers in the other room, and then we'll chat."

The couple in the kitchen seemed to be lookers only, so I went back to Betty's niece.

"I'm sorry to take your time, but when my mother died, I buried her with her favorite quilt."

I nodded to indicate that I was listening.

"My siblings objected terribly and were furious that I didn't get their permission. Was I wrong to do that? The funeral director said a lot of folks do it today."

"Yes, they do. Why are your siblings so upset?"

"They loved the quilt and hoped to inherit it. It's worth quite a bit. My mother put a lot of time and effort into making it. I'm almost sure they would have sold it, knowing them."

"Are you the executor of her will?"

"She didn't leave a will, unfortunately. Aunt Betty thought I might feel more justified about my decision if I talked to you."

"I guess you were thinking about what your mother would

have liked, which makes sense," I surmised. "Surely they can understand that."

"Yes, she was always cold. I know it sounds silly, but it made me feel better knowing that she was wrapped up in that quilt."

"I'm sure this misunderstanding will pass."

"They are pursuing legal action against me and the funeral home, if you can believe that," she went on.

How awful, I thought.

"Money. It's always about money. They know I did it without permission, and it cost them their inheritance and caused undue stress."

As the couple from the back room began to exit the shop, I wished them a merry Christmas.

"I guess what I'd like to know from you is if you would you be willing to testify that this practice is not unusual?"

I couldn't believe her question. "Beverly Sue, I don't like getting involved in domestic issues like this," I explained. "You have got to work this out among yourselves or you will all regret it in years to come. Nothing is worth this kind of drama. It should be about what your mother would have wanted. If you want me to talk to any of them, I'd be happy to."

"I see," she said sadly. "I understand. Thank you for listening."

When she left, I couldn't stop thinking about her unusual situation. How could using a quilt for comfort be so objectionable? Hopefully the holidays would mellow their family drama.

CHAPTER 42

To my total surprise, Holly and another woman walked into the shop!

"What a surprise! Why didn't you send me a text saying you were coming?"

Holly grinned. "Then it wouldn't have been a surprise," she replied. "Lily, this is Mary Beth. We swim at the club every day at the same time."

"Nice to meet you!" I said, reaching for her hand. "Holly has mentioned you."

"When Mary Beth offered to drive out here, I wasn't going to pass up that opportunity. The shop looks great, Lily."

"Thanks! My friend should be here anytime to relieve me for a while, so if you can hang out here for a bit, I'll go with the two of you."

"That would be great, because I'm not familiar with anything out here," Mary Beth said.

"Here is a brochure that tells about all the activities," I explained as I handed them each a brochure.

Holly started showing Mary Beth all the quilts in the

other room as I saw Susan approaching the shop.

"You don't know how much I appreciate this," I said to Susan. "My friends from the city just arrived, so I will leave with them to get some food."

"Sure, take your time," Susan said as she removed her coat. "This will be fun."

I took a minute to explain the checkout process to Susan. She seemed confident and excited about the idea of playing store.

I bundled up in layers and we took off to join the festivities. Our first stop was the Uptown Store so Mary Beth could meet Carrie Mae, who was very busy with customers. We headed to her quilt rack, where I was always amazed at finding something new that had been added to her inventory. I wondered if she had a good stash of quilts upstairs where she lived.

Our next stop was The Cranberry Cottage. I explained to Holly and Mary Beth about the couple who made barn quilts. Holly explained to Mary Beth what they were. We followed the slow line into the shop. I wished I had a line of folks trying to get into my shop! The Cranberry Cottage was in a prime location in the heart of Augusta. As soon as we entered the crowded room, I was attracted to an iron string holder that held scissors. I could just see it sitting on my counter. Holly found some candles, and Mary Beth found a hand-painted sign that said "Merry Christmas."

Close by was Kate's Coffee, where I suggested that we get a snack instead of getting tied up in a busy restaurant. They both agreed, since they had plans for a bigger meal in the evening.

The line was long to get into the Gallery Augusta, but

I assured them that it was well worth the wait. After we had enjoyed that experience, I decided to be on my way to Ebenezer Church so I could get some food to take back to the shop. I hated to leave such good company, but I wished them a merry Christmas and went on my way.

Before I entered the church hall, I went inside Ebenezer Church's sanctuary. I knew there would be ongoing Christmas carols and wanted to experience a part of Christmas that I loved. I made my way to the front pew and joined in as they sang. Visitors came and went as they entered to get warm and enjoy the charming atmosphere. Children were amused, and it was a good reminder of what Christmas is all about. It was the perfect time to give thanks for the many blessings I had received throughout the year. I didn't want to leave.

My stomach was growling as I headed to the church hall, eager for some of their vegetable soup. There was a line, but it was moving quickly. The smell of chili, soup, and wonderful desserts was delightful. I passed tables of cookies prettily wrapped and ready for people to buy and take home. When I spotted some snickerdoodles, I purchased two plates to add to my refreshment table at the shop. Long tables were filled with hungry customers. Children were eating hot dogs covered with chili, while others were playfully circling the tables, laughing and thoroughly enjoying themselves. How fun this must be to look forward to each year!

CHAPTER 43

I reluctantly headed back to my shop, passing many shoppers and vendors. The sign outside the tourism office advertised Santa being available for photos. I couldn't resist peeking in the window, where I saw crying babies and excited children waiting for their turn to sit on Santa's lap. I guessed individuals either loved Santa Claus or were terrified by him.

"Hi, Lily Girl!" a voice called out. It was Kitty. "I see you went to get food as well."

"Yes, and I can't wait to dive in," I said with anticipation. "I can't believe this crowd."

"It gets even heavier toward the late evening. I'm told tickets for the Snow Ball are sold out."

"Really? What is that all about?" I asked.

"It's a dance at the American Legion at nine," she stated. "They'll have a great band, which is usually country western. It's a wonderful way to keep the festivities going while tourists are here."

I nodded. "That's great," I responded as I kept walking. "Have a great rest of the evening!"

I was pleased to get into my warm shop. I saw Susan making a very nice sale to a man who was purchasing a set of antique fireplace tools. They were quite ornate and expensive.

"Thanks for helping, Susan," I said, thankful for her assistance.

"I enjoyed it, but you need to thank this nice man for helping me make a good sale!" she joked.

"This is just what I was looking for," the handsome man said. "Thanks for your help, young lady, and you girls have a merry Christmas!"

I turned to Susan and gave her a high five for the hefty sale.

"That was fun!" Susan gushed. "I only work three days at the library, so if you need someone in a pinch, let me know."

"Oh, that is so good to know!"

The moment Susan left, I dove into my food while it was still hot. Kitty was correct when she told me that the crowd would pick up in the evening. I loved to see the horse and carriage rides turn on the corner as they passed every half hour. My phone rang. It was Marc.

"How's it going?"

"It's been very busy!" I reported with excitement.

"Sorry I didn't get out there like I thought I might. We had a partner meeting and everyone wanted to go to dinner afterwards as part of our Christmas."

"No problem. I hope it was good. I could have used your expertise in handling the customers, however."

He chuckled.

"I saw Lynn at Rigazzi's during lunch today," Marc shared. "Her gallery was staying open later tonight."

"I really miss her. I look forward to catching up with her

soon. Marc, can I get back to you? I have a shop just full of folks, and Holly and her friend should be coming back here soon to say goodbye."

"Great! Call me later if you're aren't too tired."

"Sounds good."

Holly and Mary Beth came in the shop only minutes later.

"Oh, this was so much fun!" Mary Beth exclaimed. "Look at all the stuff Holly bought!"

"Wow," I said as I looked at her armful of goodies. "Are any of those for me?"

"As a matter of fact, yes, so don't ask me to show you anything," she teased. "You never told me about the amazing glass blower that's by Carrie Mae's shop."

"Yeah, we could have stayed to watch him demonstrate all night," Mary Beth added. "That was a great surprise!"

"He's quite famous and very expensive, right?" I asked.

"It didn't stop me," Holly boasted.

"We did meet your friend Judy at the coffee shop," Mary Beth noted. "What a cute place."

"It is, and it's quite lovely on the patio during the summer," I added.

"They had a fire going outside, so there were lots of people sitting on the patio," Mary Beth said.

"Oh, Lily, can I see the fireplace that you got from Marc?" Holly asked.

"Sure, if Mary Beth can keep an eye out here at the counter."

Mary Beth nodded, and Holly and I headed upstairs. Holly was impressed by how I had turned my upper porch into another room upstairs, now that I had heat in the room.

"I think this Marc is a keeper," Holly mentioned. "Try to let yourself trust someone, Lily. Not all relationships are trouble."

"I'll try. Will you be in trouble when you get home?"

"I've had enough wine tonight that I really don't care," she said with a sigh.

I knew that on the long ride back to her home tonight, Holly's lack of caring would disappear.

CHAPTER 44

At nine, I finally brought in the rocker and called it a day. I could hear sounds indicating that the rest of the town was still in a party mood. I looked at my sales stacked high on the spindle and felt that the day had been a success. I went upstairs and poured a glass of wine. I turned on the fireplace to take in the warmth and wondered if Marc would be expecting a call from me. I felt badly about putting him off earlier, so I decided to call him back. The call went to voicemail, which I didn't expect. Feeling exhausted, I fell asleep in front of the fire and didn't wake up until three in the morning. I turned the fireplace off and crawled into bed.

Since it was Sunday, I wanted to attend a church somewhere. I decided it would be Ebenezer United Church of Christ, which was within walking distance, or possibly Christ Lutheran Church, which was larger, but farther away. The more I thought about it, I found it easy to talk myself into waiting until I got back from Wisconsin.

My phone rang, which surprised me. It was Judy.

"You're up, I hope," she said.

"Sure, what's up?"

"I have the day off and wondered if you'd be interested in going to the Daniel Boone Home with me. You said you'd never been there."

"Judy, thank you, but I have so much to do before my trip. I need to be open for a while today."

"I was afraid you would say that, so If I may suggest, you could work in the shop until three, and then we'd be able to take advantage of the candlelight tour there tonight. It's a sight to behold, Lily! Christmas is not to be missed at this historic place."

I paused.

"You won't be sorry!"

"Okay," I said, giving in. "I don't want to go there by myself anyway, so I appreciate your invitation."

"So I'll pick you up at three?"

"Okay!"

I finished getting dressed so I could open the shop for any business that might come my way. After the rocker was on the porch, I checked my phone for any emails. There was a group email with an update from Loretta. She said if Sarah hadn't delivered by Christmas, they would induce labor. The thought of knowing I would likely be there for Sarah's delivery was exciting.

The morning was slow with little traffic. I put some finishing touches on my quilt block so I would be ready for class tomorrow.

"Good morning," a sharply dressed man in a black overcoat said as he entered the shop. "Are you Lily Rosenthal?"

"Yes. How can I help you?"

"I'm Detective Michael Wilbrand," he said, flashing his

badge. "Don't be alarmed. Is anyone else in the shop?"

I shook my head.

"We're looking into a theft reported by Butler Hayes," he began. "I'm told you've been made aware of the missing quilt."

He made it sound like it was a missing person. "Yes, I'm aware," I replied. "I was quite shocked."

"Why were you shocked, Ms. Rosenthal?"

His eyes seemed to stare right through me.

"Well, I got the impression that Butler had pretty good security for his high-end antiques."

"You deal in quilts. Have you experienced any theft recently?"

"Nothing like that! Last month, I had two quilts stolen, but they didn't have much value. I still felt angry, however."

He nodded.

"I understand you were an interested party in buying the quilt. Is that correct?"

I was taken aback by his line of questioning. "Interested, perhaps, but not when he showed me the appraised value. I could never afford anything like that, nor could my clientele afford anything like it."

He nodded like he understood. "Are you in a position to see quilts marketed elsewhere, in case this is advertised for resale?"

"No more than anyone else who browses the internet. My friend said there is a website called stolenquilts.com. I haven't had time to check it."

The detective wrote down the address in a little notepad. "I'll leave you my card in case you learn anything. How long have you known Mr. Hayes?"

"Not long. Carrie Mae from the Uptown Store put him in touch with me. She seemed to think well of him."

"And you? Have you seen each other socially?"

Where was this going?

"That's an interesting question, because I did go to dinner with him one night. It wasn't personal. I mostly picked his brain about the antique business."

"Do you mind showing me the quilts you have for sale?"

"Not at all. They're in here."

CHAPTER 45

"You have an interesting shop, Ms. Rosenthal."

"Thank you. I've been collecting quilts for many years."

"How is business?"

"It's been a pretty good Christmas season."

"I understand that you live upstairs?"

What else did he know about me?

"Yes, it's very convenient."

"Well, I appreciate your time. We must follow up on any lead possible. I see you are about to get a customer, so I'll leave. Call me if you find out any information regarding the quilt."

"Okay, I will." I opened the door to let him out.

I watched him go to his car as two young girls entered the shop. They were so engrossed in conversation that they didn't even acknowledge me when I asked if I could help them. They continued their conversation as they scouted the rooms and went directly out the door again. Did they know where they were or what they had missed? I doubted it. It must have been a very interesting conversation!

I called Carrie Mae as soon as they left. The phone rang and rang. Perhaps she was upstairs. She finally answered as I was about to hang up.

"Uptown Store," she answered.

"It's Lily. Do you have a minute to talk?"

"Sure! I always have time for you."

"Did you have a detective visit you about Butler's quilt?"

"Yes. He was waiting for me when I opened the shop this morning. I figured he'd come to see you next."

"What do you make of it?" Are we suspects?"

She chuckled.

"We're pieces of the puzzle, perhaps. Butler must be desperate to bring the law into this. He thought he could solve this on his own. He doesn't need the money, but he was concerned about where that quilt ended up."

"It sounds like an inside job to me," I stated.

"He claims that his nephew is the only one who has access to his security system."

"How old is he?"

"I think Butler said he's in his twenties. He took him in years ago. I think Butler helps him a lot."

"I hope they figure this out quickly."

I let her get back to her customers, and I approached an older lady who had recently entered the shop. She was carrying a large bag. I suspected that it held a quilt.

"Hello," she said.

"How are you? Can I help you?"

She set her bag on the counter. "Are you the owner?"

"I am. My name is Lily."

She smiled. "Well, as you can see, I'm getting up in age and have some things I would like to sell. I brought this in for you to look at. My neighbor said you sell quilts here for a lot of money."

I had to chuckle. "Well, let's see what you have," I replied as she emptied her bag. She pulled out a sweet quilt which appeared to be from the twenties. It was a Fan pattern made of handkerchiefs. It appeared that it had not been used.

"It's been very dear to me all these years," she noted with pride.

"It's lovely. Did you or someone in your family make it?"

She nodded. "I was a very young lady when I started this. My mother collected handkerchiefs, and when she died, I stared at them, wondering what to do with all of them. I was just going to make a few blocks, but then it grew into a quilt." She chuckled at herself. "I can tell you about each handkerchief. This quilt has been in my hope chest all these years."

"Why wouldn't you want this to stay in your family?"

"My sister has passed on and I never married. I figure if someone bought the quilt, they would love it and take care of it. I don't mind saying that I could use the money!"

My heart sank.

"Did you quilt it?"

She nodded with a smile. "My sister helped, and her stitches are better than mine."

"The stitches are beautiful. It looks like the handkerchiefs are mostly floral designs."

"That's because my mother loved flowers."

"How much are you asking for the quilt?"

She took a deep breath.

"I just can't let it go for under a hundred dollars."

"Oh, my goodness. You can get much more than that.

Are you really sure you should sell it?"

"It's given me a lot of joy through the years, and now it's time for it to move on. Would you be interested in buying it?"

"Sure, but I'll have to pay you at least two hundred dollars. It's worth more than that, but if I decide to resell it, I can't pay much more."

"That's too much," she responded in disbelief.

"It's not too much. It's quite a keepsake. I may have to keep it for myself."

Her face lit up. "That would be grand!" she said with a big grin. "I know you'd take care of it."

"I'll write you a check. I'll need your name and the information about your mother and where she lived."

She was delighted to oblige. "Oh, of course."

We chatted a bit more, and I was so touched by how happy she was to be paid for something that was so dear to her. Part of me felt badly about buying it, but I hated the possibility of someone taking advantage of her.

Before she left, she showed me the corner on the backing that had her initials and those of her sister embroidered on it. She patted the quilt in a silent goodbye. I reassured her that I loved it and would take good care of it.

I closed the shop and looked at the orphan quilt that sat on my counter. It wasn't the kind of quilt I would have ever purchased, but the story and impeccable workmanship were certainly noteworthy. I took it upstairs and placed it on a quilt rack for now. I would have to rethink its future, as it was now my responsibility.

CHAPTER 46

Judy honked her horn and I came out of the house bundled up for the cold evening ahead. The cloudy winter days brought early darkness each evening.

The Daniel Boone Home was located on hundreds of acres in Defiance, near the Femme Osage Creek, a tributary to the Missouri River. Judy briefly told me of the restoration which had been done many years ago and said that the house now belonged to the St. Charles County Park System. It was quite a national tourist spot because Daniel Boone had died there in 1820.

Judy parked the car in the crowded parking lot before we entered the tourist center. From there, I could see thousands of luminaries scattered over the entire village. It was a sight to behold, just as Judy had indicated. We went outdoors to wait for the next tour guide, and I shivered in anticipation.

The house, which had belonged to Daniel's youngest son, Nathan, overlooked the meadow. It was so charming, with each room having a lit fireplace. Seeing the exact bedroom where Daniel Boone passed away was touching.

We left the home and followed the candlelit outdoor path, which took us to each cabin in the village. The cabins, which were restored and relocated here, dated between 1804 and 1865. Their uses ranged from a general store to a one-room schoolhouse.

The most impressive building was a small white chapel. It looked like a miniature of something grander. Its tiny balcony, alter, and pews were perfect for very small weddings. Judy said the venue was very popular. Our tour guide was a young adult who obviously loved his job. He nearly made us forget about the cold as we walked through history.

When Judy couldn't stop blowing her nose and began to complain about numb toes, we decided to call it a night. We came back to the center to enjoy hot chocolate, which was a welcomed treat. When I thought about living so close to such a historic spot, I told myself I'd have to come back more often.

"I can't thank you enough for this invitation, Judy," I said when we got back to my house. "I hope you don't get sick from this outing, because I hope you'll be at class tomorrow."

"I do, too!" she said with another sniffle.

I was glad to get home and turn on the fireplace! I grabbed my robe and huddled on the couch. I dozed off seeing lit luminaries all around me.

The morning came too quickly. I jumped up, knowing I had to get ready for the quilt class. This might be the last class of the year, and I didn't want to miss it. I was feeling proud of my block. I was pleased to get a text from Marc telling me to try to carve out a few minutes for him when I came to Lynn's house the night before we'd leave for Wisconsin.

I texted back that I would try to make it happen. I then

thought of Alex, so I gave him a call.

"It's Monday morning! Are you busy writing?" I asked.

"Oh, for heaven's sake," Alex grumbled. "Why are you up so early?"

"I have quilt class. If you ever want a quilt from me, you're going to have to tolerate my journey. You're alone, aren't you?"

"Funny, Ms. Rosenthal," he mumbled. "You're making a Christmas quilt, right?"

"Yes, you remembered!"

"Is it supposed to be for me for Christmas?" he asked, laughing. "You'd better get with it, Lily Girl."

"Hey! Speaking of Christmas, when can we exchange gifts?"

"I was wondering the same thing. Let's wait until you get back from your trip. You'll have lots to tell me."

"That will work. Did you get a little something for Mindy?"

"I debated about that," he said with a sigh in his voice. "She'll be out of town with her family."

"So, are you falling in love?"

"No! I do like her sense of humor, and I'm totally flattered that she is paying attention to me."

"I think I detected something between the two of you, which was interesting to see."

"Look who's talking. If you don't commit to Mr. Rennels soon, you may lose him."

"Who says I'm not committed? I don't tell you everything!"

I went on to tell him about the visit from the detective regarding Butler's quilt.

"I warned you not to covet that quilt. I'll bet you found some nifty hiding place in that old house of yours," he teased.

"You are so cruel!"

"Have you asked Rosie where the quilt might be? She may have stolen it for you."

"Alex, you are creepy! I'm leaving for my quilt class now."

CHAPTER 47

Almost everyone was there when I entered the library.

"Judy is sick with a cold, so she won't be joining us today," Susan announced.

Everyone agreed that we were relieved that she'd stayed home so we wouldn't get her germs.

"I'm anxious to see all of your blocks," Susan said with excitement. "Let's go around the table and see what you have. Just think, by next Christmas, you'll have a Christmas quilt to display. Heidi, you go first," Susan instructed.

"Well, 'Jingle Bells' was always a happy Christmas song for me growing up," Heidi explained. "I figured that bells wouldn't be very many pieces, so it really didn't take me too long."

We clapped and complimented her block. Now, it was my turn.

"The song 'I'll be Home for Christmas,' always tugs at my heart," I announced with a big smile. "I thought of my siblings, so I decided to do this simple fireplace with their stockings. I have their names embroidered on each of them.

Our names all start with an L, in case you didn't notice."

They chuckled.

"My embroidery is still poor, but I'm getting better."

"It's very nice, Lily, and it's so personal," Susan remarked, and the others agreed.

I was so impressed seeing the others' blocks. Everyone's skill level was so different, but Edna's was perfect. Of course, we were all anxious to hear about the next assignment.

"Okay, ladies," Susan said. "A very important part of the Christmas holiday is food. Think of your favorite treat and try to create it on your block. Do your best."

Everyone seemed to love the idea. The chatter grew louder, and for a Christmas surprise, Susan had a tray of chicken salad sandwiches and Christmas cookies for us. The tray of different cookies was so colorful that I thought it might make a fun Christmas block for next month! I would have to consider the idea. We thanked Susan, and unfortunately, we hadn't thought ahead to get Susan a gift. There was a lot of conversation about the Christmas Walk, however. Almost everyone thought it was the most-attended walk the area had ever enjoyed.

"Did anyone go to the Snow Ball?" I asked.

Everyone shook their head.

"I think if you had a shop or did any vending, you were just anxious to get home," Susan remarked.

"That's because Susan had a taste of retail when she helped me out at my shop when I went to dinner," I revealed. "She did an excellent job."

"I loved it because I could go home and leave all the responsibilities to you," Susan chuckled. "I guess it's like being a grandmother. You get to have fun, but then it's nice when they go home."

Everyone agreed.

I left the class feeling excited. I was truly enjoying the other quilters and loved challenging myself by making each of the Christmas blocks. On the way home, I couldn't resist stopping at The Cranberry Cottage, since its open sign was in the window. Karen was delighted to see me.

"I'm so sorry I couldn't talk to you the night of the walk, but we were so busy," Karen explained.

"No problem." I smiled. "I was lucky enough to get out of the shop for a while. I enjoyed experiencing the walk for the first time."

"Sure!" Karen nodded. "It was our first time having the shop open. It was fantastic."

"I'm leaving town for Christmas, but I'd love to have lunch sometime."

"Yes, I would like that, because I have an idea for you," Karen replied. "I think some of my smaller quilt signs would sell well in your shop."

"Maybe for spring," I offered, remembering how broke I would be through the winter months.

"I know winter can be brutal here for businesses, so I'm glad we have the barn quilts. Lily, I know you're not married, but do you have a significant other?"

I grinned. "Sort of," I said, blushing.

"That's great. If you were available, I have a friend that I thought you would like," she revealed.

"Well, that's sweet, but this isn't a good time. I'm not sure where the relationship is going at this point."

"It's a small town, and it's hard to meet new people, so I thought I would mention it."

"Thanks."

When I left her shop, I thought it was strange that somehow everyone in town seemed to think they knew me. They obviously didn't know about Marc, and that was a good thing.

CHAPTER 48

Time was running out for packing and preparing for my trip. I called Carrie Mae to ask her to keep an eye out for my place while I was gone.

"You know I will," she assured me. "Have you heard from Butler about the quilt, by chance?"

"No, but it's always on my mind."

"I suppose I could give him a call. Since I've known him so long, I think he'd tell me what's going on. I looked at his website recently, and he seems to be dealing in more fine art these days."

"Interesting. Well, if you hear anything, let me know."

I hung up, wondering where on earth the Christmas quilt could be. I went upstairs to begin packing. One suitcase was dedicated to the gifts I was bringing for everyone. I was glad I had given Marc his gift when I'd seen him last. I thought the most exciting part of going to Wisconsin was being able to be there with Sarah when she'd have her baby. I'd bought a few small girly gifts for her that wouldn't take up much room. I wanted to do more to secure the baby girl's future.

It was about ten in the evening when I relaxed in front of the fire. I would be having wine with my family in front of their fireplace very soon. My phone rang, and I saw it was Marc calling.

"Are you getting excited about your trip?" he asked.

"Yes. I just finished packing."

"I just talked to Lynn, and she has no objection with me taking you to dinner the night you get to their place."

"I know, but I think we should make it a quick drink instead of dinner."

"That's fine. I'm just missing you, Lily Girl,"

"I feel the same as I sit here in front of this wonderful fire."

We chatted for a while. I told him about my quilt class and the details of my trip. I was tired, and my voice showed it, so we hung up.

The next morning, I had an extensive list of last-minute things to do. I was hoping for some decent Christmas sales, since it was going to be the last day of Christmas shopping before I left.

While I had my coffee, I cleaned out the refrigerator and watered my little Christmas tree for the last time. It still smelled delightful, and I decided I would keep it indoors as long as I could. I did take time to remove some of the live greenery that I had spread throughout the shop for decoration.

Two ladies came in who were happy and chatty. "I love your rocking chair on the porch," one of them exclaimed. "Is it for sale?"

"No, sorry. I use it for display. It belonged to a dear friend of mine. I do have a smaller, more primitive one for sale in the other room, if you'd like to see it. It's called a fireside rocker."

"Fine. I need one for my guest room when my new grandbaby comes to visit," she explained.

When she saw it, her friend immediately offered her opinion, and they each sat down to try it out. One said you should never buy a rocker without arms when you want to rock a baby. The other one thought it was perfect because it was small and wouldn't take up much room. They seemed to be getting distracted as they conversed, so I left them alone to decide.

Snowshoes came in with a substantially-sized box for me. I told him to just set it on the counter and asked him to hold my mail until I returned. He was happy to give me a card to fill out to put that request into action. Another couple entered the shop, so I needed to concentrate on making a sale.

"Have a wonderful trip and a merry Christmas, Lily," Snowshoes said.

"The same to you," I returned.

The couple said they were shopping for a quilt for their daughter, who was getting her own apartment. The mother said the daughter loved antiques, so I told her she was at the right place. I took them into the quilt room and began showing them quilts. The mother thought some pastel colors would be lovely, but the father thought it would be a mistake with their daughter's tendency to be careless.

I then noticed the two ladies from earlier standing at the counter waiting to pay for something. One had a couple of paperweights she wanted to buy. To my delight, the other purchased the fireside rocker. I worked as fast as I could to finish their sales as I kept an eye out for the prospect of a quilt sale in the other room.

CHAPTER 49

After I helped get the rocker to the front door for the customers, I quickly went in to check on my possible quilt buyer.

"Which one do you like?" the mother asked me. "We can't decide." They each held up a quilt for me to see.

"Both are quite nice and in good condition," I stated. "The Iris appliqué is more delicate and will not hold up as well as the strip-pieced one. They both are so different."

"Honey, you know the iris is her favorite flower," the mother reminded her hubby, using a sweet voice.

"If that one tugs at your heart the most, then go with that one," I suggested.

"I know, but my husband's right! She probably won't take good care of it."

"Oh, for God's sake, Helen, let's get both of them," the husband said impatiently. "It's Christmas, and I don't want to be hearing all the way home about how we bought the wrong one!"

I tried hard not to smile.

The wife was thrilled with the suggestion, so I quickly took both quilts to the counter before they changed their minds! I couldn't wait to do my happy dance! I saw them to the door as Carrie Mae was coming towards the shop.

"Merry Christmas!" she greeted. "I have a little something for you before you leave."

"Oh no, you didn't, Carrie Mae. I don't have anything for you. My mind has been on my siblings, I guess."

Carrie Mae laughed heartily. "Honey, I don't need a thing. You know that," she said jokingly. "I happened to remember how much you admired this when you were in the shop with your friends Holly and Mary Beth."

I tore the white tissue off the box and set the red ribbon aside. "Oh, my goodness. It's the twin doll quilts I admired."

"I bought them from a lady who said she made them for her twin girls when they were little. She said they had no interest in them now, so she decided to sell them, which is rather sad."

I held them up to examine each one. They were adorned with small lazy daisy flowers. One quilt was blue and the other was yellow. I had never seen twin doll quilts before, and they were perfect for my collection. "I can't believe you are willing to give these up! The workmanship for a doll quilt is amazing. They must not have played with these very much. Thank you so much, Carrie Mae!" I gave her a big hug of thanks.

Her eyes got misty. "I saw packages go out the door, my friend. You must be having a very good day so far."

I nodded and smiled. "Yes, I sold a rocker, and then two quilts. They were things from Rosie's inventory."

"Wonderful. You are going to have to start replenishing that inventory one of these days. Well, Betty is minding the store, so I'd better get back."

"Oh! I've been too busy to open the box that Snowshoes brought me this morning," I exclaimed. "It must be a Christmas present, because I'm not expecting any orders."

"Well, see who it's from," Carrie Mae said. "You've got so many male suitors, who knows who it could be from?" She giggled.

"Oh, so many," I joked. "I don't see a return address."

I worked diligently to get inside the box. There was a plastic bag covering something like a quilt. The pattern was folded to the inside.

"It must be a quilt return," Carrie Mae predicted.

"It had better not be," I insisted, taking it out of the bag. "Oh, my goodness! It's the Christmas quilt!" I announced aloud. "What's it doing here?"

"This is out of the ordinary! What's all this about, I wonder?"

"Why is it addressed to me?" The label with my name was typed, not handwritten.

"Would it be from Butler?" Carrie Mae suggested.

"Hardly! It's been missing! There's not even a note inside." I desperately kept looking.

"Well, you'd better call him and ask what's going on," Carrie Mae suggested. "He knows how much you loved it, and it is Christmas!" Carrie Mae laughed.

"It's not funny. I've got to find his card and call him right now. Lock the door, Carrie Mae. We can't let anyone in until I know what's going on."

"That's silly. You go call him while I watch the shop. This is not the time to turn away customers."

I nodded and ran upstairs to retrieve his card.

CHAPTER 50

The phone rang and rang. It started to go to Butler's voicemail when he interrupted with his name.

"Butler speaking," he announced.

"Butler, this is Lily Rosenthal."

"Lily, merry Christmas! Are you still in town?"

"I leave tomorrow," I replied. "I'm calling about the quilt."

He paused. "What do you know?"

I wanted to choose my words carefully. "I received a box today in the mail, and the Christmas quilt was inside."

"What? Who sent it to you?"

He sounded angry.

"I don't know. There wasn't a return address, nor a card inside. Carrie Mae happened to be here with me when I opened it. She thought you had sent it."

"There has to be an explanation," he said sarcastically. "I think you are a sweetheart, but it was not from me."

"This is frightening, Butler. Should I call the detective?"

"No, no. Let me process this. Put it in a very safe place

until I can get it. I'm in Chicago, and I won't be able to leave here until tomorrow. They've been cancelling flights right and left because of the weather."

"I'll give it to Carrie Mae to keep since I'm leaving for Wisconsin tomorrow. Is that okay?"

"Sure, but tell her to put it in her safe, if she can."

"I will. I hope you get to the bottom of this. I don't like being involved."

"I understand, Lily. I'm sorry you were put in this position. I'll call Carrie Mae tomorrow and arrange to pick it up."

"Okay." I hung up and went downstairs to tell Carrie Mae that she was going to oversee the quilt for the time being. She reacted with a nervous laugh but said she would be glad to help.

"Let's wrap it up exactly like it came, in case it will be helpful," Carrie Mae suggested.

A woman came into the shop as we were carefully folding the quilt.

"Thanks for doing this," I said with gratitude. "I'm sorry to ask you to do it, but we've got to get this into Butler's hands as soon as possible."

She nodded. "I'll guard it with my life—whatever's left of it," she teased. "Put this out of your mind and enjoy your trip," Carrie Mae insisted. She then gave me a big hug. Before she left, I thanked her again for the darling doll quilts.

I had to admit, I was very relieved when she left with the quilt. It was such a bizarre occurrence. I took a deep breath and approached the customer who was now looking at my quilts.

"How are you?" I greeted. "If you have any questions regarding the quilts, I'll be glad to help you."

She had a puzzled expression on her face.

"Where do you get all of these quilts?"

"I buy them from various sources."

"Do you sell very many?"

"Not as many as I'd like, of course," I said, smiling.

"How much do you make on each quilt?"

I paused, wanting to be polite. "Sometimes there is more of a profit than others," I said, trying not to lose my patience.

"How long have you been selling quilts?"

"Not long. I've mostly collected them through the years. Why are you so curious about all of this, if I may ask?"

"Well, I'm thinking about opening a quilt shop, but I don't want to waste my time if there's no money in it."

I smiled. "I'm afraid I can't advise you on that. Going into any business is a risk."

"What is your overhead here?"

I took a deep breath. "I think I've shared enough information with you," I responded as politely as I could. "I wish you much success if you proceed. I do have to say, retail gets in your blood, as others warned me about." I ended with a smile as I walked away, but she wasn't done with me.

"You have some serious competition with the Uptown Store," she said, following me into the other room.

"It's been here a long time," I agreed.

"You do have a cute shop. Well, I guess I'd better get going," she said, opening the door.

"Thanks, and please come back!" I said, trying to sound sincere.

She didn't respond.

I couldn't help but wonder what was really on this person's mind. Did I have to worry about additional competition? Was she sent here by someone else to question me? Had I been too rude? Dealing with the public sure was full of surprises.

CHAPTER 51

I got up early to pack my car. I walked through the house to say goodbye, hoping I wasn't going to forget anything. I whispered to Rosie to keep an eye out for me. Before I got in the car, a text came in from Marc.

Are we on for tonight?

I answered,

For a quick drink. I need to turn in early to catch my early flight.

Let me know where and when.

I found myself smiling. I'm sure that if Loretta would have invited him to Wisconsin, he would have come with me.

The sunny, wintry morning made the drive into the

city quite pleasant. When I entered The Hill area and my old neighborhood, I immediately thought of Harry. We hadn't communicated lately, but I had sent him a Christmas card.

I drove by my old apartment before heading to Lynn's house. I saw new curtains in both apartments and unfamiliar cars parked in front where I usually parked. I couldn't help but wonder if Bertie's spirit was still in the house. I decided to make an unexpected stop at Tony's to pick up some bagels. He was surprised to see me. I asked about Harry and he got a sad look on his face.

"You know that he's in a nursing home, don't you?" Tony said. "He has Alzheimer's, they say."

"Oh, I'm so sorry to hear that," I said, feeling almost ill. "The last conversation we had indicated a memory loss, but I had no idea it had escalated that far."

"We miss him, and we also miss you," Tony said with a smile. "Are you happy out there?"

"I am. It's a whole new life, thanks to Rosie."

He smiled and nodded. "Yeah, folks still ask where her shop is located."

I took my bag and left for Lynn's house feeling quite sad. Lynn saw me pull in her driveway and came out to help me with my luggage. As I handed her the bagels, I told her about Harry. She, too, was surprised and saddened.

"From the looks of all of this, you must plan to stay for quite some time," Lynn joked.

"Some things will stay here, but the gifts take up a lot of room. Is Carl here?"

"He'll be back after lunch. He wanted to finish up some things at work. Are you going to have dinner with Marc?"

"No, I told him I'd meet him for a quick drink. I wasn't

sure what our schedule would be."

"We're having your favorite pizza for dinner, so why don't you ask him to join us? Carl would enjoy that."

"Are you sure?"

She nodded.

"I'll see what he says."

It was so good to see Lynn. Our excitement about the trip had us talking at the same time.

"Oh, your tree is magnificent!"

"Thanks. It's great having such tall ceilings. There is a painting in here that I want you to see."

"Lynn, this is charming. Did you paint it? It reminds me of the wine country. I love the church steeples peeking out in the distance."

"It's yours! Merry Christmas!"

"Seriously?"

"I took it from a postcard I'd purchased when I was out in Augusta. I'm so glad you like it."

"I love it! Thank you so much!" I gave her a hug, and my eyes filled with tears.

"Well, that's one gift I don't have to drag to Wisconsin," Lynn joked.

When Carl arrived, he was in a jolly mood, which was a relief. He knew he was scoring big points by joining his wife's family in Green Bay. I went in the den to give Marc a call about joining us for pizza.

"Lily, something's come up and I have to take care of it before I leave town. I'm so sorry. I hope you understand."

"Of course, I understand."

"Hopefully, with my help, this will be resolved quickly. It's for a devoted client of mine. You don't know how much

I wanted to see you. Have a great trip, and call when you get there."

"I will."

"Hugs and kisses, sweetheart," he said, ending the call.

I felt so disappointed. I wished I could have hugged him goodbye.

CHAPTER 52

After we finished our pizza, the three of us sat by the fire with glasses of wine. The conversation was full of laughter. Since Carl was in such a good mood, I decided to share my unusual experience involving the Christmas quilt. As I relayed the circumstances, their faces turned serious.

"You never told me about any of this," Lynn scolded.

"Well, it wasn't such a big deal until the quilt arrived at my doorstep!"

"Lily, if you want my opinion on this, it sounds like someone wants to insert you into the crime."

"It feels that way," I agreed. "I felt bad leaving it in Carrie Mae's hands because I was leaving town."

"I'm glad she was there when you opened the box," Carl said.

"Me, too!" I admitted.

"At least you have a witness," Carl added.

"Don't you think it's strange that there wasn't a note or a return address?"

"Not if the intention was to unload the quilt into your

hands," Carl surmised.

"You can sure get yourself into some strange situations," Lynn said, shaking her head. "I can't wait to hear how this ends up."

"Well, ladies, I'm turning in," Carl announced. "We have to get up at the crack of dawn for that flight."

We all agreed, so I got settled in my cute guest room. It was all done in white. Lynn had such great taste. As I reclined in bed, all I could think about was the Christmas quilt. It was a good question. Why me?

The alarm on my phone went off way too soon. In silence, we all met in the kitchen for our first cup of coffee. Carl was very efficient about getting our car packed quickly. We were fortunate that our flight was scheduled to leave right on time. It had been years since I'd flown, so I was agitated with all the security restrictions.

Once we boarded, I was seated next to a sweet lady who was reading a book. Before I had my seat belt fastened, she was sound asleep. That was helpful, because I hoped to catch a few winks myself. Carl and Lynn were across the aisle. It made me smile when I saw them holding hands. I said a short prayer for a safe trip and to have a merry Christmas with all my family.

Loretta came by herself to meet us at the airport. As I hugged her tightly, I noticed some gray hairs on her that I hadn't noticed before. She wore the same perfume that our mother always wore. It was a welcome-home kind of feeling.

Bill was at work when we arrived at their house, but Sarah was at the front door to meet us. Her protruding tummy was bigger than I'd expected.

"Sarah! You are a sight to behold! You look wonderful! Are you feeling okay?"

"Oh, Aunt Lily, I am so miserable," she said with her hands on her hips. "I'm so glad you're here."

Loretta's house was a huge Victorian home built in 1898. I loved her large wraparound porch with gingerbread trim and the large live wreath she had on the front door. When we walked in the living room, she had a gigantic Christmas tree in the bay window. Since Loretta was the oldest, she had gotten all the family ornaments we grew up with. I couldn't wait to find the ones I had made.

Tomorrow was Christmas Eve, so Loretta filled us in about what to expect. Laurie would be joining us from Fish Creek in the morning and would spend the night with all of us. I felt like a child again with all the excitement.

It was good to see Bill when he finally got home. He, too, was showing his age. It was good to see the loving embrace that he and Loretta shared. The second thing he did was check on his daughter. He quickly asked if she had been having any pains.

"Daddy, this little girl is just as anxious to get out as I am to let her out," Sarah said with a sigh. "Thank goodness they will take her after Christmas if I haven't gone into labor yet."

Loretta fixed her special lasagna using Mother's recipe. She fixed it every Christmas Eve. Bill made wonderful garlic cheese bread to go with it, while Lynn and I whipped up a very large salad. Sarah stayed seated and rolled with laughter watching our antics and listening to all of us. Lynn took photos on her phone every now and then, which would make for fun memories.

CHAPTER 53

When we sat down to dinner at Loretta's long harvest table, we joined hands as Bill prayed, "Come Lord Jesus, be our guest, and let this food to us be blessed. Amen."

Everyone followed by saying, "Amen."

I knew those who were no longer with us were smiling down on us as we dug into a fabulous meal. Sarah's loaded plate looked like she was indeed eating for two. It didn't take my sisters long to start repeating our many family traditions as we laughed between bites.

"No peeking and rewrapping presents tonight like we used to," Loretta joked.

"I can't believe you all used to do that," Carl protested. "Did your parents know?"

"If they did, they pretended otherwise," Laurie said.

"Remember when we discovered that we all got bikes, and then we decided to give them a trial run in the living room before morning?" Lynn asked, laughing.

"I take it that it didn't go well?" Bill joked.

We shook our heads.

"What are you girls going to do while Carl and I go to the game tomorrow?" Bill asked with a grin.

"We're going to have a leisurely breakfast, do a bit of shopping, and have lunch," Loretta shared. "Don't forget that the Christmas Eve church service starts promptly at six thirty. When we get home, we'll have heavy appetizers and save our appetites for Christmas dinner."

"Oh, I hope I can sit through the service," Sarah complained.

"Honey, you decide whether you want to go or not," her mother sympathized. "Those benches can be pretty hard."

"Will you be singing in the choir, Loretta?" I asked, remembering previous years.

"Yes, and Bill has agreed to help usher during that service." Loretta said. "Our church does such a beautiful job of decorating with live greenery. I don't know where they manage to find such a tall tree every year to decorate."

"Okay, it looks like it's time for the cleanup crew to begin," I said as we finished dessert.

Everyone helped and complained about being tired and feeling ready to turn in.

I had just changed into my gown and robe when I heard a soft knock at my door.

"Come in," I answered.

It was Sarah wearing her bathrobe.

"I hope you don't mind if I have a private word with you, Aunt Lily," Sarah said quietly. "With all the commotion, I was worried that I wouldn't get to talk to you about my plans."

"What is it? Sit here by me."

She sat next to me on the bedside. "Mom didn't want me to bring this up while you were here, but I want you to know that I haven't changed my mind about moving to Augusta."

"Now, you know you're welcome, but there are a lot of things to take care of before that can happen," I advised.

"I know. My online classes will continue, but I want to get a job and raise my baby girl outside of Green Bay."

"What you mean is, away from your mother," I interpreted.

She nodded. "When you go home, will you do what you can to check around for a place for me? You're getting to know more people there now."

"I'll ask Carrie Mae, of course. You know I can't possibly take you in at my place, don't you?"

"Oh, I know that. I do want to have a plan before I go."

"Right now, just concentrate on having that baby girl," I said, patting her knee. "She'll be here very shortly, and you need your rest."

She gave me a hug and left the room. It was clear that she had a vision for her future, and it wasn't going to be here in Green Bay. I couldn't keep from thinking about all the problems this would create, but as with many things, there could always be a way.

CHAPTER 54

I woke up to the smell of coffee and the sound of chirping voices coming from the kitchen. Christmas Eve was finally here. I took a moment and thought of Marc at his sister's house.

Carl and Bill were busy planning their day at Lambeau Field. Carl had never been to the historic stadium, so he was extra excited to see the field as well as the Packers. They would be leaving soon so they could get lunch before the game.

"Is Sarah still sleeping?" I asked when I saw she was the only one absent.

"Yes, and I'm pleased," Loretta voiced. "She hasn't been sleeping well lately."

"Did Sarah give you any hints at all about what the baby girl's name will be?"

"Not a clue," Loretta said as she shook her head. "I sure hope she comes up with one before she leaves the hospital."

"I remember her saying that it won't be starting with an L," I added.

Everyone laughed.

Loretta suggested that we go to The Attic, which was a cool bookstore with amazing coffees. She knew the owners and wanted them to meet her siblings. She said Sarah would not be coming with us. I was rather relieved.

"It sounds great, and it'll be nice just being with the sisters," I remarked. "I want to make a call before we go, Loretta. I can't get that darned quilt off my mind."

"I don't blame you," Lynn agreed.

I went back to my bedroom and called Carrie Mae. I knew she'd be closed, so she'd be answering from her apartment.

"Merry Christmas!" I exclaimed.

"Lily, how is Wisconsin? We have snow!"

"It's a white Christmas here as well! I'm concerned about Butler's quilt. Did he show up to get it?"

"No, he didn't come. James, his nephew, came instead," she explained.

"Really?"

"I asked him if Butler was still out of town and he said yes."

"He must really trust that young man."

"I guess. He sure wasn't friendly. As soon as he got the quilt in his hands, he left immediately. He didn't even say thanks. However, I guess if Butler trusts him, so should I!"

"The good news is that it is out of Augusta."

Carrie Mae chuckled and agreed. "Has that baby arrived yet?"

"Not yet. Sarah looks like she could deliver any minute."

"Tell her good luck from me. You never know on your first delivery what you're in for."

I wanted to tell Carrie Mae that Sarah still wanted to move to Augusta, but that conversation would have to be at a different time. I knew the girls were ready to go, so I said goodbye.

We left with beautiful snow flurries coming down. It made the day that much more festive. Loretta told us that the guys would be freezing their tails off sitting on those concrete benches in the stadium today. She said the game would be even more thrilling with the snow coming down and players sliding all over the field. Boys will be boys, I supposed.

The Attic was delightful. The owner's hospitality was over the top, and they gave us complimentary tea and tiny tea sandwiches. Their bookshelves reached to the ceiling. Lynn loved their displays, and I checked out their large section of quilt books. We checked in with Sarah, and she told us she was wrapping some last-minute gifts. We left to go down the street where other cute boutique shops were buzzing with shoppers. Loretta checked the football game score on her phone. To our delight, the Packers were ahead. With that news, she had a feeling that Carl and Bill would come home early to get out of the cold.

By six, everyone gathered in the living room, dressed in our best church finery. Sarah was determined to go, but she said she'd prefer to sit in the back of the church, so she could use the restroom if necessary.

Visiting this gothic-style church was a treat. Loretta was right. The decorations were stunning. Lynn, Carl, Laurie, and I filled up a small church pew. Bill stayed in the back with Sarah. He also ushered. The choir, dressed in red-and-white robes, marched down the aisle as we proudly saw our sister Loretta singing her heart out. Loretta was the most musically inclined in the family. As we sang traditional Christmas hymns, I got chills as I hung on to Laurie's arm. Our mother and dad had to be watching. There is nothing like family.

At the end of the service, we sang "Silent Night." The lights were dimmed. After the choir passed by, everyone lit a small candle as we filed out of church. It was a perfect memory for me and my family.

When we arrived home, I helped myself to wine while some enjoyed eggnog. Sarah and Loretta had prepared trays of lovely finger food, which we eagerly attacked. Bill and Carl were mostly focused on the large tray of fresh shrimp.

"Can we just break one rule this year and open presents tonight instead of waiting until Christmas morning?" Sarah pleaded. "I told Mom that I like sleeping in. It's not like I'm a kid anymore."

"Well, I have to admit that this year is special," Loretta said, giving in. "I say we take a vote."

"Good idea, honey," Bill agreed. "All those in favor of opening gifts tonight, raise your hand."

Everyone cheered and raised their hands.

"I'll hand them out!" Sarah said, jumping to her feet.

CHAPTER 55

Sarah took command of her Santa duty and began giving out the gifts. She was still a child herself, so she showed great excitement. While that was taking place, I bragged to everyone about the painting Lynn had done for me. As we opened our gifts, I realized that she had done one for Loretta and Laurie as well. Loretta's was a field of poppies, which she loved, and Laurie's was a field of wild lavender. Lynn's gift from Carl stole the show. The beautiful sapphire ring was a shock to everyone, including Lynn. It was quite late when we opened the last gift and had our last drink for the evening. Knowing that we didn't have to get up at the crack of dawn was comforting.

Christmas morning was extremely quiet. I slept in, as did the others. Finally, I heard a someone making some noise in the kitchen. I sat up just as my phone rang.

"Merry Christmas!" Marc's sweet voice greeted.

"The same to you!"

"How are things in Green Bay?"

"Pretty good. The Packers won, we have a white

Christmas, and Sarah's holding her own. How is your Christmas going?"

"Good, like yours. We opened gifts last night and my flight leaves here in the late afternoon."

"I wish you were here. Laurie and Loretta are so eager to meet you."

"That would have been fun. Perhaps another time. When you get back to Lynn's house, maybe we can meet up before you go back to Augusta."

"Let's try to do that." After we said goodbye, I realized how much I really did want him to be here. I planned to get dressed and then call Holly and Alex to wish them a merry Christmas. I got my coffee, kissed Loretta on the cheek, and then dialed Holly's number. Oddly, it went to voicemail. Goodness knows what her holiday was like! She always hoped each year for a special gift from Maurice, but it usually didn't happen.

I sighed and called Alex. He answered, sounding happy.

"Was Santa good to you?" he joked.

"He was, and I deserved it because I had been very good. Did you get coal in your stocking?"

"I didn't even get a stocking!" he protested. "I'm going to my aunt's house for dinner, so I'm baking some bread to take with me."

"Oh, I can almost smell it from here!"

"You are so sweet to call. I take it that you are not yet an aunt, or you'd be screaming in my ear."

"That is correct. If not today, then tomorrow. It's pretty exciting!"

"When you get back, you need to come here for dinner to see my tree. I'll try to keep it up for the New Year's Eve party. I hope you and Marc will come."

"I can't speak for Marc, but nothing will stop our tradition of being together."

"Love you, Lily Girl!"

"Love you, too!"

The kitchen noise became louder, so I joined them. Carl and Bill each had on an apron. Laurie was taking their picture. Loretta was giving out jobs in preparation for the early dinner we were going to have that evening.

"I get this same old job every year," Sarah complained as she peeled the sweet potatoes. "Why do we have to have two kinds of potatoes? Why can't we have just mashed potatoes?"

Laurie was filling a large dish of green bean casserole and Lynn was helping Loretta set the dining room table. It was a picture right out of the past, since we were using Mom's Christmas china.

"What the heck?" Sarah shouted, dropping her paring knife noisily on the counter. She looked at the floor in a mixture of confusion and disbelief.

"What?" we asked in unison. "What's wrong?"

Loretta rushed to her side and noticed what had just happened. "It's just your water breaking, Sarah," she consoled. "It's nothing to worry about." Her voice remained calm as we remained silent. "It's okay, I'll take care of it. Take off your apron. This is our sign that it's time to go to the hospital."

Bill wasted no time and flew out the door to get the car ready.

"Why now?" Sarah moaned.

I stood in silence, not knowing what to do to be helpful. Lynn got Sarah's coat to put around her and Carl grabbed her overnight bag, which was sitting by the front door.

Laurie was in shock like me, so we stood next to each other watching the scene unfold.

Sarah started making quiet sounds as she leaned over slightly, bowing to the increasing pains. She followed Loretta out to the car where Bill was waiting, and the three of them headed to the hospital. The rest of us looked at each other, searching for the right words after the door closed. Sarah was like our child as well, and the concern on our faces showed.

Carl took charge in the kitchen as he decided what foods could be put on hold.

"We have got to go!" I said to my sisters. "We have to be there. Get your coats."

"I'll call for a car," Carl suggested. "You can't take Loretta's because I think she took her keys with her to the hospital. I'll stay behind and take care of things here."

Fortunately, the car came quickly as we waited by the door. I think we may have been more nervous than Sarah. We were not going to be left out of this exciting experience!

CHAPTER 56

When we arrived at the hospital, Bill was in the waiting room.

"I had to take a break," he confessed. "I can't stand to see my little girl going through that pain."

"Who is allowed to be with her?" I asked.

"You'll have to check," Bill stated. "I suppose it's up to Sarah. That room is pretty small."

Everyone sat down. Laurie went to the coffee machine to get Bill a cup of coffee.

"None of us have had any babies," I reminded Bill. "Sarah's in good hands, but I want her to know that all of her mommies are here supporting her."

Bill smiled and gave me a hug.

"Okay, folks," Lynn called out. "I just saw Loretta. Sarah's still got a ways to go. She said she just wants her mom, which is understandable. She's very touched that we're all here."

"She's in God's capable hands, and baby girl will be here before we know it," I said.

"I feel like my baby girl is having a baby girl," Bill

reflected softly. "It seems like just yesterday that she was born. Now here she is, no husband, no degree, and no job. How is she going to be a mother?"

"She'll be fine," I said, patting his hand. "She will be a wonderful mother, and she'll take the other steps one at a time."

"I agree," Laurie chimed in.

"You know, Carl and I kept putting off having a child," Lynn confessed. "There are times that I regret it when I think about how important siblings are."

We smiled at her. Then we fell silent. I found myself thinking about things I would have done differently in my life. I didn't feel badly about not becoming a mother yet. Perhaps if I had met the right person, I would feel differently.

Hours passed before Loretta reported that they may have to do a caesarian section if she didn't deliver soon. We tried to talk about other things with Bill to keep him relaxed.

It was six thirty when a nurse came into the room and announced that a baby girl had arrived and that everyone was doing well. We cheered and hugged one another. The nurse said that as soon as the baby was cleaned up, we would be able to see her.

Naturally, Bill went in first to see Sarah. After five minutes, the rest of us entered her room.

"I did it!" Sarah exclaimed triumphantly. "She weighed seven pounds and thirteen ounces. You should see her rosy cheeks!"

"I'm so proud of you, honey," Bill said, kissing his daughter's cheek.

Seeing the happiness that the next generation brought was so special. I was so glad that I did not miss this.

Minutes later, we were told to go to the window, where the baby girl was getting dressed for the first time. The tiny red-faced baby was screaming her lungs out. We stood in awe, and I found myself choking back tears of joy. Just hours ago, this tiny creature was inside Sarah. Birth is such a miracle. I thanked God for this blessing!

Lynn had been reporting to Carl on the phone. She took a photo through the glass. He told her he'd have dinner ready for us when we got home.

We waited around until the baby was brought back to Sarah's room. When Sarah finally held the wrapped bundle in her arms, her face was aglow with pride.

"I feel like I'm the only woman in the world to ever have had a baby." She smiled. "I now know her name. I want you all to meet Lucille Rose."

We cheered. It sounded perfect!

"But it's a name that starts with an L," Loretta corrected. "I thought that was a big no-no."

Sarah chuckled.

"I've always loved the name Lucy, and she definitely has rosy cheeks," Sarah explained. "I think it suits her."

We each got a chance to hold her. I couldn't believe such a tiny person could exist! I was scared to death I'd break the little thing.

The nurse came into the room and encouraged Sarah to get some rest.

"Let's go home and eat some of that delicious dinner," Bill suggested. "We just got the best Christmas present!"

As we left the hospital, Lynn called Carl to tell him that we were on our way home. I think Sarah was happy to see us leave so she could get some rest.

Carl greeted each of us with a hug of congratulations. Lynn was amazed that Carl had managed to pull the dinner together.

Our first task was get a glass of wine and toast Sarah and Lucille Rose. Everyone talked at once trying to describe to Carl what he had missed. When we sat down to amazing food, we thanked the Almighty for the generous gift of Lucille Rose.

After we finally cleared the table, exhaustion kicked in for all of us. It had been such an emotional day of waiting and then finally getting to celebrate.

CHAPTER 57

The next morning, Carl must have been inspired by his great cooking skills, because he and Lynn were making pancakes for everyone.

"Sarah had a good night's rest," Loretta reported. "As soon as we finish breakfast, I'm going to head to the hospital."

Bill suggested that everyone else go after lunch and then he'd drop us off at the airport. I agreed, but I also wanted to call Marc and Holly before I left.

Marc's call went to voicemail, so I refilled my coffee cup and went to my room to call Holly.

"Merry Christmas, girlfriend," I greeted.

"Thanks. The same to you," she responded. "Are you having an enjoyable time?"

"Oh yes. I have a new grandniece named Lucille Rose. Isn't that special?"

"Yes! I love the name. Congratulations!"

"We're going to see her before we fly home. How was your Christmas?"

"Pretty much like every other year," she reported. "My

205

job today is to take down the stupid tree first thing this morning, so that's what I'm doing."

"Already? Why can't Maurice be happy for five minutes? Did you get a present?"

"My present was a reminder that I have access to his credit card, so I shouldn't need anything."

"How awful. He said that last year, didn't he?"

"I know I shouldn't expect anything. Thanks so much for the radio. I love it. By the way, any word on the Christmas quilt?"

I started from the beginning and told her the chain of events. She almost choked when I told her about it showing up at my place.

"You should have kept it," she joked.

"You can't be serious. I will never own a quilt that expensive."

"That's why I'm making the suggestion," she snickered.

"Let's try to do lunch soon. I have to go now to get ready for the hospital."

"I'll try," she said in a hopeless tone.

We hung up. I checked on the rest of the gang. Everyone was getting ready to go.

We finally got everything into Bill's car and headed to the hospital. When we arrived, I went to the hospital gift shop to get Sarah some flowers. Laurie had some essential oils with her that she thought Sarah could use.

When we walked in Sarah's room, she was like a new person. She had on fresh makeup and a cute polka-dot robe. In a tiny crib by her bedside was Lucille Rose. She'd just had a bottle from her grandmother and was sound asleep. Sarah bragged about the baby's appetite and how she couldn't wait to take her home.

When it was time for all of us to say goodbye, I suddenly became emotional. It had been such a special visit. Sarah squeezed my hand and whispered that I shouldn't forget her desire to move to Augusta. Seeing my sister with her happy family was so rewarding.

Lynn announced that she hoped she could host next year's Christmas, but we all knew that time would tell. If Sarah did make her way to Augusta, I knew there would be many visits from Loretta, Bill, and Laurie.

Everyone was solemn as we waited at the airport. Our emotions were settling in as we remembered each moment of a very special Christmas.

CHAPTER 58

Our flight gave us a chance to doze off a bit. When we got back to Lynn's house, I called Marc and we agreed to go out for drinks later in the evening. I was happy that we could make a plan to meet since I had to leave early the next morning.

Marc enveloped me in a big hug when I opened the door. He had a brief conversation with Carl and Lynn before we left. We ended up at a small neighborhood bar that Marc liked. It was quiet, so we could talk. I immediately showed Marc pictures of Lucille Rose on my phone. He loved them and then asked what I thought about Sarah's desire to move to Augusta.

"Nothing will happen for a while, I assure you."

"How do you really feel about having that kind of responsibility?"

"I made it clear that she couldn't move in with me. We talked about the need for her to have a plan."

"You say that, but you know you'd be thrilled to have access to Sarah and the baby," Marc teased.

"No question! I could have stolen that baby right out of the crib!"

He laughed. "Well, I'm glad you didn't do that. Do you ever regret not having any children?"

"I'll answer that if you will," I challenged.

"My answer is that I have no regrets," he stated firmly.

"I'm pretty sure that I feel the same way, which almost makes me feel guilty at times."

"I know so many unhappily married men. I really feel for their kids." Mark paused as if in deep thought and then shared, "I always say I'm too busy, but I think I'd like to help some of the fatherless boys that we see at the Boys and Girl's Club. I'm on their board, which allows me to help in some ways. There are so many children in stressful family situations out there."

"I'm glad to hear you say that you'd like to help, and I encourage you to do so. I feel that way about adoption. Why are so many children brought into this world with no place to go?"

We continued talking about a variety of serious issues that we had never discussed before. The more I heard from him, the more I was convinced that Marc was very happy with the way things were.

It was nearly midnight when Marc took me back to Lynn's house. We shared a passionate embrace but were careful not to share how we felt about one another.

Lynn and Carl had retired for the evening when I entered the house. I felt that the holiday was complete now that I'd spent some time with Marc. I discovered that I really enjoyed having someone care about me. It made me feel special in a way I hadn't experienced previously.

I slept later than expected. By the time I got to the kitchen, Carl had left for work and Lynn was on the computer while having her morning coffee. She closed her laptop and wanted a report on my date with Marc.

"It was great bringing him up to date about Sarah and the baby. We have become very close."

"Close like you are with Alex?"

I chuckled. "Yes, but more than that, of course. Alex wants to exchange gifts before I go home, so I guess I'll see if we can have lunch."

"Do you have his gift?"

I nodded.

"What is it?"

"It's a vintage Batman watch."

"You've got to be kidding me!" Lynn gasped.

"Don't laugh. He will absolutely love it. He has been a huge Batman collector since his boyhood. When I saw it in Carrie Mae's shop months ago, I thought of him. It wasn't cheap."

Lynn shook her head in disbelief.

I enjoyed a bagel before texting Alex. It was nice to visit with Lynn. I reminded her that Sarah's intent was to get to Augusta.

"Part of me hopes she does," Lynn admitted. "Loretta is going to raise that baby if Sarah doesn't leave their house."

I nodded in agreement. "I know, but finding her a place to live won't be easy, much less finding a job for her."

"And who would babysit that baby?" Lynn teased.

"Not me. I don't know anything about babies, and I have a business to run."

Lynn laughed. "Exactly. That's why Bill and Loretta will

do everything they can to keep her in Green Bay."

Alex finally responded to my text.

> How about lunch at Charlie Gitto's? Let's go, Big A!

> Can I wear jeans?

> I'm wearing jeans!

> Okay, see you there at noon.

"Can I wear jeans to Charlie Gitto's?" I asked Lynn.

"Of course. Is he treating?"

"We usually go Dutch."

Lynn gave a sigh. "I love their food. Carl and I went there years ago on our anniversary."

"It was great to see you and Carl so close at Christmas."

She smiled. "I hope he's not pretending. I still feel like he has something else on his mind. I try not to think about it."

CHAPTER 59

Alex was waiting at a table when I arrived for lunch.

"I see they let you in the door," Alex teased, looking at my jeans.

"Merry Christmas to you, too!" I joked.

"Thanks for taking some time," Alex began. "I'm dying to hear how Carl and Lynn did on the trip. Oh yeah, then there's this grandniece I need to know more about. I also want to know if you saw Marc while you were in town."

I didn't know where to start, but Alex was like one of the girls when it came to talking about the latest gossip. I filled him in on lots of details. When it came to mentioning Marc, I didn't share a lot of information.

The toasted ravioli was the restaurant's signature dish. Both of us decided to order it. We continued our conversation as the food arrived. It was an hour later when we thought about our gifts. Alex opened my gift to him first. His eyes widened with surprise when he saw the Batman watch.

"No way, Lily Girl!" he gasped. "Where on earth did you find this? I've been looking for one of these!"

"I'm glad you like it. I bought it from Carrie Mae last fall. She said it actually works."

"I guess you noticed I didn't walk in with a package for you," Alex commented.

"I did! What's up with that?" I joked.

"I have a tell for you instead of a show. I never know what to get you. I am picking up the lunch tab today, however."

"So, do tell. And since you're paying, I'll have that chocolate delight on the dessert menu."

He laughed and called for the waiter, and we ordered scrumptious desserts.

"On a serious note, Lily, you and I have talked about your doing some freelance writing to supplement your income as well as to complete something on your bucket list. I have some really good news for you."

I was eager to hear more.

"I've talked about you at the magazine. I have a job for you if you want it."

"I have a job!"

"I know, but that job is really something that Rosie had planned for you. As long as I've known you, you've wanted to move away from editing and write a book."

"Perhaps that's true, but things have changed. I have a mortgage to pay. Besides, I'm not unhappy."

"Just listen. My boss, Robert Benton, knows what a good editor you are. He's looking to add a lifestyle column. You can pick the topic. You have amazing things to write about. You could cover quilts, antiques, and what it's like to live in a small community. He wants a charming title, which I'm sure you could create. It would be great nationwide advertising for your shop, which you could use."

I stared at him. "I can't believe you did that for me."

"You would do it for me. Give it a try."

I nodded in surprise and disbelief. "It does sound a bit surreal, but I'd be foolish not to try."

"That's my girl!" Alex cheered. "He wants you to email something to him that would be of interest to you. The two of you can meet to finalize the details. He's pretty committed to this idea. He was grateful that I mentioned your name."

"Thanks so much, Alex. This is a good time of year to have the quiet time to write. I hope I won't disappoint you."

"You are destined to be more than a shop owner."

"Hey!" I gave Alex a warning look. I then smiled, giving him a wink.

Our dessert was fantastic, and it felt like a good way to celebrate the prospect of having my own column. It was a long lunch, but one that held the possibility of changing the direction of my life.

I left Alex with a lot on my mind as I made the trip home to Augusta. The forecast called for snow flurries and I was not disappointed as I made my way home. When I finally pulled in front of my house and saw the Lily Girl's Quilts and Antiques sign, I felt grateful and happy. It made me think of Nick for a second. It had been kind of him to make the sign for me. I looked over at Doc's little brick house. Not surprisingly, the light was on, seemingly welcoming me home. Since I had no real explanation for the occurrence, I decided it was meant as a smile from Rosie or the mysterious doctor who once practiced there.

CHAPTER 60

After everything was inside the house, I poured myself a glass of wine and lit the fireplace. It made me think of Marc. I felt so blessed to have enjoyed a wonderful Christmas with my family. I was grateful to have a friend like Alex who "got me" when it came to my dreams. Like so many things that happened in my life, this writing opportunity couldn't have come at a better time.

I skipped dinner. After I got into my gown and robe, I looked out the window and saw accumulating snow covering Augusta like a blanket. I knew it would mean closing the shop tomorrow, but it was winter, and it was beautiful. I would use the time to think about my first column. I had so many ideas. It was great that I had the freedom to write what I wished to write. As I drifted off from exhaustion, lots of ideas danced in my head.

At seven the next morning, I awoke to more snow piled on my windowsill. I drifted back to sleep. Around nine, the phone on my bedside table rang. I opened my eyes just enough to see that it was Carrie Mae.

"Good morning," I said, my voice sounding groggy.

"Did I wake you? I'm sorry. You probably got in late."

"No, I got here before the big snow came, but since I won't be opening, I decided to sleep in. Did you have a nice Christmas?"

"Splendid! How about you?"

I yawned before answering. "Little Lucille Rose, my grandniece, was the best Christmas present ever!"

"Oh, I love that name! Is everyone doing well?"

"Yes. What's on your mind this morning?"

"I had an interesting visitor yesterday. If you had been in town, he would have visited you as well."

"Who?"

"The detective who is investigating the missing quilt."

"Why?"

"That's what I wondered. He had no idea that you had received the quilt, nor did he know that James came to pick it up after that."

"That's odd."

"Maybe since Butler's out of town, James just decided not to contact the detective until Butler got home. The detective didn't take kindly to not knowing about the update."

"I'm sure. Do you know when Butler plans to come home?"

"No, and I really don't want to know. I don't like being involved in this at all. I just want to mind my own business."

"Same here. Why wouldn't James or Butler call the detective right away?"

"I have no idea. By the way, you missed another bit of news while you were gone."

"No, what?"

"Nick Conrey passed away."

"Carrie Mae! I can't believe it. Was he in the hospital?"

"I heard that they found him in his country house. Vic came to tell me and said to let you know. Vic said that until he was told otherwise, he would continue to sell Nick's work that he has in the gallery."

"What a mixed-up guy Nick was," I sighed. "He seemed to almost want to self-destruct after he got cancer."

"I haven't gotten word of any kind of memorial service, but I'm sure you and I will both hear about it, if there is one. I'm so sorry about all this shocking news."

"Christmas cheer can't last forever," I said as we hung up.

As I took a shower, I reflected on the sadness of my relationship with Nick. He could be so kind. He seemed to take joy in making the shop sign for me. But he seemed to have a mean streak, which became evident the night of our accident.

When I got my coffee, I once again revisited what Carrie Mae had said about the visit from the detective. What was going on?

As it continued to snow, I remembered I still had to complete my next quilt block. I decided that depicting a plate of cookies was my best option. That wouldn't take much fabric or time. Before I got started, I spread everything out on the table. Having done that, I realized that my heart wasn't in this task right now. I decided instead to contact my sisters to tell them I had arrived home safely.

When I turned on the computer, I discovered that Loretta had beaten me to the punch by showing a darling photo of her new granddaughter. She said everyone was doing well. I hoped that Sarah would take a photo of Lucille Rose wrapped in the antique crib quilt I had given her.

I let everyone know that I had arrived home. I decided to wait to tell them about Alex's news until another time. I did tell them about the snowfall and that the shop was closed for the day. I mentioned to them that it would be a good day to complete block three of my Christmas quilt, which would feature a plate of Christmas cookies.

CHAPTER 61

I looked and looked for my other two quilt blocks that were kept in a bag with the next month's kit. I was certain I'd brought it home, but I finally called Susan to make sure. The phone rang and rang, which meant the library had closed today because of the weather.

I went on to do other things, like find a place to hang the lovely picture Lynn had painted for me. It reminded me of Nick once again. What would happen to all his artwork?

I went upstairs, and to my surprise, the quilt blocks were on my bed! It was surreal that a spirit could do things like that. Was Rosie trying to be helpful or annoying?

"Rosie, don't scare me," I said aloud. "Thank you for finding them."

I rummaged through the kit to see what it had that I could use. I wished for a nearby quilt or fabric shop. I needed a nice light brown fabric for the cookie base. It would be fun to embellish or decorate each cookie. I went to my laptop and pulled up some fabric sites. I spent quite a while looking at polka-dot fabric and red-and-white prints. Picking out a brown solid fabric was boring. After browsing online for quite a while, I realized that I had spent a fair amount of time without making any true headway on the project.

Perhaps I should spend the rest of the evening thinking about my first column for *Spirit* magazine. I carried a glass of wine and a few snacks in front of the fire as I gave the article more thought. My first effort had to be impressive and attract a large audience. I thought about myself and considered what I knew best. What I had learned as a quilt collector could apply to nearly anything anyone would be interested in. The title "How to be a Good Collector" seemed perfect. So many pieces of advice popped in my head, but "condition, condition, condition" was always my radar signal when making a quilt purchase. Different people could have a variety of tastes, but if the purchased piece was in good condition, it would always have some value.

Suddenly, my pen was flying, filling up page after page! Surely this was too much information, but I'd always told my writers at the publishing house to get everything out before editing anything. I reminded them to rewrite and rewrite until they achieved their best version. It was now time to take some of my own advice.

I began to ponder possibilities for the title of the column. Mr. Benton may already have a title, but I felt I should be thinking about one, just in case. I wanted to use my name in the title. Perhaps "A Word from Lily Girl," "Lily's Letters," or "Leave it to Lily" would work. Alex was so good at coming up with names for things. He was the one who came up with the name for my shop.

It was getting very late, but at least my snow day had accomplished something!

CHAPTER 62

The next morning, I peeked out the window and saw Tom and Kip clearing snow. I hoped that they would clean my car off as well. I got dressed quickly so I could pay them when they were done.

Despite the weather, I made up my mind to open the shop. I made a big sign that indicated I was having a sale and stuck it in the window. Although I didn't know if my approach would work, I was willing to try.

I opened the door to let the guys enter when they knocked on the door. They were a mess. Wet snow fell to the floor, yet I was so grateful that they had showed up to help me.

"Did the little Christmas tree hold up?" Tom asked.

"It did. I watered it well before I left town. It still smells wonderful, so it's staying right here for now."

They chuckled.

"Thanks so much!" Tom said when I handed them cash.

"Now don't forget, when spring arrives, I hope you guys save time to tear down that mess that resembles a barn and shed."

They nodded and laughed.

"You bet!" Kip said. "We'd be happy to."

"Say, we were wondering why you sometimes keep a light on in that little brick building," Tom mentioned.

"It's not my doing," I explained. "It just goes on and off from time to time."

"See, Tom, I told you the place is haunted," Kip teased, making a face at Tom.

"I love that little building, so it stays," I stated, smiling.

As they left, I realized that they would probably tell the whole town that this place was haunted. I looked up and down the street and saw that there wasn't a car in sight. As I went to get some coffee and nibble on a bagel, the phone rang.

"It's Butler."

"Oh, hello."

"Did you have a nice Christmas? If I remember, you were going away."

"Yes, I did. Thanks for asking. How about you?"

"Well, it wasn't what I'd had in mind. It was hard getting a flight back home."

"That had to be frustrating."

"Well, it's sunny today," he stated. "I just tried to call Carrie Mae to tell her that I'll finally get out to pick up the quilt. I haven't been able to get her to answer. Is she okay? I realize that she may be closed due to the weather."

"Did you say you were coming out to get the quilt?" I felt confused.

"Yeah, I know it has taken me a while, but it's the first chance I've had to do it."

"Butler, James came out and got the quilt. He told Carrie Mae that you were detained by the weather."

"I see," he said quietly.

"Didn't he say anything?"

"James isn't here. He, too, hasn't been answering his phone."

"Well, surely the quilt is with him, so don't worry," I assured him.

"I haven't looked to see if it is here. You're probably right. I just wonder where he is."

"Carrie Mae will feel just awful if she wasn't supposed to give it to him. She even thought afterwards that she wished she'd made him sign something."

"Please don't upset her. I'm sure there's an explanation."

"I hate to ask, but would you let us know if you find the quilt?" I requested.

"I can do that," he agreed. "I know how fond you are of it."

"Thanks," I said as we hung up.

I had to sit down to absorb what Butler had just said. Where was James? Did he have the quilt? Where was Carrie Mae? Why wasn't she answering? I decided to call her myself.

"Uptown Store," Carrie Mae answered after several rings.

"Did I wake you? This is Lily."

"No, I slept in because I probably won't open again today," she explained. "I still have the sniffles."

"I decided to open for a bit today. Can I bring you some soup for lunch or get you anything?"

"You don't have to do that, but it does sound wonderful. I doubt that you're going to have any customers," she warned.

"You're probably right. I'll see you at lunch."

CHAPTER 63

I was poised to call Kate's Coffee to order soup and sandwiches for Carrie Mae and me. I was so eager to tell her about Butler's call. Just then, Snowshoes came in from the chilly air and stomped his shoes on the doormat. "I can't believe you're open, Lily," he said, handing me some mail. "It sure feels good in here. Did you have a good trip?"

"Yes, I did. How was your Christmas?"

"It was very nice. My son came in from California."

"That's wonderful!"

"I guess you've heard by now that they found Nick Conrey dead at his place."

"I did hear about that. It's so sad when someone passes during the holidays."

"I guess his paintings will be worth a tad more now, they say."

"Really?"

"Well, we'll see. I guess I'd better get on my way. Thanks for clearing your sidewalks."

"You bet! Be careful out there. I hope you get a chance

to warm up occasionally." Again, I was thankful for the helpfulness of Kip and Tom.

He nodded as he left.

When I called the coffee shop to place my order, Judy answered the phone.

"Welcome home," she greeted. "How was Wisconsin?"

"It was great! I have a new grandniece and the Packers won the football game. How was your Christmas?"

"The flu hit our house, so that took a bite out of the holidays."

"It sure is going around. I'm calling to order two of your chicken noodle soups to go and two of your turkey sandwiches on that good cranberry bread that you have."

"You've got it. I'll see you in a bit," Judy replied.

The day looked like a loss, so I removed the sale sign from the window. I planned to work on my quilt block after lunch. The morning had gotten away from me entirely, and soon it was time to pick up lunch.

"I heard you were back!" Randal said as I entered his shop. "I heard you went up north because it wasn't cold enough for you here!"

We chuckled.

"By the way, I put a couple of brownies in for you that just came out of the oven."

"How sweet. Thank you. I'm on my way to share lunch with Carrie Mae."

"You tell her hello from all of us," he instructed.

I nodded. I then called Carrie Mae to tell her I was on my way. I hoped that she would unlock the door so I wouldn't have to be out in the cold very long. When I arrived, she was wearing a fluffy lavender-flowered robe.

"This is so nice of you, Lily," she said, smiling. "It smells divine! Excuse my appearance, but it's too cold to get dressed today, don't you think?"

I nodded in agreement.

When we got settled at her little table, the first thing she wanted to know was how Sarah and Lucille Rose were doing. I informed her that Sarah hadn't given up on the idea about moving to Augusta.

"I think she experienced the friendliness that so many folks encounter in this sleepy little town. Also, she wants to be on her own. She loves being by you because you won't keep trying to influence her life. If she stays under her parents' roof, she won't be free to raise that baby the way she wants."

"That's all well and good, but there are still obstacles she'll have to face. Number one, she'll need a place to live. I told her that it would not suit to have her live with me. I am willing to keep an eye out to see if something suitable opens up for her, however."

"I'll keep that in mind," Carrie Mae offered. "This is so delicious, Lily. What a grand idea you had."

"Well, I had another purpose in wanting to visit with you today."

She looked at me with curiosity.

"I had a phone call from Butler. You're not going to like what I'm about to tell you."

"Now what?"

I started from the beginning. As I spoke, her expression changed from interest to shock. There was no way to soften the story. She shook her head when I told her about James not responding to Butler's phone calls.

"You know, there was something about that young man's attitude when he was here. Butler is always so friendly. I just assumed that his nephew would be the same way, but he wasn't. I should have asked more questions."

"Don't feel bad. Butler always spoke well of him, so why would we suspect him of any foul play?"

"What can we do to help?" she asked, getting up and pacing a bit.

"Nothing! I told him to keep us posted."

"Did you ask him why he hadn't told the detective that the quilt had been found?"

"No, but I should have."

"Well, if he doesn't, the detective is going to think that Butler will try to get insurance money for the quilt and still keep it. That's not a new trick."

"I didn't think of that."

"There's something fishy going on here," Carrie Mae said with a sigh.

CHAPTER 64

I stayed at Carrie Mae's about two hours before coming home. As I was removing my coat, Alex called.

"Hey, are you all settled in?" Alex asked.

"I am. It's good to be home, but my shop is closed again because of the weather."

"Enjoy the free time. Don't you have something to write?"

"I do, I do."

"Are you still coming to my New Year's Eve party? You told Marc, didn't you?"

"I'm coming. I'm certain of that. Marc and I never firmed anything up for that night."

"You can spend the night here if you want. That way, you don't have to drive home so late at night. We have to keep the tradition, you know."

"I'll do that. What can I bring?"

"Wine, baby, wine!" he said, laughing.

"I can do that."

"We should have a nice crowd. Mindy invited a few of

her friends as well."

"How's it going with her, by the way?"

"Cool. She is a bit pushy, if you know what I mean."

I had to giggle. "As are most women, you mean?"

"Yes, exactly."

"By pushy, you mean that she wants a commitment?"

"You got it, Lily Girl. Let me know if Marc is coming, okay?"

"Will do."

Having New Year's Eve to look forward to brightened my mood. I was about to call Marc to remind him about the party when Sarah called.

"Hey, what's up?" I asked her.

"Oh, I just called to vent."

"Okay, but how's Lucille Rose?"

"That's what I called to vent about. She won't stop crying. I really don't think she likes me."

"Oh, Sarah, you're her mommy and she loves you. Her grandmother is a nurse, so what does she have to say?"

"She says it's probably a tummyache. When Mom or Dad pick her up, she stops crying. Have you talked to Carrie Mae about finding me a place?"

"I have, actually, but right now, neither one of us know of anything. I love the picture your mom sent of Lucy. She has really changed since I saw her. I really think she looks like you."

"She looks fat like her mom. If I don't shed some of this weight soon, I'm going to die!"

"The weight will go away," I assured her. "You didn't gain very much weight to begin with. It's none of my business, Sarah, but did you notify Lucy's father when she was born?"

"No. He likely knows, and I haven't heard a peep from him, which is just fine with me."

"You and Lucy have an exciting life ahead of you. You have a lot of support from those who love you."

"Don't make me cry again. It's all I do these days. What are you doing on New Year's Eve?"

"I will be at Alex's party, where I have spent the last umpteen New Year's Eves. I'm going to ask Marc if he wants to go."

"I really like Marc. Maybe he can fix me up one day when I lose this weight."

I chuckled at the thought. "You are getting ahead of yourself."

"I'll be watching the ball drop in New York, I suppose. Mom and Dad will be asleep by ten."

"Sounds pretty good to me. You take care and I'll keep you posted. Give Lucy a kiss for me."

With all I had on my mind, getting Lucy and Sarah to Augusta was the last thing I wanted to think about. Her immaturity was evident in this phone call. I wondered how much was due to postpartum mood swings. Hopefully, time would help.

CHAPTER 65

New Year's Eve day was sunny and bright, and I found myself greatly looking forward to Alex's party.

I once again tried baiting customers with my big sale sign in the window, but no one seemed to notice.

It had been several days since I'd heard from Butler. If James had deserted him, he must be feeling terrible. I still couldn't understand why the quilt was sent to me. I kept telling myself to move on from this situation, but I did want to keep Butler as a professional acquaintance.

A young couple entered the shop. They were linked arm in arm and looked very happy.

"Good morning!" Their greeting was enthusiastic.

"How are you today?" I responded. "I'm Lily, and I'll be happy to help you."

"Thanks, Lily," the young man said. "We're visiting for the weekend. It's our honeymoon."

"Oh, congratulations! This is a very romantic area with lots of wineries. Where are you staying?"

"The Red Brick Inn, which is marvelous," the woman

raved.

"Yes, it is. I hope you enjoy Augusta."

"I see you have quilts," the woman said. She had spotted the red-and-white Jacob's Ladder quilt. "I love red and white, don't you, honey?"

"Yeah, sure," he answered. "My grandmother made quilts."

"Do you have some of them?" the bride asked her new husband.

"One or two," he answered.

"Oh, look at all the red-and-white quilts, honey," she said, pulling him closer.

"So, Lily, I take it that you prefer red and white?" he asked, smiling.

"Yes, I collected them until I opened this shop," I explained.

"I think the one with stars would go great in our bedroom, don't you?" she asked her husband. "I just love stars."

"How much is it?" the husband asked.

She showed him the tag and he looked a bit taken aback.

"I'd be happy to give you a discount since it is your honeymoon," I offered.

"Really?" the bride gushed, smiling broadly.

I looked at the tag and told them I could knock a hundred dollars off the six-hundred-dollar price. The bride jumped up and down with joy. The groom looked rather helpless.

"Okay, okay," he said, giving in. "We did get money from the wedding. I think you just made yourself a sale."

"When the woman of the house is happy, everyone is happy," I assured him.

"Oh, thank you, sweetheart," she exclaimed as she kissed him on the cheek.

After they left, I had to chuckle at the thought of that being the first of many requests that poor man would have to give into. I was pleased knowing that the quilt would be in a happy home.

In my spare time, I read and reread the first effort I had written for my new column. It would be a while before any of these efforts would produce a paycheck, but it was a start.

The time had gotten away from me. It was time to get ready for the party. I wondered what Marc would be wearing. I chose a black turtleneck with black pants. I had a leopard vest that dressed it up a bit. I looked decent and thought Marc would like it.

I wanted to get on my way before it got any later. As I drove through town, I wondered what most people did out here in Augusta on New Year's Eve. The wineries would probably be busy. I'd seen several advertisements for special dinners. Thank goodness I wouldn't be driving on these roads later in the evening. The drive brought back thoughts of Nick as I drove around each curve.

CHAPTER 66

It was always a challenge to find a place to park in Alex's neighborhood. I situated the bottles of wine in a carrier and made my way down the block. As I entered Alex's apartment, he shouted "Happy New Year" to me above the sound of the loud music. He took the wine and then greeted me with a big hug. "I'm so glad you made it. Take off your coat. There's someone I want you to meet before he leaves."

As I followed him into another room, Alex's friend Dale handed me a glass of wine.

"Happy New Year, Lily," he said from behind a makeshift bar. "It's good to see you again."

"You too, Dale," I said, still following Alex's lead.

We were approaching an attractive man with dark-rimmed glasses.

"Lily, this is Robert Benton, the owner and publisher of *Spirit* magazine," he announced. "Robert, this is my friend Lily Rosenthal. She is not only a great friend but is the wonderful writer I told you about."

"Yes, I know all about Ms. Rosenthal, and I think you would be a great asset to *Spirit* magazine," he said, smiling.

"It's so nice to meet you. I hope Alex also told you that I am a shop owner in Augusta."

"He did. Augusta is a charming setting. I think our readers will be interested in hearing your perspective on living there."

I smiled. "I do have something to send you, but please be very honest about what you think of it," I requested. "I'll email it to you in a day or two."

"Excellent."

"I have to admit that it was fun putting my own words on paper instead of editing what others have written."

"I've been there myself, so just let your creative juices flow."

"Thanks, I appreciate the opportunity," I said as Marc approached me. "Robert, this is my friend, Marc Rennels."

"Nice to meet you, Marc. You are a lucky man. I look forward to hearing from you, Lily." Robert gave me a wink and turned around to talk to Alex.

"Should I be jealous?" Marc asked with a twinkle in his eye.

"You?" I smiled. "I don't think that's your style. I'm writing something for his magazine in hopes that they like it. Alex said I may get my own column, which would be a wonderful way to supplement my income."

"That's great!" Marc said. "There's quite a crowd here. Do you know most of these people?"

"Some. I'm hoping that Carl and Lynn will come."

"Let's get something to eat," Marc suggested. "I passed what looked like some great food in the other room."

Alex had put out an amazing assortment of food that was displayed beautifully. His love of cooking showed.

"Hi, Lily!" a female voice behind me said.

I turned around. "Hi, Mindy! Do you remember Marc from my open house?"

She smiled and nodded.

"Nice to see you again," Marc said, shaking her hand.

A crowd of folks gathered around us and conversations took many directions as people socialized, but I kept my eyes on Marc. He was so handsome in his white sweater that complemented his salt-and-pepper hair. The conversation soon turned to baseball, so Marc was in heaven. He loved telling the story about how the two of us met on The Hill near Joe Garagiola's house.

As it got close to midnight, the noise in the apartment became louder. I watched Alex and Mindy interact a bit from across the room. Alex, naturally, was preoccupied with guests, but Mindy seemed smitten with everything Alex said and did.

The countdown to midnight began. Marc took my hand and led me into the kitchen. I followed, feeling lightheaded from all the wine. At the stroke of midnight, Marc gathered me into his arms and kissed me. He leaned my back against the kitchen counter. To our surprise, a plate of deviled eggs came crashing to the floor! We burst into laughter and began picking them up.

"They'll never know what happened here, but you'd better get the eggs off of your back," Marc said, laughing hard.

"Hey, Lily Girl!" Alex said, entering the kitchen. "I want my New Year's kiss. You stole my best girl, Marc. I wondered where you both went."

Alex turned me around to give me a big kiss. I couldn't keep a straight face while wondering about the deviled eggs that I might be wearing. I also wondered what Mindy thought about Alex's behavior. She was watching his every move.

"Hey, you're staying here tonight, aren't you?" Alex implored. "I don't want you driving back this late."

"No, she has a place to stay," Marc answered before I could respond. "Perhaps Mindy might like the invitation," he added, just quietly enough for me and Alex to hear.

The three of us burst into laughter. I don't think Mindy heard Marc, thank goodness.

Marc squeezed my hand as Alex went on his way. "Are you okay with that?" Marc asked, his voice taking on a serious tone.

"Yes, of course," I responded. "My things are in the car."

"By the way, happy New Year," Marc said, pulling me close for another kiss.

"Happy New Year," I whispered in his ear.

CHAPTER 67

We left Alex's place about one and I got my bag out of the car to put it in Marc's. I hoped I was doing the right thing by accepting Marc's invitation. It was a twenty-minute drive to his loft in St. Charles. We laughed once again about our encounter in the kitchen.

"Does Alex call you his girl very often?" Marc asked.

I smiled. "I may very well be his best friend, so he may have a time or two."

"Do you think that you two being so close may have kept you from other relationships?"

I knew I had to think carefully about my answer. "Someone else had suggested that idea, but I really don't think so. We just have so much in common."

Marc's loft was along the river near the historic area of St. Charles. Marc said the historic building had once been a warehouse. The renovation made it very contemporary, which appealed to him.

After we walked in the cold-looking entrance, we took a large freight elevator to the second floor. The first thing Marc wanted to show me was the large window that gave him a view of the river. Another window provided a spectacular view of the historic courthouse on the hill. The city lights flickering in the distance were stunning.

The soaring ceilings were impressive. Then I saw the large painting that Lynn had done. It gave me chills. It was the one I had admired at her gallery reception. When Marc had announced that he was going to purchase it, I had been blown away.

"I thought this was going in your office."

He shook his head. "It was too large, and I enjoy it more here."

"It's perfect, and I like the way you have the light shining on it."

He nodded with pride.

I could see antiques here and there with a mix of modern accessories. When he showed me his office, the presence of the St. Louis Cardinals was everywhere. I should have known. The large room not only held an impressive antique desk, but also a large leather chair and couch that were positioned to get the best view of his large TV screen.

"This is quite the man cave," I remarked.

"I spend most of my time in here," he admitted. "I do a fair amount of law work here when it's too crazy at the office."

The next room was an extra bedroom where he instructed me to put my things. I felt myself relax, knowing that I had some options for the rest of the evening.

"Would you like a nightcap?"

"Water would be wonderful to counteract the wine."

We went into the kitchen. It was sparkling clean with the most modern conveniences. When Marc got a glimpse of my back, he started laughing.

"I think you still have some evidence of deviled eggs following you around. I promise, I didn't smell anything."

We dissolved into laughter.

"It's all your fault!" I accused him, wiping tears from my eyes.

"But it was worth it, right?"

Our eyes met for just a moment, and something electric pulsed through me. Feeling quite sober now, I told Marc I was exhausted and thought I'd try to get some sleep. He was perfectly fine with the idea and told me he wouldn't be far away. I pecked him on the cheek and took my water with me.

The guest room was very inviting. I changed my clothes and pulled down the covers. I slid between the sheets and tried to reflect on the events of the evening. Having Marc in this same large building seemed surreal. I wondered if he had gone straight to bed. Would he still be awake? I put on my robe and decided to find out.

As I went down the hallway, I saw beautifully framed family photos on the wall. It was clear that he valued family relationships. Loretta took most of our family photos after my mother died. She took many of our Christmas photos and put them in red frames, so she could display them all at Christmastime. Perhaps I should think of doing something similar in my new home.

The door to Marc's bedroom was closed, but I saw a light coming from the office. I quietly approached the open door. Marc was sitting in his leather chair, nodding as if he was about to fall asleep. I tiptoed behind him and slipped my arms around his neck. He swirled around in his chair and pulled me onto his lap.

"You didn't tell me that you walk in your sleep," he whispered.

"Only when I'm lonely."

Marc's embrace was followed by a passionate kiss. Somehow, we managed to make our way over to the leather couch. Things progressed in a way I couldn't have imagined. Intimacy wasn't something I had sought out particularly, but I found Marc to be so loving, which made me feel comfortable in his arms. The rest of the night was spent together, with a very loving man holding me close.

CHAPTER 68

The next morning, I was fast asleep when Marc woke me up, bringing in two steaming cups of coffee.

"Happy New Year!" he said sweetly. "What a way to start the new year!"

I had to laugh as I looked forward to my first swallow of black coffee. I smiled as I accepted the hot mug. "You know you have to take me to my car this morning," I reminded him.

"It's a holiday! I was hoping you wouldn't have to hurry home. I thought I'd whip up a nice little breakfast for us. I make the best French toast you've ever tasted. How does that sound?"

"Right now, I could devour anything," I teased. "What else are you offering?" That flirtatious remark delayed the wonderful breakfast, but it was well worth it.

By noon I was on my way home and had so much to think about. Marc and I had taken a big step, and I hoped it wouldn't impact our relationship in a negative or stressful way. Hopefully, neither one of us would have any regrets.

My phone rang. It was Alex, so I put in on speaker.

"I sure hope you found a place to stay last night," teased Alex. "How are you feeling today?"

"I did find a place to camp out. How about you? Did you have more than one guest stay over?"

He chuckled.

"Cute, Lily, cute!" he responded.

"Your party was great. How did the cleanup go?"

"Pretty good, but I had a little help from my friend," he teased.

"You shouldn't ask your guests to do that," I scolded.

"I think you really impressed Robert Benton, by the way."

"He may think otherwise after he reads my first column." I added, "He was very nice."

"He's quite popular with the ladies with his good looks. He's either divorced or in the process. I'm not sure."

I told Alex he wasn't my type, but I hoped he would like my work. After we hung up, I tried to concentrate on my driving since I knew I was a little tired. However, even in the dead of winter, the scenery in wine country was heaven. It was now my home.

I was unloading my car when my phone rang again. It was Kitty.

"Hi, Kitty. I just got home. What's up?"

"This morning, I delivered flyers about Nick's memorial service tomorrow. When you weren't there, I remembered that you'd told me you were going into the city. Anyway, they're having a memorial service at the American Legion hall at two. You may have mixed feelings about going, but I wanted to make sure you knew about it."

"Thanks, Kitty. I'll have to think about it."

"Sure. Let's get together soon."

I took my things upstairs and started the fireplace to take the chill off the room. Why did I have to think of Nick after such a wonderful New Year's Eve? If I went, I'd be grinding my teeth having to hear about all his wonderful attributes. Because of his drinking, a man lost his life and Nick and I were injured. I knew I needed to put it all out of my mind, but I kept thinking about it from all angles. He certainly didn't deserve to die, and he was kind enough to make my sign, after all. What should I do?

I took time to send Marc a text telling him that I was home safe and sound. Thinking of our time together got my mind off Nick. Now, back to making some decisions.

CHAPTER 69

The next morning, I sent my first column to Robert Benton. I wanted to show him that I sincerely appreciated the opportunity.

Carrie Mae called as I was finishing an English muffin. "What are your plans today, honey?" she questioned.

"Well, if you're calling to see whether I'm going to Nick's service, the answer is yes. I just don't see how I cannot pay my respects."

"Well, that's nice of you, but it's not why I'm calling."

"Oh, sorry! What's going on?"

"I would rather talk to you about it in person, but if today is too busy, I understand."

"I am never too busy for you. Let me take care of a few things before I leave the house. Put the kettle on. The service isn't until later this afternoon."

She seemed to be happy with that, but now I was worried about the subject matter she wanted to discuss. It was good to look out the window and see Kip and Tom come by and do some more shoveling of snow. A little while later, they knocked at the door, ready for their payment.

"Ms. Lily," Kip asked again, "do you have an electrical problem? While you were away, lights were flashing in your house occasionally. I see you have a light on sometimes in the little brick house, but we didn't know whether to be alarmed or not."

I smiled. "I suppose this old house has a lot of oddities," I answered. "Thanks for being concerned, however. I'm giving you a little extra today since I wasn't here at Christmas to see you."

"Oh, gee, thanks," Kip responded as Tom stood near him, shivering.

I closed the door and wondered what Rosie had been up to while I was gone. I went upstairs to dress for the service and my visit with Carrie Mae.

"I hate winter, I hate winter," I chanted musically as I entered the Uptown Store.

Carrie Mae agreed and quickly shut the door behind me.

"This hot tea will warm you up," she said as she filled my cup.

"Why does tea taste so much better in a china cup than in a mug? I just marvel at all the pretty patterns and shapes on your beautiful cups."

"It's the English way, and I don't think I've ever had tea in a mug before. You have some pretty ones from Rosie's inventory, if I recall."

I nodded and smiled. "So, what's going on?"

Carrie Mae took a deep breath. "I had a very disturbing conversation with Butler."

"What about?"

"He was rather emotional, I'd say. When he returned from being out of town, James was gone. Not only James, but other valuables that included the Christmas quilt."

"Gone, as in moved out?" I gasped in disbelief.

She nodded.

"Did he say why?"

"He was beside himself trying to think of reasons. He said they argued occasionally. Evidently James used to be on heavy drugs when he first came to live with Butler. Butler and AA helped him recover, but now Butler's very worried about his nephew's state of mind and health."

"Did he report that to anyone?"

"No. He doesn't want the law involved. James is like a son to him. I'm sure he hopes James will return in time and will feel foolish about his actions. Butler doesn't think James has too much money with him."

"That has to be devasting to Butler. I'm surprised he shared it with you."

"Perhaps he thought I could give him some insight as to what James might do. He asked us to call him if we heard anything. I'm sure it was good for him to vent because he knew I wouldn't tell anyone."

"Anyone but me, of course," I quipped. "Do you think James stole the items in hopes of selling them?"

"Why else? He knows all of Butler's contacts, so I hope they will check with Butler first if he tries to sell them anything."

"Who knows where that pretty Christmas quilt will end up!"

"Well, Lily Girl, you had your chance!"

I loved her sense of humor. "Yes, I did. Maybe if I

would have offered to pay him twenty dollars a month for the rest of my life, he would have agreed to it. Then again, I could have remortgaged my house for a quilt. What would you have thought of that?"

We both broke out in laughter.

CHAPTER 70

It was too cold and icy to walk up to the American Legion hall, so I drove. The parking lot was already becoming crowded. I tried to brace myself for some awkward moments ahead.

When I walked inside, I was grateful for the heated building and the availability of some empty seats towards the back of the room. I recognized several people, most of whom were business owners. We were handed a pamphlet with information about Nick. It included a recent photograph. The back featured some of his paintings. There were flowers in the front of the hall and a couple of Nick's paintings on display. A container at the front and center of the room presumably held his ashes. Someone had given this service some thought. There were many folks I didn't recognize who were sitting up front, and I assumed they were relatives and close friends.

A man stood and introduced himself as Nick's brother. The physical favorance was remarkable. He thanked everyone for coming and then described what it was like growing up with such a talented brother. He said Nick had a real love for the community, which inspired his creativity.

The next person to speak was Vic from the gallery. He claimed that he met Nick on the first day he came to wine country. He added that they shared their love of good art and that he had been honored to sell Nick's work.

A niece did a heartfelt closing prayer. After ending the prayer, she invited everyone to a reception downstairs. Feeling I had fulfilled any sense of obligation, I headed straight for the door before anyone could talk to me. I walked out with Johann from the hardware store. We exchanged greetings as I made my way to my car.

I took a deep breath when I closed the car door. My duty had been fulfilled. I had been seen by the locals and had signed the guestbook. There was no reason to socialize and answer questions about how I knew Nick or provide any details about the accident. Feeling relieved, I stopped at the cookie shop to get bread, breakfast rolls, and a few cookies.

When I arrived home, I turned my phone back on. I'd missed calls from Marc and Robert. Seeing the call from the publisher made my heart begin to race as I thought about how quickly he'd responded. He'd left a message with his phone number and instructed me to give him a call. I decided to do that immediately.

"This is Lily Rosenthal," I greeted after he answered. "I'm sorry I missed your call. I was attending a memorial service."

"Well, I'm sorry to hear that. I received your email. Lily, I liked your article very much. The topic you chose was rather universal, which will capture the attention of a wide variety of readers."

"Oh, I'm so glad you liked it. I have so many questions for you."

"Sure! How about lunch? I want to see your shop and that charming small town of yours. Your website doesn't give much information."

I heard myself give a nervous laugh. "I know. I'm not very savvy when it comes to technology. It's on my list of things to work on."

"Well, we have someone who can help you with that. It's very important that you have an appealing website because a lot of our subscribers are online. They will want to communicate with you."

"When do you suppose the first column will appear?"

"If we can agree on terms, it could be as early as next month."

"I see. So, when are you free to come out?"

"How about tomorrow? The sooner we get this rolling, the better. I have your address. You pick the restaurant. I know there are a lot of wineries around there, so I hope you can show me around a bit."

"How about noon?"

"Splendid. I will let you know if I'm running late."

I hung up with a case of pure anxiety. What was I getting into? I immediately called Alex to get his reaction.

"Is sounds like things are progressing just as they should," Alex said when I shared the news. "I told you he was looking for someone like you. Your timing is great."

"What's he like? He sounded so aggressive."

Alex chuckled. "That he is! Frankly, I'm surprised he's taking the time to come out and check everything out. He might be taking a personal interest in you, so be careful!"

"What's that supposed to mean? I hardly think I'm his type," I responded. "Plus, I'm sort of seeing Marc."

"Sort of?"

"No, I am, I guess."

"You guess?"

"Yes, I'm seeing Marc."

Alex roared with laughter, pleased that he'd made me completely uncomfortable.

CHAPTER 71

The next morning, I woke up tired, having gotten very little rest. What was I so worried about? Should I bring up the subject of payment with Mr. Benton or leave it to him to broach the subject? Was there more that he was expecting from me? What did Alex mean when he'd said to be careful?

I was starting to feel guilty about not responding to Marc's call until now, but my mind had been on other things. After I had one of my newly-purchased breakfast rolls, I decided to call him.

"Are you angry with me?" I began.

"Should I be?" he joked.

"I'm sorry, but I've been so distracted."

"With what?"

I told him about Nick's funeral service and then let him know that my column had been accepted. It was a lot of information, but he seemed to be following me just fine. When I told him that Robert Benton was coming out for lunch to talk about details, he became quiet.

"It's all happening so fast," I said.

"You'll be fine, and the extra income will help you out. Alex would not have hooked you up with Mr. Benton if he didn't think it would be a win for each of you."

"I guess you're right. It felt so good to write something creative. The column could be great for my business, and they're even going to help me improve my website."

"That's awesome. Just be careful about the content of the contract before you sign it."

"Good advice, Mr. Rennels. I may need legal advice."

"Can you keep the weekend free, so we can get together?"

"Sure!"

"I'll drive out Saturday and arrive when you close. We can have dinner somewhere."

"Sounds great. I miss you."

"I miss you, too."

I hung up, smiling. I was so lucky to have Alex and Marc in my life. They had such confidence in me. Now I had to think of what to wear and what to say.

Robert called and said he was running late, which didn't surprise me one bit. It gave me time to email my sisters and tell them I was going on a real job interview. It didn't take long to get a response from Laurie, who wanted more details. I didn't have time for that now.

Finally, Robert arrived. I opened the door to greet him.

"You're so right. You have the bright yellow house down the hill," he teased.

I began by giving him a condensed version of how I ended up in Augusta. It was probably more information than he wanted to hear. He did seem impressed with the large inventory I had in the shop.

"Where are we going for lunch?"

"My favorite place is Wine Country Gardens, which is up on the hill in Defiance. You drove past there on your drive in. I called for reservations, but they are closed today for a private event. We'll go to Chandler Hill instead. You'll love the view and how expansive it is."

"Yes, I saw their sign. I was invited to a wedding there once but couldn't go."

He assisted me with my coat and we were off. He had a sharp sports car with a make that that I couldn't identify. It sat low and felt very cushy.

I suggested that we first take a quick drive round Augusta to see some of the local wineries. He commented about the charm and wondered how they survived during the winter. I didn't pursue that line of conversation. I had often wondered the same thing myself.

"Have you felt restricted out here since you left the city?"

"That's a very good question. When I lived in the city, I loved to come out here and visit often, but it's different when you live here. Everyone thinks nothing about driving into the city for the least little thing. I'm not that adventurous after having an automobile accident shortly after moving here."

He didn't ask about the details, thank goodness.

"I think the area will provide a good background for your columns. I could never live out here, but I can see you having a following of fans who think you live in paradise. They will want to see your shop and pictures of the area's scenic views. I'll have Kelly from marketing give you a call, so we can get some good photos to use."

"Okay. That will be great."

CHAPTER 72

As soon as we arrived at the restaurant, Robert began giving me flirtatious smiles. I couldn't determine whether it was to put me at ease or flatter me. I wasn't sure how to react. He was interested in trying the wine, but I told him I only had wine at cocktail time. He quickly reminded me that it was cocktail time somewhere.

"I'll be recording some things if you don't object, Lily," he said, catching me off guard. "I don't usually ask this question, but would you rather be paid by the column or by the word?"

"By the column. Some will vary in length, I'm sure."

He nodded as if he approved.

Being recorded quickly made me uncomfortable.

"We'll decide if something is too lengthy. What compensation do you have in mind?"

I hated this conversation so far. "I didn't really have a set amount in mind," I admitted. "I will appreciate the extra income. When I left Dexter Publishing, my goal was to write a book. Then the opportunity to open a shop came about, and

I honestly needed a job. I enjoyed writing this first column very much."

He smiled and winked. What did that mean? Our food arrived, so our conversation turned to Alex.

"Alex began to fill me in on your personal life, but he never said if you've been married."

I knew he shouldn't be asking such a question, but I shook my head.

"Any close calls?" he said with a chuckle. "I hope you don't think I'm getting too personal, but your column will reflect your background, so I'd like to know a little more about you."

"I've led a rather sheltered life, if you really want to know. It seems to be a trait among many editors that I knew."

He chuckled like he agreed.

"It just seems that I don't know too many happily married couples."

"You've got that right. I'm going through my second divorce now, and I'll never make that mistake again."

"I'm sorry."

"Back to the column. I want you to make it as personal as you can. I like how you came across in this first column. Folks love that kind of warmth, but it's got to be real or they'll pick up on it. You live and work in a charming environment. Writing about that will really appeal to our audience. You know the drill as a former editor. In the process, we'll have our own professionals make changes, and then we'll get your final approval."

I nodded and smiled.

We were about to leave when he mentioned the amount per column. I was stunned. No wonder Alex liked his job!

Alex had never revealed what he made, but I knew that he was very pleased.

"Thanks, that will be fine," I said. "I hope I don't disappoint you."

I was on cloud nine as we began the drive back to Augusta.

"So, Lily, I would like to get to know you better."

There was that uneasy feeling again.

"I like what I see so far," he said confidently.

What did that mean?

"Just so we're clear, I don't date anyone associated with the magazine, in case you misunderstood me. I confess that you have piqued my interest. Alex didn't say if you were seeing anyone."

"I am. I'm surprised Alex didn't tell you."

"He may have," he admitted, shaking his head.

"So, in return, may I ask if you have a significant other?"

He smiled and gave me that wink again. I couldn't believe I'd asked him that question.

"No, I do not, so don't flatter me, Ms. Rosenthal. It won't get you anywhere."

We chuckled.

When we got to my place, I told him to just let me out. He agreed and said he would be emailing me a contract and that I should return it as soon as possible. Unexpectedly, he took my hand and kissed it rather than shaking it. It felt weird.

When I got inside, I leaned against the door to collect my thoughts. He was something else! Perhaps that was the way business was done these days. Should I share with Alex the things he'd asked me and what he'd offered to pay me?

As I went upstairs to bed, I got excited thinking about my next column. Was the monetary reward influencing my creativity? I undressed, slipped into a robe, and snuggled in front of the fire. In my mind, I replayed the evening repeatedly. It had been creepy and wonderful at the same time.

CHAPTER 73

It suddenly dawned on me that we didn't discuss the name of my column. Every name I seemed to come up with seemed silly or too serious. It was no wonder that Alex had been the one to think of the name for my shop.

I was too emotionally drained to report my evening to Alex or Marc. I thanked God for giving me the resources to make my financial ends meet during the winter months. How did shop owners survive out here? I finally dozed off in pure exhaustion.

I was still on the couch the next morning when I awoke at seven. The sun was up and shining right through all the glass windows. Today, I had to get back to being a shop owner. Perhaps the sunshine would bring a few folks in the door. I also needed to work on that silly cookie quilt block.

Alex didn't waste any time calling me early in the morning. I'd poured my first cup of coffee when the questions started.

"How did it go?"

"Very well, I think. I've never met anyone like him."

"He didn't hit on you, did he?"

I had to chuckle. "There were times when I didn't know what to make of his mannerisms. He did make a point of saying he doesn't date anyone from the magazine. That was a bit awkward, but I was glad to hear it."

"He's probably correct about that. What about the details?"

I felt that I had to be careful about what I said. "He's emailing me a contract today. He also has someone who can help me with my website. He thinks I'll have a following."

"He liked your first column then?"

"Yes, very much!"

"And the name of it is?"

"Don't ask. It didn't come up, and I was so distracted by other things."

Alex roared with laughter. "I guess you'll find out from him. I'm sure he has something in mind."

"I felt somewhat intimidated. He is so charismatic."

"I've never known you to be that way, Lily Girl," he commented. "Hey, I'm afraid I have to run. I have an interview in thirty minutes."

I hung up feeling even more silly about my meeting with Robert. I hoped Alex didn't think I was ungrateful for the opportunity.

I wasn't in the mood to talk to Marc, so I put the rocking chair on the porch and covered part of it with a scrappy wool quilt. Perhaps someone would stop. Having customers would be a welcomed addition to my day.

I played some music and tried to think positive thoughts. I turned on my computer and saw a group email from Laurie. She had a photo of some new yard ornaments she'd ordered in for her spring inventory. Next was a darling photo of little Lucy being held by Grandpa Bill. I supposed he would have to be the daddy for now. I quickly responded to both emails, sending compliments to both. I wondered what Lynn was up to. I was about to send Sarah a short email when one popped up from Robert.

Sure enough, it was about *Spirit* magazine. It was a contract. Robert instructed me to read the document carefully and email him back promptly if there were any changes. He said he would write an introduction when my first column was printed.

After I got my copy printed, I sat back to read it. That's when I noticed my title of "Living with Lily Girl by Lily Rosenthal." I repeated the title to myself. It was a "one size fits all" sort of title. I now could write about the birds in Augusta or small-town politics. I had to chuckle to myself. I thought I could live with that. I wondered what Alex would say.

CHAPTER 74

As I reread the contract, I wondered if I should have Marc or Carl look it over. My preference would be Carl, since he was family. I was suddenly startled by a young woman rushing into the shop, shivering from head to toe.

"Good morning," I said.

"Good morning! I'm glad the snow stopped, but it sure is freezing out there. I am so glad to see that you are open."

"Wonderful! What can I help you with today?"

"My name is Gracie Hammond. Since you sell quilts, I thought I would get your advice about something. I stopped by here during the Christmas Walk, but you weren't here. I loved seeing your quilts." She then took time to blow her nose.

"Thanks. I'm sorry I missed you."

"I'm a friend of Susan, your quilt teacher. Just like her, I'm a quilter. So many of us who quilt are frustrated about the lack of a quilt or fabric shop nearby."

"I agree, but there are plenty of reasons why there are none here, I'm sure."

"To get to my point, I'm thinking about opening a quilt shop."

"Really? Wow, that would be awesome."

"It's not that simple, of course. Do you think a business like that would survive in this small town?"

"Good question. It isn't easy, especially through the winter, and what you would be selling is for a rather specialized clientele."

Her face showed disappointment.

"Just so you know, I wouldn't be competition. I wouldn't sell quilts. I'd be selling fabric and quilting supplies. However, I do have a friend, Charlotte, who makes cute little gifts out of fabric. I might carry a few of her things."

"There sure isn't anything like it around here, and Susan's classes would be good for your business."

She nodded.

"Augusta seems to be the best location, but finding a suitable building could be a challenge."

"It's not easy. Without the help of Carrie Mae at the Uptown Store, I wouldn't be here."

"Your shop is so cute. Do you have any regrets?"

"Not at all. This shop wasn't my dream. It came about through a series of events."

She looked puzzled. I didn't want to share the whole story at this point.

"When I was here last, I remember you had a cute wooden sewing box that still had all the thread inside. Do you still have it?"

I smiled and went into the quilt room. "Yes, and I think it's from the 1920s."

Gracie opened it up and her face brightened. "I love this.

I didn't notice this needle threader in here before."

"Perhaps you should have it," I joked.

"I agree!" she said, handing the threader to me. "I've seen these going for a lot more money than what you're asking."

"My things are reasonably priced. You may be my only sale today, so thank you."

"I want to leave a card I had printed in case you hear of a building that may be available. I have a relative who has offered to help me get started financially, but that picture hasn't been completed, if you know what I mean."

I looked at her card. It just had "Gracie's Quilt Shop" and her phone number printed on it.

"I have another question for you. Do you feel a presence here? I felt the same thing when I was here last time."

I smiled. "I think I brought a spirit with me from The Hill where I used to live, but it's a long story."

"Does that scare you?"

"No, not at all," I said as I wrapped up her sewing box. "I think you were also supposed to have this."

She smiled. "I will think of you when I use it," she said.

"I wish you well with your idea. Perhaps Susan will have an update for us at the next class."

"I hope so. I told her to ask her students for suggestions. Nice to meet you, Lily. I'm sure I'll be back again."

CHAPTER 75

I called Carl at his office and left a message requesting that he look at my contract with *Spirit* magazine. With confidence, I attached my contract.

Next, I decided to text Marc to get his reaction to the title of my column.

> What do you think of "Living with Lily Girl" as the title to my column?

It didn't take long for him to respond.

> "Living with Lily Girl" sounds very provocative to me! I have an idea of what that would be like. Just kidding! It sounds fine. I hope the meeting went well.

I blushed, knowing what he was thinking.

> When will you arrive on Saturday?

> I see you want to change the subject. How about five?

> Great! See you then!

Marc always had a way of putting me in a good mood. They say you should always be around the people who bring out the best in you. That would be Marc.

I got out my quilt block and decorated the last cookie. I put different colored circles on it, thinking it looked like M&M's. It felt awkward doing the satin stitch, but it made it look better. I followed the embroidery chart that Susan had given us.

As I stitched quietly, I thought of all the folks who sensed Rosie's presence here. Why did some have that gift and others didn't? Why couldn't I understand her better? I should be able to at least know what she meant when the lights begin flashing. Nevertheless, I felt safe with Rosie.

"Hello!" someone called from the front room. "Delivery for Lily Rosenthal!"

When I came around the corner, I saw a large arrangement of white lilies and baby's breath.

"For me?" I gasped in delight.

The deliveryman nodded as I signed his clipboard. Before he left, I retrieved some cash out of my drawer for a tip.

The aroma was overwhelming. I was pleased to see that the orange lily centers had been removed, because I knew from experience that they stained whatever they touched. I looked at the card, and it read, "To Lily Girl, Welcome to

Spirit magazine. I'm sure that 'Living with Lily Girl' will be a tremendous success. Robert."

This was certainly a surprise. I placed the flowers on the counter so everyone could enjoy them. After all, it was a business gesture, I reminded myself. Do I thank him now or when I see him again? As I was giving that some thought, Kitty walked in.

"What are you doing out today"? I asked, curious.

"I'm delivering copies of *Boone County Connection*," she said, handing me a stack. Her eyes immediately caught sight of the beautiful flowers. "What's the occasion, Lily? They sure smell good."

"They are from *Spirit* magazine. I'm going to be doing some writing for them."

"You don't say," she responded with a big smile. "What will you be writing about?"

"Quilts, antiques, and life in wine country."

"That's awesome! What great advertising that will be."

"I'm hoping it will be good for the whole area."

"Well, with this horrid winter, you'll have plenty of time to write."

"That's for sure. Thanks for the newsletters. I always read every word."

CHAPTER 76

Since today was Saturday, I not only hoped for a good retail day but was also looking forward to a great evening with Marc.

I put the rocker on the porch and placed a bright yellow-and-red Four-Patch quilt on the seat. The batting was thick and heavy, which no one seemed to like. As a result, the quilting stitches were primitive, to say the least. I could only picture children loving this bright quilt because it was warm and happy. Oh my, if quilts could talk.

Snowshoes met me as soon as I opened the door.

"Good morning," I said as I took my mail from him.

"It's a beautiful day in the neighborhood," he sang. He must have watched *Mister Rogers' Neighborhood* like I did when I was a child.

"Yes, it is. I hope we'll be busy. Say, Snowshoes, do you know of a little place to rent?"

"Not right off the top of my head. Are you thinking of a second location?"

"You're too funny," I joked.

"I think some of the bigger places would sublet, especially this time of year," he said. "The problem with those is that the utilities can eat you up."

I immediately thought of Kitty's large antique shop and Carrie Mae's gigantic Uptown Store. I'd have to tell them about Gracie looking for rental space.

As he left, I welcomed a group of ladies who were very anxious to get out of the cold. One said they'd left their car on Walnut street and were walking from shop to shop.

"Welcome, ladies," I said. "Let me know if I can help you with anything."

They all seemed to head to the quilt room, which pleased me.

"Do you just carry old quilts?" the tallest of them asked.

"Yes; are you looking for a new one?" I questioned.

"I would really like to find a Christmas quilt," the tall lady said. "My friend had one at Christmas, and I envied it so much. A red-and-green antique quilt in decent condition is hard to find."

"Yes, I know," I replied, thinking of Butler's wonderful quilt. "I do have a few that are green and red hanging on the end of the rack, if you want to take a look."

"I have a wonderful Variable Star quilt that I put under my tree every year," the shorter woman bragged. "I have a weakness for anything Christmas, I guess. You look like you prefer red-and-white quilts, from the looks of things here."

"Yes, it's a weakness of mine," I admitted.

While the others separated, I continued showing the tall lady my green-and-red quilts. I wished I had a better selection. She was knowledgeable enough that she knew all about the fugitive green fading on most of them. When I showed her the best of them, which was a Carolina Lily, her face lit up.

"This is so soft and lovely," she said, holding it close to her. "I've always loved this pattern, and it looks like it's been loved a lot. The binding is really worn, but it's still beautiful."

"It was probably made around 1850 to 1870, when so many red-and-green quilts surfaced."

"Do you remember who you purchased this from?" she asked.

"No. It came with the inventory I purchased to open this shop," I explained.

I let her ponder over the quilts so I could help a lady that came in looking for paperweights and butter pats. Those items were displayed in the glass case by my counter.

By the end of the day, I had managed to sell the Carolina Lily quilt, two paperweights, a glass pitcher, antique music sheets, and a small oil lamp. That wasn't bad for a Saturday during the winter. I locked the door and proceeded to go upstairs to get ready for my big date.

Marc arrived early. I ran downstairs to let him in. It didn't take him long to notice the lilies on my counter.

"I got these from the owner of the magazine. How about that? The smell is pretty strong, isn't it?"

"These are from the man who hired you?"

I nodded. We went on upstairs and Marc didn't comment any further. He went to warm up in front of the wonderful fireplace.

CHAPTER 77

"I have a surprise for you, and I hope you won't be disappointed," Marc announced. "You know how much I enjoy cooking, so I brought some things to make dinner here tonight."

"You did what?"

"It's a simple meal," he explained. "All I need from you is a pot of hot boiling water for my pasta, two plates, and two wine glasses."

"You're serious, aren't you? You are something!"

He grinned.

"That sounds great!"

"I have a basket in the car that I need to bring in. Just pretend we're having a picnic in front of the fire."

"Well, that's an offer I can't refuse. Bring everything to the kitchen up here. I think I can manage boiling water."

"Awesome!" he said as he headed downstairs.

What man does that? I did have a large pan I had used for pasta, and I could certainly pull china, silverware, and crystal to use on the table. I went downstairs to the kitchen to retrieve what I needed. Marc came in the door with a large picnic basket and followed me upstairs. I took an antique folding table that I'd had sitting in the corner of my sitting room and placed it in front of the fire. I was reminded of our makeshift pizza picnic when the lights went out at Rosie's shop. Marc had been there helping me, so we'd spread out a tablecloth and had had a picnic on the floor with candlelight. While Marc busied himself in the kitchen, I prepared an intimate table with two candlesticks in the center. I was almost giddy with happiness.

"Do I need to open my wine, or do you have some you prefer?" he asked from the kitchen.

"Whatever you brought will be fine," I assured him. "What else would you like me to do?"

"Pour some wine and water," he ordered. "I also brought fresh bread from Al's that I thought you would enjoy. I don't think you've had my homemade salad dressing before, so prepare yourself!"

"Marc, you are amazing. How do I deserve a man who likes to cook? I thought Alex was the only man in the world who loved to cook."

"I'll put Alex to shame before I'm done."

"I'll bet you will!"

I went downstairs to get matches from behind the counter. When I returned to the porch, the candles were already lit. Well, that meant we weren't alone. Should I mention that to Marc?

Fifteen minutes later, Marc had prepared pasta con broccoli with large chunks of chicken. He said it was a simple recipe his mother always made, and he'd learned to make it from memory. His mother was Italian, and he loved her cooking. The salad dressing on a simple lettuce wedge was both sweet and spicy. It was such a treat. Marc broke Al's crusty Italian bread, which made my mouth water. The aromas drove me crazy. We smiled at each other as we sat down to indulge. This was so much better than I'd anticipated for the evening. Maybe it was the Italian menu that I missed from the The Hill that got me so excited.

"Here's to a wonderful chef who makes house calls," I said, raising my glass.

Marc burst into laughter.

"How do you like the wine? It's a bit heavy, but I like it with nearly everything," Mark said.

I was perfectly happy with the choice. I wasn't very talkative, but I thoroughly enjoyed every moment. Marc seemed happy to share about how each thing was prepared. I loved hearing him talk. When we finished, we cleared the table and Marc poured us another glass of wine.

"I'm afraid I left your kitchen in a bit of a mess," Marc said apologetically. "I'll help clean up."

"Please stop and sit. This was so lovely. I can't thank you enough."

When we sat in front of the fire, Marc admitted that he knew the two of us would enjoy his gift of the fireplace.

"I was set up?" I teased.

He nodded and kissed me on the cheek.

Marc was the most talkative I'd ever seen him. He shared stories about his mother and sister being good cooks. Of course, baseball worked its way into the conversation.

"I think I am seriously going to make an attempt to get to the Baseball Hall of Fame this year," he stated. "If you are really nice to me, I may ask you to come along."

"That would be a remarkable trip. Cooperstown is so charming, from what I've read. I'll have to think about that."

"Baseball brought us together, remember?" he said, smiling.

"Oh, I thought it was when we were admiring Lynn's painting at the gallery."

"Well, you may be right, but there was something about when I first saw you sitting on that park bench by St. Ambrose Church that sticks in my memory."

How sweet.

The candles were burning lower as we snuggled by the warmth of the fire. In my mind, there was no question that Marc would be spending the night. Sharing my bed was a huge step for me. I felt extremely lucky that we'd taken time to develop our relationship.

CHAPTER 78

Marc left early Sunday morning. I cleaned up the kitchen and then decided I would complete my quilt block. I would open the shop at noon like the others did in the area.

Two women were my first customers. One was tall and heavy and the other was short and thin. The smaller one was quite talkative, and they soon separated to shop in various parts of the store.

"I'm looking for smoking memorabilia," the shorter woman requested. "Do you have anything at all?"

I had to think. "There are few unusual ashtrays, cigar boxes, and some cigarette advertising posters around here somewhere."

When I walked away from her to check on the other woman in the quilt room, I was almost certain I saw the taller woman slip a doll quilt into her coat. I asked if I could help her and gave her a look that revealed my angry feelings. She shook her head and moved towards the front door.

"We'd better get going, Marge," she said to her friend.

"I'll take these ashtrays," the smaller woman said.

As I wrapped her ashtrays, I wondered how I could approach the one who was stealing. She looked nervous. I surely didn't want her to get out the door.

"Thank you very much," I said as finished up the transaction with the paying customer. Then I addressed her friend. "Do you want pay for the doll quilt you have under your coat, ma'am?"

They both looked shocked at my question.

"What are you talking about?" the tall woman asked.

"I believe that you have something that belongs to me."

"Are you accusing me?" she shot back. "You'd better be careful!"

"I'm simply reminding you to pay for what isn't yours. I saw you put the quilt in your coat. I hope we can resolve this before I call for security."

She burst into laughter. "Security? What a joke!"

"Please feel free to show me that I was mistaken by opening up your coat."

"I beg your pardon," she said defiantly. "I will do no such thing!"

"You have no idea about my security here," I said, glaring at her. "I have a camera that will support my accusation, and then I'll alert the other shops," I said calmly before reaching for my phone.

"Leave it!" her friend demanded.

The larger friend gave her a dirty look and turned towards the quilt room.

"I'll take that," I said, approaching her.

She pulled the quilt from underneath her coat and threw it in the opposite direction from me without saying a word.

"Please leave," I commanded. "Don't return to my shop again."

As soon as they left, I called Carrie Mae.

"I actually think they've been in here before," she recalled after she heard my account of the experience. "You were awfully brave. You must be very sure before you accuse anyone." She paused. "You really don't have a camera, do you?"

I chuckled without answering. "My eyes and my gut said what I saw."

When I hung up, I became very angry at the idea of someone just taking another person's things. It was so hard to keep track of customers who separated in the store.

Lisa, a new friend of mine and someone I'd met through Carrie Mae, walked in the shop. She loved quilts. I greeted her warmly.

"I wish you'd come out to see me, Lily," she said. "Carrie Mae thought you might be in the market to add to your quilt inventory. I need to unload some of my quilts."

"It's not a good time of year for me to be buying, but do you have any red-and-white quilts to sell?"

"I believe so. I have some of the usual patterns, and my favorite is Hearts and Gizzards. Do you know of it?"

I nodded and smiled. "Do you have a Feathered Star?" Of course, I was still thinking of the Christmas quilt.

"I believe that I might. Isn't it pathetic that I don't even know what I have? If I recall correctly, it's in excellent condition."

"Do you think you could ever part with it?"

She paused. "Maybe. That's a very good question when it comes right down to it." She giggled to herself.

"How many quilts do you think you have?" I asked, curious about her collection.

"Don't ask me that. I tell folks not to ask my age, how old my children are, and how many quilts I have."

We laughed heartily. I could certainly understand her position!

CHAPTER 79

"Welcome, everyone!" Susan called above the talkative students in her quilt class. "It looks like everyone's here. Candace, I'm glad you're feeling better." Candace smiled and nodded. "Snow is predicted this afternoon, so we want to start on time," Susan warned. "I can't wait to see your show and tell of your favorite Christmas food. In case you haven't heard through the grapevine, someone is looking into opening a quilt shop here in the area. She wants your thoughts. It's not definite yet."

"Oh," Marilyn gasped. "That would be wonderful, wouldn't it, Mother?"

"Yes," voiced Edna. "It's those spur-of-the-moment needs when it would be most helpful."

"I can't imagine anyone not thinking it's a clever idea," Judy added.

"I will pass on your response," Susan said with a smile. "Okay, why don't you start the show and tell, Judy?" she suggested.

"Don't laugh, but we had Brunswick stew every Christmas

Eve," Judy began. "Of course, I was challenged regarding what to put on my block, so I appliquéd a soup tureen. We always served it in something fancy like that."

Everyone complimented Judy on her block.

"Judy, you put me to shame," I said sheepishly.

"Well, Lily, we'll be the judge of that," Susan said with a chuckle. "Let's see what you made."

When I pulled out my block, the looks on their faces said it all. At first, no one said anything.

"We all love cookies at Christmastime, that's for sure," Marilyn said politely.

With that first remark, they all followed by giving me suggestions about what I should have or could have done differently. No one said they liked it.

Next was Edna, who always had the perfect block with the most work. She had appliquéd a turkey on a platter and added all the trimmings with embroidery. Praises came from around the table. Candace said it looked good enough to eat.

The longer the class went on, the more I realized how inadequate I felt about my aptitude. I think they thought I wasn't taking the class seriously enough.

When show and tell was finished, Susan showed us how a lightbox would be helpful as we designed our blocks. If we didn't have one, she told us how to make one with glass over a light. It did look like it would make things easier.

"Your next block will be fun," Susan announced. "Think about your favorite Christmas character. I don't want everyone to make a snowman, because that's just a couple of circles."

Everyone chuckled. She was probably thinking of me.

"Just think, you're about half done with your very own Christmas quilt!"

I left the group feeling a bit down. Getting approval was a big part of being in this group. Most of them had more experience than me, that was certain. Maybe I was just not meant to be a quilter. Maybe I should just write about it.

Today's feeling of disappointment reminded me of other groups where I'd fallen short. I'd wanted to play an instrument in grade school but failed at that. I did succeed in creative writing in high school, but it made me an unpopular nerd. When I joined a book club at Dexter Publishing, I'd failed to enjoy any of it. I found myself editing every word while forgetting about the story. I'd decided to drop out. When do adults decide something is over and quit? Why was getting approval so important, even as adults? I wondered if my quilt class would let me write about them in my column. Fitting in not only applied to this little group; fitting into the community was another challenge. I wondered how they'd react if I did include my feelings and experiences in the quilting group as part of my column?

I knew Carrie Mae could lift my spirits, so I stopped in to say hello. However, there wasn't the usual "Hi, Ms. Lily" I typically heard. Instead, she looked so down and forlorn.

"You look like you're having the kind of day I'm having, Carrie Mae," I confessed.

"Perhaps. How was quilt class?"

I took too long to explain to her why I wasn't cut out to be quiltmaker. It was a whiny report, and she didn't make any effort to reassure me. I wasn't sure she was even listening.

"I have some sad news about someone who likely never did fit in," she announced.

"Who are you talking about?"

CHAPTER 80

"I got a call from Butler earlier this morning," she said, not looking me in the face.

"About what?"

"He got a call from his brother about his son, James."

"Were they estranged because of James?"

She nodded.

"James died from an overdose," she stated, her eyes filling with tears. "Isn't that sad?"

"He was that troubled? What else do you know? That is horrible news."

"James had gone to New York. He'd gotten heavily involved in drugs again and hung out with the wrong people, which was Butler's greatest fear when James left. The police notified Butler's brother. They are going to bring him back to St. Louis."

"Where does Butler's brother live?"

"I'm guessing not that far, but Butler never said. I feel so bad for him. He is taking this as hard as if he'd lost a son."

"Of course. I hate to ask, but what about all the stuff he

stole from Butler?"

"I just couldn't ask about that," Carrie Mae said sadly. "If he was into drugs, he likely sold what he took from Butler."

"Maybe this will bring Butler and his brother closer again," I suggested. "What is his brother's name?"

"I think he said Brad, as in Bradford," she recalled. Carrie Mae paused and heaved a big sigh. "Would you like some tea?"

"That would be nice. This has not been a pleasant morning. Do you think I should call Butler and give him my sympathies?"

"I don't think it would hurt."

"Okay, I will. Back to my experience this morning, have you ever felt criticized or felt like you didn't fit in?"

She chuckled. "Lordy, girl, just most of my life. You can't let it get to you, or you will lose yourself. Look at you. You didn't have much going for you when you decided to take on Rosie's inventory, but your gut said you could do it and here you are. I came from a dirt-poor family, and I liked pretty things. Those two things didn't go together. When I discovered I could make a profit selling pretty things, I became hooked on retail. I learned as I went, just like you. I feel retail is a win-win, don't you?"

"I see what you mean. I was asked for some retail advice recently. A woman by the name of Gracie wants to open a quilt store in the area and wondered if I thought it was a promising idea."

"I think she's been in and out of here looking at quilts a time or two. By the questions she was asking, I figured she was going to open a shop of some kind."

"Her biggest problem is the location. There's nothing

available. She said she had capital from a relative."

"I know you said to be also thinking of a place for your niece, but I don't know of anything right now."

"What if you let Gracie clear out your basement and let her sell her things downstairs?" I suggested.

Carrie Mae gave me a strange look.

"You could get some rent and a chance to clear away what you don't need or want anymore. It could be a safety measure, too. Maybe that would allow you to spend more time upstairs."

"And where do you suppose I should go with all of my junk, Lily Girl?" Carrie Mae replied, sounding a bit perplexed.

"I could buy some and you could squeeze some in up here. I'll bet there would be a pile to just pitch."

She laughed. "You come up with the craziest ideas sometimes, do you know that?" I chuckled and nodded. "Will you at least give it some thought? Remember, the last idea I presented to you worked out pretty well."

"Okay. It doesn't hurt to think about it, I suppose."

"Remember, someday you may decide to retire, and she could buy you out. How about those bananas?"

"Out with you, Lily Girl! You're trouble, do you know that?"

CHAPTER 81

By late afternoon, Marc and I briefly connected by phone. He was heavily involved with a case that could take him out of town. I hesitated to go into my grief over James's death and my disappointment over my quilt class. I decided to say nothing about either topic to Marc.

It was seven that evening when I got a call from Kitty. We exchanged greetings and she explained her reason for calling.

"I promised my husband that after the holidays, I would close our shop and the B&B down so we could take a couple of months to travel. All of his family is out west, and he still thinks we need to go to Scotland."

"How nice! What's wrong with that?"

"I sure don't want folks to think we are going out of business. I need a break, don't get me wrong. I'm happy to get away from changing sheets and waiting on customers. My request to you is to check on our places while we're gone. I can't just ask anyone. You walk or drive by more frequently than most. Wc are keeping the utilities and the lights on."

"Of course, I'll do that for you," I said.

"That would be wonderful. Are you sure?"

"Of course. When do you leave?"

"Next week, if you're on board."

"I know you have a nice RV. Will you be traveling in that?"

"Yes, and then we'll leave it at his dad's when we go to Scotland. I'll keep you posted and give you all of our contact information."

"You won't miss much business this time of year, that's for sure. I wish you safe and happy travels!"

"Thanks so much, Lily. I'll see you before we leave."

When I hung up, I felt pleased to be able to do something nice for someone who had been so nice to me when I moved here. I envied their ability to pick up and go.

I poured some wine to get myself relaxed and began to focus on my next article. From my recent experience, it would have to be called "Where Do We Fit?" Or maybe it could be called "Fitting In." I started by stating that it's difficult to leave our comfort zones and venture out to new places with unfamiliar faces. I added that it's nice to have a connecting person or experience to make the transition easier. I was thinking of Carrie Mae, who had helped me so much when I moved to Augusta. Putting oneself in new situations is a risk that can lead to heartbreak or happiness.

My handwriting went on, page after page. I knew immediately that writing this column would be therapeutic for me on many levels. I didn't want this column to suggest that we had to fit our square lives into a round hole. When I finished my lengthy rant, I read it through. I liked it.

After a good cleanup, I thought it would work for column number two.

I went to bed with thoughts of Butler and his family. What if James's death was due to a combination of the wrong drugs? In situations like this, the family and friends left behind feel so helpless and guilty. For what it was worth, I planned to call Butler to let him know that he had my sympathy.

CHAPTER 82

The next morning, I gave serious thought to my next Christmas block. I was going to have to step up my game or quit the class. As I looked out the window, snow flurries were hitting the ground. I might live in my pajamas today, from the looks of things.

I received a call from Sarah. "What's wrong?" I asked, certain that there must be unwelcome news.

"You respond just like my mom," she mocked. "I am fine, with the exception of being sleep-deprived."

"I take it that Lucy isn't sleeping through the night?"

"No, and everyone blames me."

"Well, that's not fair. Is she growing?"

"She is turning into a butterball like me. She'd better not have a weight problem."

"That is the least of your worries. How is everyone else?"

"Fine. They are finally planning a little trip, so when they return, I thought Lucy and I might come for a visit."

"Are you serious?" A visit was not really what I felt ready for at this point. "Did your folks go away for a particular reason?"

"Dad's goddaughter is getting married."

"Is the baby up for travel?"

"I take her everywhere I can."

"How are your classes coming along?"

"I'm doing them online, and I'm doing just fine."

"That's good. How long would you stay if you came here?" I wanted to know that ahead of time.

"As long as you'll have us!" she answered. "Are you still hanging out with Marc?"

"I am. I think he's a keeper."

"A keeper—as in marriage?"

"Oh, no. Marriage will not be an option for either one of us."

"That's a relief."

What did she mean by that? "You keep me posted on your timeline. I'll have to make some arrangements."

"Don't worry. I'll bring everything. She has her little seat that she's in most of the time, and we can make her a place to sleep somewhere."

"Tell everyone hello and that I wish them a safe trip."

When I ended the call, my heart was racing. The thought of Sarah visiting seemed to heighten my anxiety. I'd ask Carrie Mae if she had a crib in her inventory. I wondered if Loretta even knew Sarah had invited herself.

I got another cup of coffee and thought about my favorite Christmas character. Of course, there was baby Jesus, Santa Claus, the three wise men, and even Scrooge. If I did Scrooge, the class would kick me out for sure. I did love the story of *The Christmas Carol*. I had several old books by the title, and I loved the movie. Maybe if I did Tiny Tim, I would get approval.

I looked out the window again and studied the snowflakes

landing on the window. It made me think of Jack Frost. What would a Jack Frost look like? Would anyone know? He could be a stick man with lots of snowflakes around him. I could put everything on a dark background. I was certain no one else would have a Jack Frost block. So far, it was my most creative thought.

This crazy Christmas quilt was going to mean more to me than I'd originally thought. Getting approval for each block was not fun, since I was a real beginner. I did like Susan's suggestion of using a lightbox for tracing, so tracing snowflakes might work. I wondered what Edna would end up doing. I couldn't compete, so why should I care?

Once again, I was interrupted by a phone call. This time it was Loretta. I should have assumed as much.

"I heard you got a call from Sarah," Loretta began.

"It's fine. Don't worry. We'll work everything out."

"Well, I'm glad you understand. Frankly, it may do her good to get away. I don't think she realizes how much Bill and I do for her. I also worry that she has started communicating with Lucy's father."

"Is he still married?"

"Yes."

"Has he seen the baby?"

"Not that I'm aware of, but Sarah doesn't tell me everything. Who knows where she goes with Lucy every day when I'm at work."

"That's a tough one."

"I have to admit, she is a pretty good mother. I was concerned about it at first."

"We can thank Lucy for that. What's not to love?"

She agreed.

CHAPTER 83

Before we hung up, Loretta reminded me of Lynn's birthday next week.

"What in the world do I give the woman who has everything?" Loretta asked.

"That's a good question. Try to think of something personal. I just hope Carl remembers. You guys have a good trip. I'm sure Sarah is looking forward to some time alone with Lucy."

"Well, she won't have a babysitter when she decides to go here and there. I will miss that little granddaughter while we're away, though."

After we hung up, I could certainly identify with each side of Sarah's living situation. Hopefully after her visit here, she would appreciate her home.

Before I could forget, I called Lynn to set up a birthday lunch. The call went to voicemail, so I tried her landline and left a message.

My next call was to Butler. I didn't want too much time to pass after James's death before I gave him my condolences.

"Lily, how good to hear from you," he answered.

I guessed that my name showed up on his phone. "I just felt I had to call you after Carrie Mae shared the horrible news about James."

There was a pause.

"There are no words for this, Lily," he said sadly. "I don't know what made him go back to using drugs. I'm haunted by whether he intended to end his life or if it was an overdose that was done mistakenly. We do not have an autopsy report yet."

"You did a lot for him, and you should feel very good about giving him a home with unconditional love."

"Well, whatever, but it wasn't enough. Thank you for your kind words. How are you doing?"

"I'm fine. The sooner winter passes, the better."

"Don't say that. Each day is precious."

"You are so right. Look, I don't know if I can do anything for you to make this time easier, but I just wanted you to know that I care."

"Your call means a lot. We need to talk quilts, don't we? It would do me good to get my mind on something else. How about I take you and Carrie Mae to lunch soon?"

"We would love that. She is taking your loss pretty hard."

"She is a gem. She has given me good personal and business advice through the years. The two of you should pick a time that's good for you and we'll talk quilts."

"We will. Please take care," I said before hanging up. I felt so much better after I'd called him. With Butler not being James's father, he likely did not get condolences from many people.

The morning passed quickly and soon it was the afternoon. Should I try to open the shop or work on my quilt block? The ground was covered in white crystals. It was becoming a winter wonderland outside. Why did I have such a love-hate relationship with winter?

I was boiling some eggs to make egg salad when my phone rang.

"It's your favorite brother-in-law, Lily," Carl greeted me.

"So it is!" I responded.

"Hey, I heard your message, and I wondered if you would agree to coming to a little intimate birthday dinner for Lynn. She hates surprises, so I think she'll go for that."

"That is so sweet, Carl," I replied. "Who are you inviting?"

"You, Marc, Alex, Mindy, and Connie and her husband," he answered. "Have you met Connie? She helps Lynn out at the studio."

"Yes, I believe so. That sounds nice. You know my other siblings would give their eye teeth to be there."

"I know. It would be awesome, but the distance is just too great. She loves Charlie Gitto's, so I thought I would make reservations there. What do you think?"

"Perfect."

"Hey, how is 'Living with Lily Girl' doing?" he asked politely.

"Are you teasing me?"

"No. I seriously think you are going to become quite well-known," he responded kindly.

"Thanks, Carl. Let me know for sure about the dinner arrangements."

It was comforting to know that Carl was going to do something special for Lynn. I could only hope it was out of love and not guilt. The occasion was also another good excuse to see my Marc.

CHAPTER 84

By the next day, there were at least six inches of snow for Kip and Tom to clear. After I got dressed, I called out the door to ask if they could clean off my car. I had to get out of the house! I thought I would go to Kate's for coffee.

"Good morning, Lily," Randal greeted me when I got there.

"Good morning," I responded. "I'll take the hottest coffee you have."

"Coming right up! How have you been?"

"Good!" I smiled as I eyed the fresh cinnamon rolls in the counter display. "I'll also have one of those yummy rolls."

"Sure! Hey, Judy tells me you are a writer and have a column in a magazine."

I nodded, suddenly feeling a bit shy. "I was an editor in a previous life," I explained. "We'll see how good of a writer I become."

I took my coffee and bun to a table in the next room, where a newspaper had been left behind by a previous customer. The people at another table looked familiar, and I nodded hello to them. The cinnamon bun melted in my mouth. It was hard to compare this place to Al's Bakery, but it was just as good.

"Well, look who's here," Kitty greeted me.

"Good morning!" I responded. "Would you like to join me?"

"Sure!" she agreed. "Lily, have you met my husband, Ray?"

"Not officially, but it's nice to meet you," I said, extending my hand.

"Kitty said you have agreed to keep an eye on our places while we're gone," he mentioned. "That is very nice of you."

"It's no problem," I responded modestly. "I'm glad to be useful. Kitty has been wonderful to me since I arrived here."

"It's just best to not try to keep it all running while we're gone," Ray explained. "If something would go wrong, it would cut our trip short. By the way, feel free to use the guest house if you want. Kitty said you really enjoyed staying there."

"Oh, I did indeed! It was perfect for one person."

As we munched and chatted, I brought up that Gracie was looking for a quilt shop location. I mentioned that I thought Carrie Mae might consider renting part of her place downstairs.

"Carrie Mae is not getting any younger," Kitty said. "I can't imagine this community without the Uptown Store."

"As a new quilter, I hope I can help Gracie find something," I added.

"You are the fresh eyes that this area needs," Ray commented.

"Thanks, Ray."

"Why don't you just take my set of keys since you're here?" Kitty suggested. "Remember, we will keep the lights and utilities going. Since you've agreed to do this, we may leave sooner."

"I'm not going anywhere, and I'll check on things each day," I confirmed. "My niece is threatening to visit with her new baby, so I'm trying to figure that all out."

"Threatening?" they questioned with a laugh.

"Yeah. I'm not sure it's a promising idea," I acknowledged. "She wants to get away from home and thinks she would even like to live here. I work and live in my house, so her visit will be a challenge. She cannot stay with me."

"Lily, why don't you just have her stay at our guest house?" Kitty suggested. "We won't charge you a dime since you're doing this favor for us."

"You mean it?" I asked in disbelief.

"Why not?" Ray said. "We have a crib in the attic that we can bring down. We have had a guest or two use that crib in the past."

"That would be great!" I said, feeling a great deal of gratitude towards them. "The problem will be getting her to go home."

They chuckled.

"Okay, honey, we need to go," Kitty said. "Just tell us if she'll be staying there."

"Nice to see you, Lily," Ray said as he got up. "We've got to stop by Johann's to get some things."

"Thanks again," I said with sincerity.

"That goes for us as well," Kitty said.

As they left, I couldn't believe my luck! The guesthouse would be perfect for Sarah and Lucy.

CHAPTER 85

I refilled my coffee cup. As I stood to leave, I noticed that the snow had stopped. I wanted to skip and slide home because I was so happy with Kitty and Ray's offer.

To my surprise, a car was pulling up in front of my place when I got home. I unlocked the door.

"Is this place open?" the man in the car asked, opening his car door.

"It is now! Please come in."

I turned up the heat and removed my coat.

"Man, this weather is frightful," the woman with the customer said. "I'm surprised you're open today."

"What brings you folks out?" I asked, warming my hands.

"We're staying at the Clay House B&B, and my wife said she saw your quilt sign yesterday," he explained. "She loves quilts, so we were hoping you'd be open today. By the way, she makes the prettiest quilts you've ever seen!"

"Oh, honey," she said, blushing.

"That's wonderful." I nodded. "I'm learning to quilt, and it's been a real struggle for me."

"Well, I got better with practice," she stated. "I just decided I was going to do my thing and not worry about the quilt police."

"There's such a thing as the quilt police?"

"Years ago, there sure was," she stated, absolutely serious. "I've always hated following directions, so now I just figure it out myself."

"Well, that's good to know," I said with a smile. "I prefer antique quilts. I don't sell new quilts here. Do you sell yours?"

"No," she stated firmly. "My sweetie bought me a fancy machine, so I can quilt them myself. I'll master it one of these days."

"I told her she has to quilt a lot of quilts for others in order to pay for that darned machine," he joked.

"Many of the old quilts have unusual and pretty quilting designs. Have you noticed?" I asked the woman as she got closer to the quilts. Her husband went on to look at some other items in the shop.

"Yes, I always pay attention to the quilting designs," she said, looking closer. "I sure wish this town had a quilt shop."

"I agree. There is interest, but I'm not sure it will happen. Where are you from?"

"Perryville," the woman stated. "Do you know where that is?"

Before I could respond, her husband shouted that it was the county seat, like I needed to know that.

"Sure." I nodded. "Where do you buy your fabric?"

"We have a nice little department store that carries some fabric now," she explained. "It's call Rozier's, and it's on the corner of the town square."

"Now, let's be honest, honey, you buy fabric everywhere we go," he joked.

She giggled.

"I like this wholecloth quilt," she said, unfolding it. "It's quilted really nice and close. Would you take any less for it?"

I looked at the tag. It was one I'd bought at an antique mall years ago because of the great quilting.

"I'm afraid I can't," I said, shaking my head. "I've priced this as low as I can. You don't see these every day."

"For heaven's sake, Betty. If you like it, buy it," the husband argued from across the room.

"I know I shouldn't, but I can just see this at the bottom of the bed in our guest room," she reasoned.

"It sounds like it would have a very good home, which makes me happy," I shared.

"Okay." She nodded. "I'm going to take advantage of my husband's good graces."

By the time they left, the clouds had gotten darker. The check for four hundred and ninety dollars made my day. The sign in the window hadn't been turned to open, so I just left it as it was. When I looked out the window, Old Man Winter seemed to be flexing his muscles.

I got on the computer and saw a darling picture of Lucy that had been posted by Sarah. What a cutie! I couldn't believe Sarah had her baby dressed like a little adult. I was reminded of the Christmas photos I had taken in Green Bay. There was a good one of all of us that I should have gotten printed. I decided I should have that framed to give to Lynn for her birthday.

CHAPTER 86

The next day, I was determined to open the shop. I was debating which quilt to put out on the rocker when Alex called.

"What's up?" I asked.

"I just got to read your first column," Alex told me. "It's going to press soon. I liked it."

"Thanks. Believe it or not, I've started on the second one. What are you writing?"

"Destruction in cemeteries. Can you believe it?"

"That's a dark, cold subject for this time of year."

"My thoughts exactly."

"How is Mindy?"

There was a pause.

"She's fine, bubbly, and a bit too much to handle at times. What does that tell you?"

"Alex, she adores you!"

"I think you're right, but I don't think I'm the adoring kind. She knocks herself out to please me and agrees with everything I say."

"That is the pits!" I joked. "Did you just hear yourself?"

"I know. I'm a thankless creep, but I don't see this going anywhere."

"Then you'd better be honest with her. She's a sweet girl!"

"Easy for you to say. It will break her heart, and I'll end up taking everything back."

"Well, maybe in the meantime, she'll pick up on your feelings."

"The other night, she said she always wanted to get married and have a lot of kids. I pretended I didn't hear her."

"That can be the kiss of death for a woman to do at times. From what I hear, insisting you don't want to ever marry makes it more enticing for the other partner."

"Are you speaking from experience?"

I chuckled. "I have some good news to share before we hang up."

"Great! What?"

I told him about getting a call from Sarah and how her plans to visit concerned me. When I repeated the good news from Ray and Kitty about using their guest house, he agreed that it was a miracle windfall.

"You are always so lucky, Lily Girl," Alex teased.

"That's what my sisters always say, but I'm not so sure."

My talks with Alex were always so honest and real. I hoped he would handle the situation with Mindy with grace and kindness.

I finally got out the rocker for the porch and placed a pastel Grandmother's Flower Garden on it. It made me think of spring. Perhaps that would entice someone to come in. Just then, Carrie Mae drove up in her 1980s Lincoln.

"Good to see that you're open for business!" she called from her car.

"Come on in! How about some coffee?"

"I've already had my tea, thank you."

"If you don't mind, I need to pour myself a cup."

"I came to tell you that Gracie is going to come take a look at my place today. She came in to look at quilts again, and I said I may be open to renting the downstairs."

"What did she say?"

"She didn't jump up and down. I think it'll be a stretch for her to be down in that dungeon without her own entrance. She said she'd think it over, and if she was interested, we'd discuss more details."

"By the way, while Kitty and Ray are out of town, I'm going to be checking on their places. They also offered the guest house to Lucy and Sarah when they come to visit."

"How nice! That's perfect. When are they coming?"

"I'm not quite sure, but I wish she'd wait until closer to spring."

"Well, I cannot wait to see little Lucy."

"I know. Me too. Sarah is anxious to get away from her folks, but I think she'll realize rather quickly how much they have been doing for her."

CHAPTER 87

Before I opened the shop the next day, I organized everything for my Christmas block. As I thought about how I was going to achieve the snowflakes, I was reminded of some of the crocheted doilies that I had. Few customers had even looked at them, and they seemed to always end up in a messy pile. I went to take a closer look at them and noticed several sizes of motifs in some of the crocheted designs. I placed them against the dark background fabric and was pleased with the look. I could see where I could cut them apart very carefully with my tiny embroidery scissors. It would take me forever to apply them to the block, but I was prepared to spend more time on this assignment.

My rocker and quilt were sitting silently on the porch until nearly lunchtime, when the door finally opened. I was pleasantly surprised to see Holly with her friend Mary Beth.

"What a surprise! Why didn't you let me know you were coming?"

"Again, I wanted to surprise you," Holly said with a giggle. "Actually, it was a last-minute decision. Mary Beth said she would drive and would have me back in time for Maurice's meal."

"Be sure to do that, Mary Beth, because I don't want her killed for being late," I joked.

Mary Beth nodded her head as she smiled.

"It's my birthday today, so I made her feel guilty for not celebrating with me," Mary Beth stated with a wink at me.

"Well, happy birthday, Mary Beth!" I exclaimed. "I'll be happy to give you a birthday discount if you buy anything today."

"Great!" Mary Beth responded as she started towards the quilts.

"I need to see the quilts, too," Holly said, following Mary Beth.

The two immediately dove into looking at their favorites as they pulled them off the rack. Holly was adept at educating Mary Beth on all the quilt patterns.

"Anything new with Marc?" Holly asked out of the blue.

"We are a couple in progress, I suppose," I answered. "He brought dinner the other night and cooked it for me. That was pretty special."

"Wow," Mary Beth said. "Holly, are you going to tell Lily about your lunch date?"

Holly shook her head and blushed. "Oh, stop! Quit teasing me. He is just a friend."

"Well, I want to know more," I said, eyeing Holly with curiosity.

"What are you talking about?" Holly said, giving a wave of dismissal with her free hand. "He's an interesting guy who loves the arts as much as I do. I love talking to him about all the things I never get to talk to Maurice about. He actually listens and cares what I think."

It sounded like an affair might be brewing. "Oh, great," I said in jest. "That's a good thing. You need to get out and about. Is he married?"

"No. His wife died years ago. He's pretty lonely, I think."

"Well it sounds like both of you could use a good friend."

"Doesn't it?" Mary Beth chimed in. "I hope she keeps seeing him."

"Maurice would really and truly kill me if he knew, so please don't tell anyone."

"Mum's the word. I'm so glad you can talk to him. I feel like I have let you down a bit by moving out here."

"Don't be silly. You are busy and have a life," Holly said, sounding suddenly serious. "I really envy you making a new life for yourself."

"Maybe someday you'll join me," I teased.

"Don't go there," Holly warned. "No one can know about Ken. You both understand, right?"

"Oh, his name is Ken," I said with a sheepish grin. "That's good to know."

"Stop it, you guys," Holly said, anchoring her hands on her hips. "You'll never know his last name."

"I think I'm going to have to buy this cute little crib quilt," Mary Beth said, changing the subject. "I think I can make a pattern off of this."

"I'll buy it for your birthday if you lend me the pattern," Holly teased.

"Are you serious?" Mary Beth asked, surprised.

"I'll give moneybags here a discount," I said to encourage the purchase. "Happy birthday, Mary Beth!"

They laughed.

They stayed a bit longer, and I also talked Holly into buying a blue cross-stitched tablecloth that looked just like the blue in her kitchen. When they'd left, I realized how fun their visit had been. Maybe this Ken guy could give Holly the self-esteem she needed so she could leave the monster.

CHAPTER 88

The photograph of my family at Christmas arrived in time for me to take it to Lynn for her birthday. I had the perfect antique frame for it. I'd thought about giving her some of Rosie's jewelry that she'd admired, but the photograph was much more personal.

I'd told Marc I would meet him at the restaurant. I had options to spend the night with Alex, Lynn, or perhaps Marc. As I got ready for an elegant dinner on The Hill, I wondered if Mindy would attend with Alex. I also hoped that Carl would be attentive to Lynn, so she could have a wonderful birthday. I decided to wear a simple black dress with a vintage pearl and ruby necklace from Rosie's inventory. The necklace was a statement piece, which was just what the outfit needed to set it off.

I drove into the city as the sun was setting. What a sight it was! I loved the charming residential area where the restaurant was located. I used their valet parking, thinking how I appreciated the convenience. I was starting to miss my old neighborhood.

"Good timing!" Alex called as he arrived just behind me. I turned to look, and there was Mindy, all aglow for the occasion, hanging on his arm.

"Good to see you again," Mindy said cheerfully.

"It's good to see you, too!" I replied as the maître d' took us to the back dining room. It was evident that Carl had pulled out all the stops for this occasion. Marc was already there and greeted me with a warm hug. I made my way to Lynn. She looked gorgeous.

"Happy birthday!" I said as I gave her a hug.

"Good to see you, Lily," Carl greeted me, giving me a hug as well. "I'm afraid it's just the six of us. The other couple couldn't make it."

"That's okay," Lynn commented. "My family is here."

"Have you heard from the others?" I asked Lynn, referring to our siblings.

"Yes!" Lynn said as her face lit up. "Loretta sent these flowers and Laurie sent me a bird feeder that also has chimes. It's very clever. I already have it out on our patio. Sarah sent me a framed photo of Lucy. It's so adorable."

Carl pointed out that we had place cards to tell us where to sit. Candles on the table set the mood as soft music played in the background. Carl officially welcomed us and graciously made the first toast to the birthday girl.

"I'd like to wish my beautiful and talented wife a very happy birthday!"

Lynn beamed as we raised our glasses.

Alex followed with a comical toast that I wasn't sure I understood, but everyone laughed. I was next, and I struggled to say even a short toast to my sweet sister as tears filled my eyes. Marc's toast followed. Lynn was touched by all that each of us had shared.

The first course began with a platter of Italian delicacies that Carl had chosen beforehand. The conversation was light and there was a good dose of humor, thanks to Alex. I watched Mindy relish each word that Alex muttered. She laughed at his remarks more than the rest of us. The conversation went smoothly until the topic of marriage came up.

"Well, who at this table is going to enter wedded bliss next?" Carl joked.

Yikes! Why did he say that? He and Lynn had been far from experiencing any marital bliss. It seemed an odd turn for the conversation.

"Don't look at Lily, and don't look at me!" Alex responded. "Lily and I made a pact years ago that we'd run away together so we wouldn't have to marry anyone."

I couldn't believe he'd said that! Everyone was in stitches except Mindy, who barely had a smile on her face. Marc knew it was simply a joke.

"Well, you and Marc will have to be on your own," Lynn kidded, looking at Mindy.

"How about those Cardinals?" I asked loudly to change the subject. Thankfully, Marc took the bait.

"I can't wait for the season to start," he began. "Lily and I may make a trip to Cooperstown this summer." That comment certainly got everyone's attention.

"That would be awesome!" Alex agreed. "I've always wanted to go there myself. Do you have season tickets again this year?"

"Yes, but I split them with others from the firm," Marc explained. "Lily also gave me some tickets for my Christmas present."

"Can I open presents before dessert arrives?" Lynn asked impatiently.

We all gave our approval. She chose my gift first, and her reaction was heartwarming. She passed the photo around as she bragged about our awesome Christmas in Green Bay.

"I'm having Christmas next year," Lynn announced. "Get ready to party!"

To my surprise, Alex broke his wallet by giving Lynn a new iPad. Even Mindy was surprised at his generosity. Everyone knew that Lynn wasn't particularly technically inclined, so he made some humorous remarks about that. Regardless, Lynn was totally impressed by his generosity.

"By the way, I love your jewelry, Lily," Lynn mentioned.

I smiled. "Yes, I wanted something unique for this special occasion. I'm glad you like it."

CHAPTER 89

To my surprise, Marc gave Lynn two tickets to a ballet she'd been wanting to attend. I noticed that Carl had a funny look on his face as she opened Marc's gift. Perhaps Carl didn't want to take in the ballet and now felt obligated to be her escort.

Mark commented, "Don't worry, Lynn, if Carl won't go, I'll be happy to take you."

Lynn threw Marc a kiss of thanks.

Last but not least, Carl presented Lynn with a tiny gift box. She blushed.

I knew she would get more diamonds. If Carl really knew his wife, he would know that diamonds weren't really her style. She liked unique pieces of jewelry that had been handcrafted by artists. She loved wearing artistic jewelry, but in Carl's mind, that would not reflect his success in business.

"Oh, how beautiful!" Lynn exclaimed as she held up a diamond bracelet.

"I'm so glad you like it," Carl replied. "Here, let me help fasten it."

"It's lovely, Lynn," I said as I admired it. I wondered how

many similar bracelets she had.

"Now, I told Carl I didn't want a birthday cake because I adore the Grand Marnier soufflé," Lynn announced. "It's their signature dessert here at Charlie Gitto's. If you haven't had it, you'll find it heavenly."

Soon, an elegant tray of soufflés arrived. Each one was placed in front of us on a glass plate. The waiter gave a quick cut to each center of the crusty tops and poured in a delightful vanilla sauce that looked scrumptious. We were eager to enjoy this special dessert.

It was a lovely dinner in many ways. As everyone discussed leaving, Marc asked if I would come to his place, where we could have a nightcap. Everyone wished each other a good evening as we parted.

On the drive to Marc's place, Marc mentioned how smitten Mindy seemed to be with Alex.

"I'm afraid the feeling may not be mutual," I sighed.

"That was my impression. Well, everyone knows I'm smitten with Ms. Rosenthal here," Marc said as he squeezed my hand.

"Not as smitten as Ms. Rosenthal is with Mr. Rennels," I teased back.

"I felt you squirm when Carl brought up the m-word," Marc joked.

I giggled. "So how about those Cardinals?" I teased once again, playfully changing the subject.

The next morning, we walked down to Main Street to have coffee at a cute little coffee shop called Picasso's. It was very crowded, but we found a table for two by their large front window. I loved St. Charles and all its history and charm.

"Are you going to open today?" Marc asked.

"Yes, I think I should," I said, taking another spoonful of my vanilla yogurt with fruit.

"By the way, have you told Sarah about her getting to stay at the Cottage Guest House when she comes for a visit?" Marc asked.

"No, but I will soon," I said with a nod. "I worry that she won't want to go home again."

"Will it make you feel like a grandma?" Marc teased.

"I wonder." I grinned. "I haven't been around a baby, so that alone will be a new experience. Here is the latest photo I have of her," I said, getting out my phone. "She is so cute!"

"Well, you're acting like a grandmother," Marc chuckled.

After hugs and kisses, I headed home to my happy place in wine country. I decided to stop at Robins Nest to get a cup of coffee. It reminded me of the first time I ran into Nick.

When I arrived in Augusta, I parked my car in front of the Emporium Antique Shop to see if everything was okay. The town was quiet, with only a few cars moving here and there. I walked across the street to the Cottage Guest House. I decided to go inside and check it out to see if it would suit Sarah's needs. Kitty had remembered to get the crib. It was placed in the corner of the sitting room area. I felt envious of Sarah's being able to stay here. I saw Kitty's guest book sitting on the side table. It had so many wonderful compliments from her many guests through the years, including me. I closed the door with a smile on my face and headed to my yellow house on Chestnut Street.

CHAPTER 90

It was early afternoon when I opened the shop. Before a customer could arrive, I emailed my second column to Robert. Now I could begin thinking of my next one! As I was straightening up the quilts, I noticed how my inventory was getting lower and lower. I heard the door open. When I looked to see who it was, I was surprised to see Korine.

"Hi, Ms. Lily!"

"Well, what's going on with you these days?"

"Not very much. It seems like it's turning into a very long winter."

"I agree!"

"Carrie Mae said that in the spring, you'll be tearing down those dilapidated buildings on your property."

"That's right. I'm dreading the mess, but I'm also looking forward to having them gone."

"I know her boys are going to do it, but if you need any help with the cleanup, I'll be glad to offer my services in the yard, or wherever."

"I'm sure I will need some help, and I appreciate your offer.

I must get Doc's house cleaned out, which will be a dirty job. After they carry the debris away, I'll want to do some planting. Maybe you can help with that."

"Has there been any activity from your invisible friend?"

"Don't you worry about such things. I could still use you to clean here occasionally. I took on a writing job to make a little extra money, but it takes time."

"I do need the money. If I did clean inside the house, you would be here, right?"

I nodded.

"By the way, did you know that Kip had a run-in with the law?"

"No. Carrie Mae didn't say anything. What did he do?"

"Both those boys run with a rough crowd, so there were probably drugs involved."

"I sure don't like hearing that, especially if they are going to be around here."

Her explanation reminded me of James and how it all went bad with him.

"You're a writer?"

"So it seems. I used to edit other people's work, but now I get to write my own column."

"That's awesome. I never knew anyone who was a writer. What's your column called?"

"Living with Lily Girl," I stated.

"But no one lives with Lily," she teased.

"That's what you think," I teased back. She didn't get my joke about having a spirit around here.

"You don't even have a cat or dog. How come?"

"Well, I've always rented, and most landlords don't allow pets in the city. My previous landlord had a cat named Sugar.

In the end, I was always glad I didn't have to take care of an animal. Do you have a pet?"

"No. I figure it's just another mouth to feed. We do well to feed ourselves. Carrie Mae keeps her dog upstairs. She said she worries that it may slip out when the shop door opens and closes."

"I don't blame her."

"I sure like that quilt you have on the rocker outside. It's really faded and worn, but it's a pretty pattern."

"It's seen a lot of love and use. It has a low price on it. You never know what folks are looking for."

"That one corner has a pretty bad tear. Have you seen it?"

I nodded. "Yes, some of the older quilts got caught on the old bed springs they used to have."

"Oh, I remember those squeaky bed springs. I slept on those growing up."

"If quilts could talk, right?"

"Right! Well, give me a call if you need me. I need to get home."

After she left, I poured myself some iced tea and opened the door to see if anyone was walking around. I glanced again at the worn quilt. Its pattern was called Broken Dishes. I wondered what it would say about its past. I started thinking about what quilts really might say if they could talk. In fact, that might be a good title for my next column. No, perhaps "Living with Quilts" might be better.

I pictured my previous apartment, where my quilts had their own room. They were my collection of friends, not my merchandise like most of them are now. Since most of them were red and white, they complemented one another. They became a family, with each of them having their own history and characteristics. They received individual care according to their needs. I treated each one with love and dignity. On occasion, they would get their photo taken or get chosen for a trip outside of the quilt room. I needed to start writing these thoughts down. Would anyone besides me think of quilts as living things?

CHAPTER 91

My phone indicated that I had a new text message. It was from Kelly, Robert's assistant at the magazine.

> Robert thinks your second column needs to be more positive. Also, check your website for some of the changes I've made. Let me know your thoughts.
> Kelly

I didn't respond. What did he mean about being more positive? Fitting in wasn't always easy. I went onto my website to see her changes. I was pleasantly surprised to see more photos of wine country and a lovely photo of my shop. It had a place to subscribe to *Spirit* magazine, where you could read all about "Living with Lily Girl." It all looked amazing. Kelly was good.

My concentration was interrupted by a phone call from Sarah.

"How are you?" I greeted.

"Pretty good. You may already know, but Mom and Dad have approved my trip when they return."

"Yes. Loretta said she thought it might be good for you."

"Little does she know! They have been calling a ton of times just to check on us."

"Well, I have good news for you!"

"What? What?" she asked anxiously.

"The Cottage Guest House is closed while the owners travel, so they said you could stay there while you visit."

"Seriously? Is that the cute place you stayed one night?"

"Yes. They even have a crib for Lucy that they have used for some guests."

"Goodness, I can't wait! Aunt Lynn has agreed to pick us up at the airport and drive us to Augusta, just like before."

"That is so helpful. You have no idea."

"Oh, Aunt Lily, this will be such a vacation for us."

"Both of you stay well, okay?"

"We will!"

I hung up and planned to get back to writing down my thoughts for the next column. Robert wanted me to be more positive? I pulled up the "Fitting In" column and reread it. I couldn't see the need to change anything. I felt that I needed to stand my ground in this particular case. If he had given a specific suggestion, I may have considered making a change.

I emailed Robert and told him that the column should stay as is. I then reported to him what the third title would be. I was testing him.

Carrie Mae's name displayed on my phone.

"How's your day going?" she asked.

"Busy, but not with customers. I had a visit from Korine today. She wants to start working here again."

"I told her to give you another try. It's a perfect way for her to make a little extra money. The reason I'm calling is that

Butler called and wants to have lunch with us at Chandler Hill Vineyards tomorrow. Do you mind closing to have lunch?"

"I mind, but no one else seems to," I joked. "I would love to go! I can pick you up."

"That would be great. I'll call and tell him. Perhaps the two of us can cheer him up by talking about quilts and antiques."

"I hope so. I am anxious to hear if he tells us more about James and what really transpired in that situation."

CHAPTER 92

The quilt class was going to be meeting again soon, so in the evening, I pulled out the crocheted pieces and started to dissect them. There were all sizes and shapes. I didn't know if I was committing a crime with the crochet police, but I was making better use of these forlorn doilies than letting them sit at the bottom of a pile. I wondered how long Rosie had had them.

I pinned them in place on the dark blue background fabric that looked like a dark sky. I would have to carefully attach them with very tiny stitches. This was going to be time-consuming, but I had to prove to my classmates I was up to the mission.

I worked diligently, determined to make this block something I could present to the group and feel confident about. I took pleasure in placing the crocheted pieces in a design that I felt was attractive. When it came to the intricate stitching, I found that I actually enjoyed the challenge. The more I applied myself to this project, the more convinced I became that I was moving in the right direction.

It was close to midnight when I decided to quit working on the project. I checked my phone, and there was a sweet text from Marc.

> Got on a plane today for Chicago. I'll be back in a couple of days. Behave yourself. Love and Kisses.

I had to think about how to respond to this love stuff.

> Safe travels! Love you back.

Did I just put in print that I love him?

CHAPTER 93

The next day was cold and there was a light drizzle. I decided to keep the shop closed and just enjoy lunch with Carrie Mae and Butler. As always, I was interested in Butler's opinion about the quilt market and his thoughts on current trends.

I took extra care in getting dressed. I wanted to look professional today. I chose a suit I hadn't worn in some time. I didn't think I recalled seeing a woman in a suit since I'd arrived in wine country.

I knocked and knocked on Carrie Mae's door until she finally appeared. "Oh, you look very nice!" I told her.

"I can clean up when I need to. I don't wear jewelry much anymore, so I feel dressed up when I do happen to put it on."

"It's gorgeous. I know you love jewelry. You should enjoy wearing it more often."

She blushed. "You certainly got some splendid jewelry from Rosie's inventory that I wouldn't mind owning. You got a good buy on most of it."

"I know, and I haven't changed the prices either. I know

I probably should. Maybe you could advise me on some of it."

"I'd be happy to help you with that sometime. Let's get going so we're not late," Carrie Mae said, taking the lead.

Butler was waiting at a table for us when we walked in.

"Over here, ladies!" he called out. "You both look lovely on this dreary day. I hope this table is suitable."

We nodded and sat down after he gave us each a polite embrace.

A handsome man came over to take our coats. A waitress named Marge said she would be our server. Butler began to study the wine list. To my surprise, Carrie Mae said she would prefer champagne over wine. I said that sounded wonderful as well. When I looked closer at Carrie Mae, I realized what a beautiful lady she must have been in her younger years. Today, she wore more makeup and had jewels near her bun instead of flowers. I could tell she was planning on an enjoyable lunch.

"I can't thank you enough for your support since the loss of James," Butler began. "It has really been tough."

"When there are drugs or alcohol involved, you certainly can't blame yourself," I stated. "It's a disease of desperation."

He nodded.

Our drinks were served. Butler picked up his wine glass and made a toast. "Here's to my fine lady friends who love quilts!"

We chuckled and clinked our glasses.

"I know you want to move on, but I hope you and your brother were able to reconcile things," Carrie Mae said gently.

Butler paused before speaking. "For the most part, we have," he said quietly. "I can only imagine the pain he is feeling as the father since he and James were estranged. I don't know when he last saw James."

"That is so unfortunate," I said, feeling sad for the whole situation. "I hope something good comes from all of this."

"Thanks," Butler said as he smiled and nodded.

We placed our orders and knew we had to change the subject.

"Lily says you have been here before," Carrie Mae mentioned.

"I have, and I like the food, sweeping views, and atmosphere," Butler said as he looked around. "There are so many wineries in the region that I'm not sure I'll ever be able to visit them all."

"I feel the same way," I agreed.

"Has there been decent business through the winter months?" Butler asked both of us.

"I have nothing to compare it with, but I can't complain," I commented.

"Well, quilts are not my major income, but I think the traffic has been about the same as other months," Carrie Mae added. "How about yourself?"

"I see the market coming back," Butler said with confidence. "I think I can honestly say that. You see antiques and vintage items in more and more home decorating ads, and fashion icons are promoting them as well. That's what gave us the surge in the 1980s. Furniture we may call antique is being repurposed and painted. It's how the new generation has embraced the future. I'm not worried at all about the industry. It's just changing."

"I remember buying an antique kit to paint my dresser when I was a teenager," I said. "I hate myself for doing that. It was a horrid pea green!"

Everyone chuckled and nodded.

"Yes," Carrie Mae laughed. "Those were the days, my friends."

Our food was served. We marveled at the presentations on our plates. I enjoyed the champagne immensely. It reminded me of Christmas dinner at Loretta's house.

"Our Lily Girl here is about to become famous, Butler," Carrie Mae bragged. "Did you know that?"

"What's that all about?" he asked.

"She's referring to a column I'm writing for *Spirit* magazine."

"Congratulations," Butler said. "I like that magazine."

"I'm glad to hear it, because I plan to write frequently about quilts," I announced.

"Her column is called 'Living with Lily Girl,'"Carrie Mae stated proudly.

"I like it!" Butler grinned.

"I hope it will benefit the whole region, and hopefully bring in more business," I said. "I think I may bring a fresh perspective to life here in wine country."

"Well,, now I'm going to subscribe to it for sure," Butler revealed. "I usually just pick it up when I see it in the stores."

"That's great!" I replied.

"Now," Butler said, "I have something important to tell you." He toyed with his napkin for a bit before speaking again. "When James's possessions were inspected, a receipt was found. It was from the post office. Lily, I had told James about your connection to the red-and-green quilt after we first met. I suppose it didn't take much for him to get your address and send the quilt to you to cast suspicion in your direction. In his mind, perhaps that made it easier for him to concentrate on selling the other items he had stolen. Then, when he had the opportunity to get the quilt again, he picked it up from Carrie Mae with the intent of selling it, presumably to get money for drugs. In any case, I apologize for the stress this has caused you and Carrie Mae. Obviously, my nephew was troubled and was not thinking clearly."

I was dumbfounded. I looked at Carrie Mae, and her expression was one of shock. It was honestly too much to comprehend except to surmise that James had probably led a secretive life outside of the watch of his caring uncle.

I was eager to return to the peaceful atmosphere of my home and consider all that Butler had just told us. We parted ways amicably. My head felt like it was spinning.

When I got home, I wanted to take a nap due to all the champagne and the distressing news. Instead, I put the finishing touches on my quilt block for tomorrow's class. It was good therapy for me and required that I concentrate on something other than what Butler had shared at the end of our lunch.

CHAPTER 94

I had to admit that I was a bit nervous and anxious before I went to the quilt class. I did feel good about my block, but I still felt inferior to the others. Would they think my block was goofy for having doilies on it? Did quilters ever do such a thing?

Candace and I walked into the library together. She seemed very happy. I surmised that it was because she had a cool block to show.

"Good to see you all again," Susan said. "Judy brought us some treats from the coffee shop. Please feel free to help yourself before we begin."

I got some coffee and said hello to everyone. I sat down next to Edna, who was the queen bee of the class by far.

"I'm going to show you an interesting technique today. Some of you may want to use this method for your blocks instead of sewing them together first," Susan announced. "It's a quilt-as-you-go method. That means you will quilt the three layers of each block individually and then attach them to the other blocks to make your quilt."

Everyone looked puzzled.

"This method is great for those of you who may not have or want to use a quilting frame."

"Can I still quilt mine by machine?" Candace asked.

"Oh, yes!" Susan assured her. "It's a bit tricky when you join the quilted blocks. You must make sure that they turn out the same size. I've joined a few of the blocks together so you can see what I mean."

It took quite a while for her to explain the method. There were many questions. I couldn't see that I would ever use this method, but it was interesting to hear about it.

"Who wants to show the block they did for a favorite Christmas character?" Susan asked, looking around the table.

"I'll go first, because I may have to leave before we're done today," Candace said. She pulled out a cute red-nosed reindeer. It was a very simple deer appliqué that sported a big red nose. So far, I didn't feel intimated. Everyone approved of her choice, it seemed. Candace also included a cute explanation about why she chose that character.

"I'll go next," Marilyn offered. "I hate following my mom because her block is always so much better."

Marilyn's block was an old-fashioned Santa that she said she'd copied from a coloring book. That was a great idea.

"What did Mama do today?" Susan teased, looking at Edna.

Edna blushed as she displayed a simple manger scene with Mary and Joseph standing behind a baby Jesus. I knew someone would pick that idea. Edna's embellishments were always the finishing touches that made her blocks special. We all praised her workmanship.

"You're next, Lily," Susan directed.

I told them that my character was Jack Frost, so they would know my thought process regarding the snowflakes. I proudly placed my block on the table and waited for a reaction.

"You did that?" Edna asked.

I nodded.

"What a clever idea. I hope you weren't the one to crochet those tiny pieces!"

I chuckled and shook my head. "Are you kidding?" I joked. "I did well to get them sewn on!"

Others joined in and complimented my work.

"I love the dark background," Judy said. "The snowflakes really jump out."

"That is a very clever idea, Lily," Susan said. "I'm proud of you. I know this took a long time to complete. You hid your stitches really well."

"I think it's my favorite so far," I admitted. I was starting to breathe easier as we looked at the last few blocks.

"Ladies, ladies!" Susan said, trying to get our attention among the chatter. "Next week's block is to be your favorite Christmas ornament."

Susan received several puzzled looks.

"I know what mine is," Edna announced.

The rest of us remained stumped.

After we adjourned, I stayed to help Judy gather up the leftovers to take back to the coffee shop.

"You had the best block today, Lily," she whispered.

I beamed with pride.

"Are you going to open your shop now?" Candace asked.

"Yes, I'd better. Why?"

"I am looking for something with cameos for my sister's birthday," she replied. "Do you think you have anything? I don't have much time."

"I do, as a matter of fact."

"Good, I'll stop by."

CHAPTER 95

When I got back to the shop, I realized that I had gotten a text. It was from Robert Benton at the magazine.

Okay, have it your way. Just want "Living with Lily Girl" to make folks feel good.

Well, I'd won that one. What if "Living with Lily Girl" wasn't always so good?

Thanks!

Candace walked in the shop and reminded me that she was in a hurry.

"Well, this is what I have right here," I said, pointing out the cameos in the case.

"Oh, that bracelet is precious. May I see it?"

I gently took it out of the glass case and placed it in her hand.

"This is set in gold, and even Carrie Mae bragged about how delicate it is," I noted. "Is it big enough? It looks like it

333

was made for a tiny wrist."

"Yes, it'll be fine. I sure didn't expect to pay this much, but it's darling."

"I can take twenty percent off if that will help," I offered.

"That would be great. Thanks, I'll take it. Can you tell me about the person who owned it?"

"No, I purchased it with Rosie's inventory."

"Okay. Here's my charge card. I have to go."

As she flew out the door, Judy came in.

"I meant to ask you at class if you take anything on consignment."

"I've never thought about it, but I guess it depends on the item."

"I have some quilts that were in my mom's estate. I doubt that they were made by any family members. They aren't red and white, but would you look at them if I brought them in?"

"Absolutely! I need to bring in some different merchandise. It's tough coming up with the extra cash during the winter. Consignment would actually help me out."

I walked out the door with Judy as we watched the sky clear.

"What are you going to do with this little building that you refer to as Doc's house?" Judy asked. "It sure is cute!"

"I need help cleaning it out, so it's a spring project. There's so much junk in there now."

"Randal said lights go on and off in there, which is weird, don't you think?"

I nodded and smiled. "Do you want to see inside? I can get the key."

She looked hesitant.

"Okay, I guess."

I went to get the key and hoped that when Judy saw inside she would notice something I hadn't.

As I turned the key, Judy stood back like she feared something might explode. I motioned for her to go in first.

"Go in!" I encouraged. "I'll be right behind you."

When we both got in, side by side, very bright lights flashed like fireworks. We both ran out of the place like it was on fire, and the door closed automatically! This was not good, and it was also rather embarrassing.

"Lands, girl!" Judy yelled, making a beeline towards her car. "What's going on in there?"

"I'm sorry, Judy. I've never experienced that before."

"Good luck getting that cleaned out," Judy warned. "Someone or something doesn't want you in there!"

"I don't know what to think. Please don't tell anyone about this."

Judy shook her head in disgust as she got into her car.

"Bring the quilts whenever you want," I said rather weakly as she drove away.

I was shaking when I went inside. What was going on? Who could I talk to about this? I had to fix it, or rumors would fly. I was in no mood to keep the shop open, so I brought the rocker and quilt inside and locked the door at three.

CHAPTER 96

Despite a restless night, the next morning started with some good luck. A nice gentleman and a young man who had been to the shop previously came in to purchase a Victorian dresser from Rosie's inventory. The gentleman paid my asking price and carried it out. The vacant space gave me a chance to rearrange the shop after I vacuumed up the dust. I was beginning to move a hope chest to the vacant spot when the front door opened. I looked, and to my surprise, it was Mindy.

"Mindy, it's so good to see you," I greeted. "What are you doing out this way? Is Alex with you?"

"No, it's just me. Are you busy?"

"I'm just rearranging things."

"That's wonderful. Is anyone else here?"

I shook my head. "What's going on?" I put down the dust rag in my hand.

"Something's going on with Alex," she said, looking at the floor.

"Really?"

"He's not been himself," she said with a big sigh. "He's distancing himself from me. He just talks about how busy he is. We used to see each other at least once a week."

I nodded.

"He isn't seeing someone else, is he?"

"I'm sure he's not," I said, shaking my head.

"Well, that's good. I know how close the two of you are. He thinks the world of you. Would you mind talking to him to see if you can find out what's bothering him?"

"Sure," I agreed.

"I think he would tell you. Most of the time that we're together, he talks about you and your shop. I know there are times when I feel like he compares me to you."

"Don't be silly. We just happen to have a history and share the same sense of humor. Hey, how about a cup of coffee?"

"That sounds good."

She followed me into the kitchen and commented on the beautiful things she saw displayed. I needed to steer the conversation away from Alex and was thinking of how to do that when we were interrupted by an older man looking for old records. I didn't have a single one to show him. He exited immediately, leaving me to my conversation with Mindy.

"Alex tells me you will also be writing for *Spirit* magazine," Mindy mentioned, which brought us back to the subject of Alex.

"Yes. I'm enjoying it a lot, and the extra money will really come in handy."

"He is talented like you," she continued. "He never talks about his previous relationships. Was he ever close to getting married?"

"Alex?" I chuckled. "Not that I'm aware of."

"Do you think he'll ever want to get married?"

I was beginning to feel uncomfortable. I thought back on conversations Alex and I had shared concerning marriage; how should I answer? "Oh, I can't predict his future. I think he's happy with the way his life is right now. He seems to be enjoying your company."

"I used to think so, but now I feel like I'm wasting my time."

"Wasting your time? How?"

"About marriage, of course."

"If that is your goal for the relationship, you need to talk to him about it. We are all different. It's certainly not my goal, but don't get me wrong, I suppose it works for most folks."

"I'm not getting any younger," she admitted.

"None of us are, but aren't you giving yourself some unnecessary pressure? Isn't your life pretty good right now?"

"Perhaps, but I'm just looking ahead at my age." Mindy breathed a deep sigh. "Hey, I'm keeping you from your work. Thanks for the coffee. If you can share anything about Alex, please let me know."

I nodded. "It was good to see you again," I said as she opened the door to leave.

The visit left me feeling sad. What did she think I could do to help? I was going to have to tell Alex to either treat her better or be honest with his feelings and talk to her. I knew I wouldn't be able to keep this visit from Alex.

Before I went back to rearranging, I thought I'd better check my email. I had a group email from Loretta announcing her trip with Bill. Laurie responded by saying she would pay a visit to Lucy and Sarah while Loretta and Bill were gone. Laurie also commented that her winter sales were awful, but today she'd had a huge essential oil sale that she was sending to a customer. Her special note to me said I should carry some items that were related to lilies. Leave it to Laurie to think of clever ideas. I decided to keep it in mind.

Lynn was the last to respond. She said she was proud of me for writing a column, and then she described a black-and-white painting she was working on called "Zebra."

I responded to all of them by wishing Loretta safe travels and saying that I was excited about the opportunity to write. I ended by mentioning how much I missed each of them and asked Loretta to hug and kiss Lucy for me.

CHAPTER 97

My last sale of the day was an old cabinet that was so brittle I was afraid it wouldn't make it out to the man's truck. He loved it and I loved getting rid of it! After he pulled away, I closed the shop for the day. Clouds had darkened the sky and the temperatures were dropping. I poured myself a glass of wine and took it upstairs. I turned on my fireplace as well as the TV and saw a news report of a shooting. It reminded me of poor Rosie. I quickly turned the TV off.

I received a text. It was from Alex.

> I just wondered if you knew about Harry passing away two weeks ago.

> What? No!

> I was in Al's Bakery and I asked about him.

> That's awful! I wonder why someone didn't tell me?

Sorry.

Call me. I want to talk.

Okay.

Seconds later, he did just that.

"I'm so sorry that you didn't hear about it," Alex said. "Al said the funeral was over before most of the people in the neighborhood had even heard about it."

"Poor Harry." I paused and then continued, "Interesting news on my end is that Mindy came out here to see me."

"Really? She drove to Augusta?"

"Yes, and I was very surprised to see her. She's picked up on your behavior and wanted to know if I knew what was wrong with you."

"Hmmm," Alex responded. "What did you tell her?"

"I acted ignorant, which wasn't hard," I joked. "You really need to put the girl out of her misery, one way or another."

"I like her, I like her, I really do," he insisted. "I just don't like talking about the future with her. She was fun at first, but then she'd misinterpret my words and actions. I've ridden in this rodeo before. She wants to plan my future."

"I understand. She evidently wants to get married. It happens to be her goal, so if it's not yours, you need to tell her."

"That is what I hate about seeing just one person," he complained. "Why doesn't she just play it cool and see what happens?"

"So, if she played hard to get, you might show more

interest?" I smirked.

He chuckled. "Maybe. Who knows? I honestly do not know her very well, and this is really a turnoff."

"Not my monkey, not my circus, as you like to say," I joked. "I'm just the reporter."

"I know, I know. I'll deal with it. She's asked me to go to a fundraiser tomorrow night for Habitat and I've agreed to go. I'll tell her then."

"Good luck. Hey, and thanks for letting me know about Harry. I wish I knew a family member to contact. I guess Harry's up there flirting with Bertie."

Alex chuckled. "You're such a romantic," he teased.

After hanging up, my mood became quite somber as I thought of Harry. It's hard to think of someone being so strong and vibrant, and then the next moment, he's gone.

I wondered what Alex would do about Mindy. Had he really given her a chance? I'd watched Alex do this routine over and over. Did she put the cart before the horse when it came to marriage? She should have been more patient. It hadn't been a year since they'd started dating. He'd seemed to like her attention until he picked up on her motivation. Alex and I had never had a secret between us, so I'd needed to tell him about Mindy's visit. I was glad I did.

I started to compare their relationship to the one I shared with Marc. I thought Marc and I were both on the same page, which gave me comfort. Things go haywire when one of the two wants more.

The thought of Marc made me miss him. Should I call him in Chicago? He'd be coming home soon, so I decided not to bother him. I was feeling mentally exhausted, so I decided to retire for the evening.

CHAPTER 98

I checked my quilt kit the next morning to see what I had to work with for the next block. The only ornament that came to my mind was a handprint ornament from my childhood. Our mother had done one for each of us when we were in the first grade. When the ornament box came out each year, we each would frantically search for our own ornament. Mother let us place them wherever we wanted on the Christmas tree. As we grew older, it was hard to believe that our hands were ever that little.

How could I possibly make a block that did justice to that memory? It needed to look like Christmas. Who would have thought that so much work could go into a Christmas quilt? There was no question that each of us was going to end up with a very personal quilt!

My phone rang. I was pleased to see that it was Carrie Mae. She'd called to tell me that she and Betty were going into the city and that her shop would be closed. I appreciated her telling me, so I wouldn't think something was wrong.

"Betty wants to visit a friend at Mercy Hospital in

Washington," she explained. "After that, we'll have lunch and shop a bit."

"That's great! You deserve a day off. I'm sitting here struggling with the Christmas block for my next quilting class. I sure wish I had a bigger fabric stash."

"Well, I think you're going to a have a longer wait to get any quilt shop out here," she said.

"Did you meet with Gracie? What happened?"

"Yes, we met. She decided rather quickly that the arrangement wouldn't work. She's probably right. She was overwhelmed when she saw my basement, as I thought she might be. She said she'd keep looking for a suitable location."

"I hope she doesn't end up opening one far away from here."

"She was going to look closer at Defiance, so maybe she'll come up with something there. If you need fabric, I'll look upstairs to see if I can find a box of scraps I may still have from years ago. I used to make little outfits for my teddy bears."

"You and your teddy bears! I hope you will show them to me someday."

She chuckled but didn't agree to let me see them. "I'll let you know if I find the box."

"Thanks! Have a fun day today!"

After I hung up, I was a bit sad knowing that Gracie's shop wouldn't open soon. I also felt a little down about Betty and Carrie Mae having a day out. It made me miss the people I was closest to on The Hill. I abandoned my quilt kit and decided to reread my next column for Robert before submitting it. What should I write about next? I knew Robert would want me to include the wineries out here, so

I might have to start checking them out. Wine dinners and clubs were picking up in popularity, so I might have to look closer at that type of cultural activity.

I continued to feel unsettled, so I decided to close the shop for a bit and take a walk. I needed to check on Kitty's guest house and antique shop, so a walk would do me good. I bundled up and thought about picking up a cup of hot coffee at Kate's.

Forcing my body up the hill, I realized that I was getting quite out of shape. I needed to get up earlier and walk these hills every morning. However, that idea might sound a little better in the springtime.

Cars were coming and going, but it didn't appear that any of them were stopping at the shops. I stopped at The Cranberry Cottage to say hello to Karen. It was an absolutely darling shop.

"Hey, come on in, Lily," Karen said.

"I'll just stay a minute," I said. "I'm on a mission. I just wanted to say hello while I was on my walk."

"Did you make a decision on a barn quilt?"

"No, it'll have to wait until spring, I'm afraid. I have enough challenges ahead and putting up the barn quilt isn't a priority just yet. Don't worry, I'm sure I'll display one at some point."

"If you need some help, let us know. We can put them up quickly."

"Thanks, I will. I'd better be on my way!"

Arriving at the antique shop, I looked in the windows first. Then I entered the picket fence gate of the guest house. Despite the lingering wintry weather, I saw a few tulip leaves peeking out of the ground. I picked up some mail on the porch and unlocked the door. I placed the papers on the table and took a quick look around. I wondered who built this charming little house.

After I left the guesthouse, I went by Johann's and picked up some things. When I left, the wind was fierce. There must have been a storm ahead. I tightened the scarf around my neck and headed home as fast as I could. As I got closer to my house, I saw Judy's car parked in front. I called to her as I got closer.

"Hey, I'm coming. Don't go away!" She was holding a large trash bag. That led me to believe that she had brought her quilts for me to see.

"It's about time you got back to work!" Judy joked.

I unlocked my door, and we were both glad to get out of the wind.

CHAPTER 99

"I brought you some quilts to take a look at for consignment," Judy began as she pulled them out of the bag.

"Well, let's have a look. We can spread them out on the kitchen table in the other room. Oh, you have a Flying Geese," I said as I rolled out the first one.

"I do? Are all of these triangles supposed to be geese?"

"Yes, from what I know. These are arranged a little differently than most."

"I hate these colors," Judy said, shaking her head in disgust.

"Judging by this pink and black, I'd guess it was made in the 1950s. I love black in a quilt. Do you know who made it? It sure wasn't used much."

"Somebody in the family made it, most likely, but I don't know who. How much do you think I can get for it?"

"The good news about this quilt is that it is in good condition. Condition is key. The colors may be challenging, but the right person may love it. How much do you want for the quilt? I'll add a thirty percent markup for the shop."

"I really don't care. Whatever you think. I want it to have a reasonable price, so it will sell."

"Okay. I'll try pricing it between two and three hundred dollars."

Judy nodded her approval. "You may not want the next one at all. We really wore this one out when we were growing up."

"Well, look at this," I said with amusement. "It's a single Log Cabin."

"A what?"

"It's just one large block of the Log Cabin quilt pattern. You're right, it is in poor condition."

"I told you so."

"Okay, I will pass on this one, but what a cool quilt it would have been in its day! Wouldn't you want to hang onto that one, with all the memories you have with it?"

"It's worn out!"

"Well, we don't always get rid of things because they're worn out. It's still in one piece and can keep someone very warm. It's so soft and cuddly." I held it close.

"You're comparing this quilt to a person who's getting old and worn out, aren't you?"

I laughed and nodded. "Maybe so. I hope no one gets rid of me when that happens."

"Okay. I feel guilty. I'll keep it. Here's the last one."

"My goodness! This is a Mariner's Compass."

"It does look like a compass, doesn't it?"

"Yes, and it's an intricate pattern that you don't see much here in the Midwest. I love the red and green."

"That's not red. It's tan, don't you think?"

"It was a nice red at one time. Holly, a friend of mine

who lectures about quilts, calls the red dye that turns tan 'Congo red.' The early Turkey red was dye-fast and stayed bright, unlike this red. The green here used to be darker. Green dye was terrible back then. They called it fugitive green because it escaped and faded in stages. It will likely get worse. Regardless, this is a wonderful graphic quilt."

"What's wonderful about it?"

"Look at the intricate piecing and tiny quilting stitches. Someone put a lot of work into this. This is the oldest one you have by far."

"How old?"

"Maybe 1850 to 1870, when many red-and-green quilts were made. It may be a hard sell because of the faded colors, but folks like me see other things that we're attracted to."

"Okay, that's great. Get what you can for it."

I created an agreement that explained the asking price and the price she would get when it sold. This would be an experiment for me as well as for her. She left, happy to have found a place to consign her quilts.

That same afternoon, a couple entered the shop. They said they were staying at a nearby bed and breakfast for their wedding anniversary and were just browsing through the local shops. They were quite lovely. I enjoyed visiting with them even though they did not make a purchase.

That evening, I finally heard from Marc. He was glad to be home and said he was anxious to see me. I told him I would consider taking a day off and coming into St. Charles to meet him for lunch. I also thought about going to The Hill to see Alex, Holly, and Lynn, but I realized that it was Marc who was on my mind and in my heart.

CHAPTER 100

It was a brisk, sunny day when I left for St. Charles. I'd told Marc I would spend the morning shopping and would meet him for lunch. He suggested the Mother-in-Law House Restaurant because it offered a quiet atmosphere for conversation and was a favorite of his. I had been there with Lynn many years ago.

The time to shop by myself was a treat. The shops were just beginning to open as I arrived. I parked in front of a shop called The Flower Petaler. Attractive flower arrangements were attached to the green shutters. That told me that spring was alive and well in this shop. I went inside and lost track of time as I meandered through their many rooms. Easter ideas galore were displayed beautifully. There was one room filled with clothing and accessories, followed by a room full of Christmas goodies. I could have spent my entire morning in that shop.

I walked out with a door wreath adorned with lilies, which was perfect for my shop door. I also chose a white knit top and two brightly-colored scarves, which would be perfect for spring. I placed my items in the car and felt my spirits lifted. I spotted The English Shop across the street and decided to take a closer look.

A pleasant lady with red hair greeted me with a delightful English accent. The shop had shelves stocked full of food, tea, and gift ideas from England. I thought of Carrie Mae and her love for tea, so I asked for some help as I chose a box to take back to her. I also added boxes of tea biscuits and shortbread cookies to my checkout pile.

Leaving there, I looked down the street to see a shop called The Quilted Cottage. Curious, I got in my car and was able to park right in front of the cute Victorian building. A tall, cheerful lady named Pat was eager to help me. I told her I needed some basic solid-colored fabrics for my stash, and she found the perfect pack of half-yard cuts to suit my needs. Christmas fabric was on sale, so I took advantage of the opportunity and purchased some for my Christmas quilt.

The shop's four rooms were filled with awesome quilts and projects that were finished products in case the customer preferred to purchase a kit. One of the rooms was only wool fabric and related patterns, which I knew were quite the rage with some quilters. Pat's personality had me buying things I'd never thought about! I splurged on new scissors that I would only use to cut fabric. I added another pair of small stork scissors for my embroidery work. There were so many nifty gadgets. Gracie might do just fine with her new little shop in wine country after all.

It was such a happy place that I hated to leave, but time was running short. Pat assured me they were just a phone call away and would send me whatever I needed. I signed up to receive emails from them, took a few photos, and then went to meet Marc.

Marc was already seated at a table when I walked into the

restaurant. He stood up when he saw me enter the fancy, ornate room. His hug and the glimmer in his eyes made me feel very cherished and loved.

"You have no idea how happy I am that I took the day off," I said as I sat down.

"You had some luck, did you?" he asked with a grin.

"My back seat is full. What else can I say? I can't believe I found a quilt shop. I think the trip here will be worth it if I need anything for my quilting hobby."

The waiter filled our water glasses and took our drink orders. The special of the day was quiche and salad, and the soup was chicken chardonnay. Marc said he'd tasted the soup before and that it was awesome.

"I love their food," he commented. "I think everything here is homemade."

"Be sure to save room for our famous coconut cream pie," the waiter suggested.

"Sounds great!" I responded. "Save me a piece."

Marc chuckled and told him to make it two.

"This is such a great historic area. I wonder if the shops make twice the income that I do with all this traffic."

"Sometimes traffic is deceiving. There's a lot of competition here for tourist dollars. Business owners need to be really good at what they do."

"Good point," I agreed. "Holly is going to be so jealous when I tell her I came here to shop. I would have invited her, but I just really wanted to shop alone. Perhaps I can meet her here for lunch sometime."

"How is your abused friend? Oh, I'm sorry, that didn't come out right."

I smiled with understanding. "Nothing has changed,

except one thing," I said with a grin.

"What's that?"

"Well, she went to lunch with a man the other day. His name is Ken, and it's someone she's known for a while."

"From what you've told me, it sounds as if she could use the experience of being around another man. Are they having an affair?"

"No, no, I didn't mean to insinuate that at all," I explained. "She's lonely and craves intelligent conversation. I'm going to encourage her to keep seeing him. The monster will find out at some point, so I don't know what that will mean."

"This is where I'm supposed to ask why she doesn't leave him, but I know how all of that works. Enough about Holly. I want to talk about us."

I smiled.

The food arrived at just the right time. We were hungry. My soup and the house salad were delicious. I particularly liked the salad dressing.

"I'm free the rest of the day, so what would you like to do?" Marc asked, touching my hand.

"Right now, I just want to enjoy this delicious pie," I teased.

"Wait until you try that pie crust. I thought my mother's crust was the best in the world until I tasted this."

As I tasted the first bite, I agreed that it was indeed delicious.

"Lynn talked about the Foundry Art Centre out here by the river. She is having an exhibit there in the spring. I wouldn't mind seeing it."

"Excellent. It's sad that I don't go there more often, since it's so close to my loft. You'll love it."

CHAPTER 101

The Foundry Art Centre was just what the name indicated. It was a gigantic foundry that had once made railroad cars. The first level was where the galleries were located, and above that was a balcony of working artists' studios. I told Marc I wanted to visit some of them, and we headed in that direction. Some artists were in their studios and some were not. I was surprised to know that Marc knew so much about art. It was no wonder he took a special interest in Lynn and her work. We visited with a delightful man who made exquisite pottery. Marc bought me a unique teapot, and I was touched by his kindness. As I looked down into the open gallery, I knew it would be a prestigious place for Lynn's artwork to be shown.

As we left the gallery, we noticed that the Katy Trail was to our left. We decided to take a walk despite the very brisk wind. It was wonderful to see the riverfront uncluttered by advertising or commercial structures. Seeing nature reminded me how close we are to our Maker each day. As we passed a couple of walkers and runners, I felt happy that they had this scenic location to enjoy while exercising.

At four, I told Marc that I needed to head home. His invitation to spend the night and go home in the morning just didn't seem right today. It was hard to turn his offer down. I knew I was falling more and more in love with my baseball man.

When we got back to my car, his goodbye embrace almost had me second-guessing my decision to leave, but I held fast to my decision. I headed home knowing it would be dark soon. I smiled, thinking about my new purchases and my time with Marc. The day had been so relaxing, and the change of place had been good for my soul.

All in all, it was good to be home. I entered the house in a hurry to escape the dropping temperatures. When I went upstairs, I was shocked to see the fireplace already turned on. Was that Rosie's idea? I kept it on as I snacked on a dinner of fresh fruit and yogurt and reflected on our wonderful lunch. Another piece of that coconut cream pie sure would have hit the spot!

Alex called around eight, and I knew right away that it must be important.

"Well, I'm on the bad boy list now," Alex stated.

"You broke up with Mindy?"

"Pretty much. I know I broke her heart, and I'm not proud of it. She tried to back off about her feelings like it didn't matter, but it was too late."

"That's unfortunate, but I'm glad you were honest with her."

"I'm actually relieved," he admitted. "If we're supposed to be together, it will happen."

"Oh, and how is that supposed to work?"

"I don't know. It's just what I hear. Did Marc get back in town?"

"He did, and I went to St. Charles to see him today."

"Well, if that doesn't sound a bit serious!"

I described our day, and Alex encouraged me to take off work more often.

"I wish Augusta could attract some of the shops I saw today," I complained.

"It wouldn't be Augusta if it did," Alex argued. "That's what makes your quiet village so quaint and attractive. You are nestled in the wine country hills, and St. Charles is located along the river."

"You're right. That's the reason I escaped here all the time. I like a smaller community. Now it's my home. We do have more wineries, though. However, in St. Charles, I passed a winery located on their main street."

"Yes, I've been there."

"Back to you and Mindy. Is Mindy going to be okay?"

"I hope so. I wouldn't be surprised if she calls you."

"You may feel sorry about breaking up with her and be the one calling her," I teased.

"I don't think so. I don't think I'm good boyfriend material."

After a few more minutes of conversation, I told Alex I was very tired from my day. Part of my heart felt sorry for Mindy.

I realized that I was too tired to open my packages. I piled everything on the couch upstairs. I couldn't wait to hang my lily wreath on the door tomorrow when I opened the shop. As I was ready to change clothes and get ready for bed, I got a text from Marc.

Home safe and sound?

Made it!

Enjoyed the day.

Me too!

Goodnight kiss!

Back to you!

I turned off the fireplace and got into bed. I spent a few minutes glancing at the day's mail. There it was! A real copy of *Spirit* magazine with my first column! I nearly tore the pages getting to page twelve, where "Living with Lily Girl" took up a whole page! Soft lilies in a grape vineyard decorated the background. I loved seeing my contact information at the bottom. After I read and reread my column, I turned to the introduction that Robert had written about me. He was complimentary of me and wished me and my column much success.

CHAPTER 102

The next day I had an unexpected visit from the Kentucky quilt buyer, Chuck Waller.

"I see you're still in business," he joked.

"I'm trying. How are you?"

"I'm hitting the road again now that most of the winter storms are over," he reported. "I just stopped at Carrie Mae's. She made me sip some tea with her before she gave me a discount."

I chuckled. "Good for her."

"You got some good buys for me?" he asked as he walked into the quilt room. "Hey, your inventory's getting low. Are quilts selling for you?"

"I can't complain. I do need to buy some things, but it's winter. Money's tight right now."

"I can add to your coffers if I find something here," he said as he quickly went through my inventory.

He pulled out the Flying Geese quilt that Judy had on consignment as well as the two red-and-white quilts I had for sale.

"Cut the price in half on these and you've got a good sale for the day," he said confidently.

I shook my head. "I can't do it. First, I took the Flying Geese on consignment for a friend. I didn't mark it up much. Red-and-white quilts are getting harder and harder to find, so I can't discount them. I can do a standard dealer discount, but that's it."

"Okay, keep your red-and-white ones. What does your friend have to have on this Flying Geese quilt?"

"I have a 30/70 consignment agreement."

"Okay, I'll pay her price and the two of you will be happy."

I paused, knowing it would be great for Judy.

"Deal."

"You'd better stock up, Lily Girl," he said as he carelessly pushed Judy's quilt onto the counter.

"So someone like you can come along and pay me half of what they're worth?" I joked. "No thanks!"

"Don't bother with a bag. Here's your cash. I'll be back in the spring."

I didn't respond with a smile. After he left, I had mixed feelings about what had just happened. I put Judy's cash in an envelope for her. That was not how I wanted to do business. How I wished Rosie was still around. Well, maybe she was.

Before someone else came in, I left a message on Judy's phone to tell her about the quilt sale. As soon as I hung up, Lynn called.

"Congrats, Lily. I read your column. I'm so proud of you. I bought copies to send to Laurie and Loretta."

"Oh, thanks. I'm very pleased. I hope the publisher will always be happy with what I write."

"What great advertisement for your shop."

"I hope so. We'll see if it'll help."

"I enjoyed Alex's article."

"Speaking of Alex, he just broke it off with Mindy."

"How is she taking it?"

"Not well. She came out to see me last week to see if I knew what was wrong with Alex's behavior regarding their relationship. I didn't know what to say, but I knew Alex did not want to get serious."

"So many women feel their clock ticking and feel pressure to get married. Before I forget, I did talk to Vic at the Gallery Augusta about putting a few of my pieces in there to sell."

"Wonderful. Let me know when you're coming out and we'll go to lunch. Marc and I went to the Foundry Art Centre yesterday. What an awesome place for your exhibit."

"I know. I can't wait. I can't believe you came in to see him either."

"I shopped on the street and then we had lunch at the Mother-in-Law House Restaurant."

"I love that place. Did you have the coconut cream pie?"

"Of course."

Lynn's call certainly lifted me up for the day. It was exciting to know her paintings would be out here in Augusta.

I saw that I had gotten a text from Alex.

Got free copies of the magazine for you. It looks great! Congrats!

Thanks! Save them for me!

It was starting to feel official. Lily Rosenthal was a writer, not an editor.

CHAPTER 103

To my surprise, Betty stopped in the shop the next morning.

"Oh, I need to sit for a minute," she said, puffing to catch her breath.

"Betty, are you okay?" I pulled a chair to the door so she could sit down quickly.

"Sure," she said, sitting down. "I left my car at Carrie Mae's and told myself that you were just down the hill. Well, it's colder and further than I thought, and now I have to walk up the hill to get to my car."

"No, I'll drive you. Was Carrie Mae open?"

She shook her head. "She'll be open when I get back. We're having lunch in Washington today. We have a friend who lives there who's not in good health."

"How about a cup of coffee?"

"No thanks. The real reason I'm here is to remind you that Carrie Mae has a birthday this month. Did you know that?"

"No, I didn't. I'm glad you said something."

"Well, I want it to be special. Do you have any idea about what I might give her? I know she admired much of Rosie's inventory."

"I am going to have to think about it, Betty," I responded. "I'm going to have the same problem as you. How old is she going to be?"

Betty chuckled. "If I told you, I'd lose a longtime friend. No one knows that answer except her daughter and me."

"That's a pretty hard secret to keep in this day and age."

"Don't I know it! If you have any ideas about what to do for her, let me know."

"Absolutely!"

"She's closer to you than her own daughter, by the way."

"That's not true," I protested. "Betty, on another topic, you might be able to help me with something."

"What would that be?" she asked as she spotted some old postcards on the counter.

"Well, Carrie Mae may have told you that I have a lot of activity over in Doc's brick house."

Betty gave me a puzzled look. "She mentioned that she thought Rosie had followed you here. What else is happening?"

"Just flashing lights in a building with no electricity."

"Well, there have always been rumors about that place. Growing up, we were told that Doc died in his little office. Some say he hung himself, some say he overdosed on his own medicine, and some even say he may have been murdered."

"Wow, I've never heard any of those rumors."

"You are new to the area and too young. Who knows what's true? Evidently Doc was a real character. He scared a lot of folks, especially if he had been drinking. He had his share of enemies. Can you imagine having to go into that little room as a child to get a shot? Doctors were never our friends years ago. I have my own nightmares about men in white coats."

"I never thought about all of that. I would really like to know what's happening so I can have some peace."

"Be careful as you try to find out. You may not want to know. You won't be able to tear it down, plus it won't solve what really happened there. It's on the list of historic places here in Augusta. You're lucky you haven't experienced any crime or homeless folks in there or in your sheds."

I nodded. "I'm glad we had this talk, Betty. I feel like I'm supposed to be here. Does that make any sense to you?"

"Sure! We're glad to have you, Lily!"

"I've had so many good experiences here, like the wonderful Christmas in this town. Come spring, I hope to refurbish things around here that I couldn't during the winter."

Betty smiled. "We need your generation to bring a fresh perspective and hope. My generation is dying off, but we did our part while we were here!"

CHAPTER 104

After Betty left, I felt more uneasy than ever about the mysterious house on my property. How would I ever know the truth about this place, and would it even matter?

It was sweet of Betty to think about Carrie Mae's birthday. I remembered Carrie Mae admiring much of Rosie's inventory, but I didn't pay that much attention at the time. Part of me said Carrie Mae didn't need more jewelry. I also knew how much she liked it. Would it be the same situation as someone deciding that I had enough quilts?

I opened the shop door and carried the rocker to the porch. I placed a pink-and-white Jacob's Ladder quilt across it. It looked like Easter, so I went inside to bring out a ceramic rabbit and placed it next to the rocker. It made me smile.

"Good morning, Ms. Lily!" Snowshoes said as he approached me with a stack of mail. "How's it going today?"

"Pretty good. Snowshoes, how old are you?"

He scratched his head and smiled. "I'll be sixty-five in April, but I'm still not sure when I'm going to retire."

"You are amazing. I think the exercise keeps you young."

He chuckled. "Well, there are many days when I have aches and pains, but I tell myself that I'll just walk them off."

"What a great attitude. Did you grow up in Augusta?"

"Thereabouts. Why?"

"What can you tell me about Doc's house over there?"

He chuckled to himself. "You are hearing stuff, are you?"

I nodded.

"Well, this has been a colorful corner for as long as I can remember. The place sat vacant for so long after Doc died that it became mysterious to folks around here. When Carrie Mae bought it, there was some sense of relief that this bright yellow paint would go away. People hoped something would change for the better. I think everyone knows now that things will."

I smiled. "I'm not changing the yellow paint!"

Snowshoes chuckled.

"Betty Bade said she thinks Doc died in that building."

"So they say! I do think he was a little tipsy most of the time, so who knows what really happened?"

"You heard that too?"

He nodded. "You haven't discovered a lot of liquor bottles around the property? I'll bet when you start tearing down those sheds that you'll be surprised."

"I did see bottles inside the brick building. I thought they were medicine bottles."

Snowshoes gave out a good belly laugh. "He probably did take a lot of his own medicine, if you know what I mean. Like most folks, I have a feeling that he's still hanging around, but I think he's harmless. I'll bet he is mighty pleased with the likes of you on the property, Ms. Lily."

"I sure hope so," I said as Snowshoes turned around and

went on his way.

Why didn't Carrie Mae tell me about all of this before I purchased the house?

I needed to get my mind on something else until I had a customer. I took some glassware into the kitchen to give it a good scrubbing. Some of these items hadn't been washed since I'd bought them. I knew it would make an enormous difference.

The front door opened, and Susan entered.

"Well, look who's here! Are you off today?"

"I am." She nodded. "I never take the time to look around in here, and you know how much I love quilts. I also wanted to talk to you about Gracie's idea of opening a quilt shop. From your business perspective, do you really think she can make it? I wouldn't want her to have false hopes."

"I don't honestly know, Susan. My friend says that quilt shop owners today need from fifty to a hundred thousand dollars in capital to get a good start. Customers can have it all these days by buying on the internet."

"Goodness. I wonder if she knows that?"

"She's probably looked into it. She would have the advantage of being convenient for quilters out here, plus it would offer some social opportunity for women."

"It's her dream, so I guess we'll see. I just don't want it to turn into a nightmare for her."

"Let's look at the quilts," I suggested. "I just sold one on consignment for Judy."

"That's great. I might have one or two for you to consign as well."

"I'd like to have the class over to see my quilts at some point."

"Lily, that would be awesome!"

CHAPTER 105

"What is the most amazing quilt you've ever seen as a collector?" Susan asked.

"I can answer that right away!"

"Seriously?"

"A high-end quilt dealer brought a quilt to show me that was for sale for eighteen thousand dollars, and he had an appraisal with him to prove it."

"No way! Was it stitched in gold?"

I smiled at the thought. It took me quite a while to describe the awesome Christmas quilt Butler had showed me. I could tell she was trying hard to visualize it.

"Did you buy it? Just kidding, of course."

"No, and unfortunately it has been stolen from the dealer."

"Good heavens!"

"It's a long story, but it gave me the chills since I love Christmas so much. If I owned it, I would decorate my entire house around it."

Susan's eyes got big. "Well, quilters copy and reproduce

antique quilts all the time. Why don't you try to make it yourself? It would be cheaper!"

I agreed with that!

"I do well to get my little quilt block done each week for class."

"You're too hard on yourself. I think you could do anything you put your mind to. I could help you."

"I've never really learned to piece well. It wasn't just the pattern that was neat, it was the incredible small quilting stitches and visual impact that were overwhelming. Butler, the owner, felt my sincere reaction and even offered to discount it for me."

"What kind of discount?"

"Believe me, I still couldn't afford the quilt."

"Well, that was nice of him to offer."

"It was, and as a dealer myself, I know we like to put a quilt or antique into the right hands. We want to know it's going to be taken care of. I have one customer who couldn't afford the quilt she wanted, so I'm letting her pay ten dollars a month until it's free and clear."

"You really have an appreciation for these quilts, don't you?"

"So do you, Susan. I just happen to be drawn to antique quilts. I seem to sense their past and always want to know more. I'm writing a column now called 'Living with Lily Girl' for *Spirit* magazine."

"It is wonderful that you can share your knowledge in that column."

Just then, an older couple entered, so I left Susan to look at the quilts by herself.

"We're just browsing, but we're both antique lovers,"

the man announced.

"Well, you came to the right place. I'm Lily. This is my shop, so please take your time as you look around."

"Thank you," the woman said.

Susan came to the counter to purchase a doll quilt that I had for sale.

"This little Four-Patch quilt is too cute for words," Susan noted with a smile. "I've never owned a doll quilt before. I never realized how pricey they were, either."

"It's something, isn't it? Not many survive in good condition. I'll give you a discount. I'm glad you will be the proud owner."

She smiled.

"I'm not so sure my husband will feel the same way," she joked. "Lily, I'm serious about helping you make that Feathered Star. Maybe if we just made one block, it would inspire you to continue."

"Or not!" I joked. "I may take you up on that. Right now, I'm stumped regarding what I want to do for my ornament block."

"Candace said the same thing," Susan acknowledged. "Don't beat yourself up over it. Perhaps think of another idea. Surely there were several ornaments you admired."

"You may be right." I nodded. "I really do want it to mean something, however."

"I'd better get going," she said, moving towards the door.

"Thanks for the purchase, and I'll think about your offer."

How sweet of Susan to make that offer. Maybe I should rethink my block. After the couple left the shop, I grabbed some celery and carrots for lunch as I thought about other possibilities.

It was starting to sprinkle outside, so I got the rocker and quilt display items moved inside. If it rained any harder, I was going to close.

I opened my laptop and observed an extensive list of emails. They were all coming from my Lily Girl website. The first one was touching.

"Thank you, Lily Girl, for your good advice on collecting. I will now have to focus better," said Alice from Austin, Texas.

I scrolled to the next one.

"How can you upgrade your collection if you have no money?" asked Thomas from Clarksville, Tennessee.

"I want to come to your lovely shop and quaint little town! Thanks for your useful information," wrote Brenda from St. Petersburg, Florida.

There were ten emails to boost my ego. I couldn't believe it! Robert had said I would get a response. Hopefully, it would all be good. I was determined to answer each message.

CHAPTER 106

I closed the shop and dedicated the rest of the day to answering emails and posting responses on my website. How did shop owners run their businesses and promote business at the same time? A lot of time could be wasted staying on social media. "Living with Lily Girl" would give me the exposure I couldn't afford to buy.

I couldn't wait to call Alex and tell him what was happening.

"I got mail," I cheered in his ear.

"Well, I'm glad Snowshoes is still delivering," he joked.

"No, I meant emails from my first column."

"Great. Any threats?"

"You're funny. No. All good so far."

"Robert will be glad to hear that. I get a few emails occasionally, depending on how controversial my subject matter is. I think you are supposed to be the warm and fuzzy writer."

I chuckled.

Alex continued, "He wants your readers to fall in love with you."

"I don't think that will happen, but I'm just glad they're reading it. Enough about me. How is Mindy doing?"

"Pray for me tonight. I'm going with her to that fundraiser."

"I will. Be nice but honest."

"Yes, Mother Rosenthal."

"Just have fun."

"If she has wedding bells on her mind, I won't."

"Well, I kind of admire a woman who knows what she wants."

"I'll get back to you on that. I have to run."

After I hung up, I wrote a group email to my sisters to catch them up on the news. I wanted to give them an example of one of my fan letters.

The first to respond was Laurie. She exclaimed that it was a sign of good things to come. She added a P.S. that said she'd had a drink with a new shop owner on the street. She wasn't sure, but she thought he liked her. He'd suggested having lunch with her next week.

I responded with excitement. Laurie never mentioned men. She didn't share that subject with her sisters, anyway. I asked more about the guy but knew she wouldn't tell me. At the end of her message, she mentioned that she was going to see Sarah and Lucy tomorrow.

I went back to moving furniture around. When I moved a Christmas plate to another location, I noticed it portrayed a pine tree with a branch that held only one ornament. It was simple and attractive, and it gave me an idea for my ornament block. I could even be ambitious and do four of them representing my sisters and myself. I put the plate aside to use as a resource.

After I closed the shop, I went upstairs and started sketching something similar to the plate design. Most of it would have to be embroidered.

I thought about Susan's visit. I should really take her up on her offer of making a Feathered Star block. I liked the idea of her showing me, since I was a visual person. I hated following directions.

I had nothing exciting to eat for dinner, so I decided to go Ashley Rose Restaurant on Walnut Street. I could just have a sandwich at the bar. I decided to walk, despite the cold temperatures. I really needed the exercise. If I had enough energy after dinner, I'd walk by and check on Kitty's guest house and the antique shop.

I was the only one sitting at the bar. As I looked at the menu, I decided that I wanted more than a sandwich. Everything looked so good. The waitress was friendly and asked where I was from. I was sure that was part of the small talk she likely engaged in with most of her customers. When I told her where I lived and the name of my shop, she recalled the bright yellow house down the hill. I nodded and didn't tell her much more. As I gave her my order, another person sat down a stool away from me.

"I'll have the usual, Sally," he told the waitress.

When I glanced over, I saw an older, distinguished-looking man with a beard. He was wearing a business suit. One didn't see that every day in Augusta. He saw me staring at him and nodded a polite hello.

"You must be a regular here," I said, starting the conversation.

He smiled and nodded. "Every Thursday when I'm in town," he assured me. "And you?"

"I rarely come here," I said. "I have a shop nearby and didn't feel like cooking anything."

"What shop?" he asked with interest.

"Lily Girl's Quilts and Antiques," I stated proudly.

"A quilt enthusiast, huh?" he asked with a smile.

"You might say that. Do you like quilts?"

"I do. My mother and grandmother made them," he said.

How many times had I heard that response?

My meal arrived, and I told the waitress I'd changed my mind and would go ahead and have a glass of their house merlot.

"If I may interrupt, you might reconsider and try a merlot called Vintage Rose. It's a little on the heavy side, but if you're a red wine person, it would be a better choice. My first suggestion would have been their Winter White for the chicken, but I know how you red wine lovers are."

I was impressed.

"Oh, you do? What makes you such a wine connoisseur?"

He chuckled with embarrassment.

"It's what I do for a living," he explained. "This place is one of my accounts, along with many wineries around here."

"A wine salesman, huh?"

He nodded and grinned.

CHAPTER 107

"I am indeed a wine salesman, and I have the pleasure of coming to this beautiful wine country very often," the man said warmly.

"Well, thanks for the wine tip. I'm sure I'll like it."

"My treat," he said kindly. "You look like a hardworking young lady who deserves a good wine at the end of the day."

"Not that young, but thank you." I blushed. "I've never turned down a good merlot—or any merlot for that matter."

He got a kick out of that.

"You're welcome. Next time, try the French dip. It's the best I've ever had."

I did enjoy the wine he'd recommended. As I savored the delicious meal, I found myself enjoying my dinner partner every bit as much. His was charming and delightful company, and I was always a sucker for a sexy Italian accent. A second glass of merlot seemed to disappear as we finished our meals amid a flurry of interesting conversation.

"I'd really like to know your name," he said finally. "Could it possibly be Lily?"

I smiled. "Lily Rosenthal. What's your name?"

"Anthony Giuliani," he stated as he reached out his hand.

"As in the New York Giuliani?"

He laughed. "Afraid so, but not related."

"It's nice to meet you, Anthony." I could feel the effects of the wine hitting my system. "I seldom have a dinner partner, so this was nice. I really need to know more about wine. Personally, I am easy to please, so I've not made it a priority to learn much about it."

"You must learn!" he said convincingly. "I grew up where wine was just as important as bread and meat." He talked with his hands, using a heavy Italian accent.

"You are so Italian," I replied with a giggle in my voice. "Tell me more."

"My ancestors are still in Italy. My education was over here before I started my own business. I retired early because I could, but then missed being around the wine and its people. I do this part-time, you might say, because I love the area out here. I love the rolling hills of the vineyards and the aroma of good wine. The wine around here is just has good as in Napa Valley."

"You don't look old enough to be retired. Do you sell to any customers on The Hill?"

His face lit up and he smiled broadly. "There are some, but this is technically my area. I do live on The Hill, however."

"You live there?" I asked in disbelief. "I moved from there months ago so I could be out here."

"That is really something! You left the home of Ted Drewes Frozen Custard to live out here?"

We both had to chuckle.

"I know, and I miss it, among many other things," I

admitted.

Another hour later, we were still talking about the people and places we knew on The Hill. He knew a lot of old-timers like Harry. Despite this man being older than me, he was handsome, charming, and sexy. Most Italian men were, come to think of it. I decided if anyone was going to teach me about wine, he was the one to do it! He was independent from the winemakers out here and had the background to be an expert.

When Sally put another glass of wine in front of me, I knew it was time to go. I looked at my watch and started to reach for my purse to pay.

"No, let me," he insisted. "I haven't enjoyed a meal like this in a long time. My treat!"

"Thank you so much. I enjoyed it as well."

"You said you walked here?" he asked, sounding concerned.

"Yes, but it's not far."

"I'll walk you. It's rather late to be walking alone."

"No, no, I'll be fine, but thank you for offering," I said sincerely. "It's very safe here, and I've done it before."

"Very well, brave lady," he joked. "Do you have a business card?"

I nodded and pulled a card from my purse to hand to him. He reciprocated by placing his card in my hand. It was a touching, sensitive moment, or had my imagination had too much wine?

"Thank you again, Anthony," I said, touching his shoulder. "It was nice to meet you and revisit The Hill with someone."

I walked away feeling lightheaded but was determined

to make myself think straight. I could have easily been persuaded to stay longer with that wonderful man, but I knew the right thing to do was to head back to my yellow house down the hill. I didn't even consider checking on the guest house or Kitty's shop. I just wanted to slip into my bed.

After struggling with my key, I made it safely inside. I slowly walked upstairs and flopped across my bed, not wanting to undress. I kicked off my shoes and sat up, seeing my face in the mirror across the room. I was smiling. Why was that? How could I have had such a great evening with a total stranger? Was I missing The Hill more than I realized? Why didn't I meet someone like him when I lived there?

As I undressed, I repeated the name Vintage Rose because I wanted to order it again. Was I really attracted to Anthony, or was it just the effects of the wine combined with memories of The Hill? Should I feel guilty that Marc was not in my heart the whole time I sat there with Anthony? No. No one could replace my baseball man.

When I finally got comfortable under the covers, my phone rang. Could something be wrong with Marc or my family at this hour? It was late.

"Lily," the familiar Italian voice said. "This is Anthony. Did you get home safely?"

"Oh, sure," I responded, surprised.

"I just wanted to make sure. I felt guilty not seeing you home at this hour. I'm driving home as we speak."

"Thanks, Anthony. I appreciate your concern. Keep your eye on those roads this time of night."

"I'm on it! Thanks again for a great evening."

"Goodnight," I said, already half asleep.

CHAPTER 108

The next morning was not pleasant for me. I woke up later than usual and grabbed an aspirin from my bedside table drawer. Despite my headache, I felt alive and independent for some reason. As I showered and dressed, I reviewed my memories from the previous evening. What did I do with Anthony's business card? I wanted to have it. I quickly looked in my handbag and found it tucked in a side pocket. Did I imagine the lovely dinner I had experienced last night?

I practically gulped my coffee down as I looked out the window to observe the weather. Snowshoes was approaching my door, so I opened it up to greet him.

"Good morning, Ms. Lily," he chirped with his familiar chuckle. "It's a sunny day for a change! How about that?"

"I'm ready! I'd told myself that the sun would come out tomorrow, and it appears that it has!"

"You've got a lot of mail today," Snowshoes announced.

"That's a sign that I'm getting a lot of bills," I complained.

"You must be a baseball fan," he teased. "This time of

year, we see a lot of baseball material come through. You attend many of the Cardinal games, by chance?"

"I am a Cardinals fan, but don't go to many games. How about you?"

"I'm a fair-weather fan most of the time, but if they have a day game, I try to listen on my earphones."

"Great! Who is your favorite player?"

"Is there anyone but Molina?" he joked, revealing a little sarcasm.

"I like him, but Carpenter and Wainwright get my attention, if you know what I mean. I may go to Cooperstown this summer."

"You don't say! What a thrill that would be. Well, I'd better be on my way. Enjoy this sunshine!"

"You too!"

I looked at all the envelopes when I got inside and saw one from *Spirit* magazine. It looked like a check. My hands started shaking. This could be my very first paycheck!

It was indeed a check, and the amount still astonished me. How could I be paid for something I enjoyed so much? I put it in my cash drawer with other checks that needed to be deposited. I knew it would come in handy for a few bills I'd put aside to pay. I felt like celebrating until I was reminded of my headache.

The door opened. It was Carrie Mae.

"Aren't you opening today?" she asked, immediately concerned. "Did you sell the rocking chair?"

I laughed. "I'm running a little late due to an unpleasant hangover," I confessed.

"You? Should I ask for more details?"

"You'd better not," I advised. "I have to admit that I

would do it all over again."

"Girl! To be young again!" she teased.

"I'd bet you had many callers in your day, Carrie Mae."

She smiled. "Some I remember and some I don't. It seems like another life."

"What brings you in this morning?"

She paused. "I've heard from Butler."

"Any news there?"

"That sweet man wants to a have a little luncheon for my birthday that's coming up," she revealed modestly. "He said he wanted me to include you and Betty. Remember Susie, my daughter? She will be in France, so she can't go."

"France?"

"Yes, she left Monday and she'll be gone for three weeks."

"Well, we'll all be happy to help you celebrate. Betty and I were just discussing your birthday recently. She wanted to make sure we did something special for you."

"I know, she told me. I think she thinks I'm going to kick the bucket sometime soon."

"Oh, I doubt that. She thinks the sun sets and rises on you. What did Butler have in mind?"

"He wanted to plan a dinner, but I told him I rarely go out at night anymore, so he agreed to a lunch."

"What plan did you settle on?"

"He's quite impressed with Chandler Hill Vineyards. I think he's very comfortable there. Honestly, Lily, I think he needs folks like us right now. Getting together and being able to talk about James is helpful to him. I'm not sure who else he has to lean on."

"You may be right. Your birthday will give him a happy reason for a lunch, and hopefully he can fill us in on the latest."

"I'll tell him we're on board, and hopefully Betty will be over her cold by then."

After Carrie Mae left, I brought out the rocker to begin the business day. The sun was bright. Despite my headache, I had a happy face.

CHAPTER 109

As I was carefully arranging a quilt on the rocker, a young man pulled up and got out of his car.

"Are you Lily Rosenthal?" he asked as I headed inside.

"Yes."

"This is a special delivery for you from Ashley Rose Restaurant. I work there." He handed me a beautifully decorated box.

"Are you sure you have the right person?"

He grinned and nodded.

After he left, I looked at the box and wondered what surprise awaited me this early in the day. I anxiously opened it and read the card. It said, "To my new friend Lily. Enjoy! Anthony."

In the package was a bottle of the Vintage Rose merlot that he'd recommended the night before. It was in a single bottle holder and was lovely in its paper wrapping. That man was something! The thought of having a glass of merlot right now was not appealing, however. As I put the wine in the kitchen, I wondered if Anthony expected a response. The thoughtful surprise made me smile.

"Anyone here?" a voice called from the front door.

"I'm here!" I answered as I saw two young boys enter. "What can I do for you?"

"Our mom is having a birthday," one of the boys said. "We're looking for a present for her."

"Well, maybe," the other boy said with hesitation. "Everything here might be too expensive."

"Well, maybe not," I countered. "What are you looking for?"

They look dumbfounded and seemed speechless.

"What does she like?"

"She cooks," one said proudly.

"Duh!" the other responded. "She goes to antique shops a lot, so that's why we came here. Our dad is going to pick us up pretty soon."

"Well, as you look around, do you see anything that you think she would like?"

"Her favorite color is pink," one son volunteered.

"I don't think so. She has a lot of blue stuff," the other boy argued.

"I see," I said.

"Look at this cat statue. It looks like our cat, Stinky," the first boy said, showing his brother.

"Yeah, it does! She'd like that. How much is it?"

I turned the vintage cat upside down to check the price. "It's twelve dollars," I reported. "How much can you spend?"

"Dad gave us each a five-dollar bill, so that's too much," one boy said, disappointed.

"I think your two five-dollar bills will take care of it," I replied cheerfully. "I think this cat needs a loving home."

"Really?" they both asked in unison.

"Would you like me to wrap it up like a present for you?"

"Sure," they agreed as they got out their five-dollar bills.

The satisfaction in their eyes was priceless. They left happy, and I told myself that this was a first for me. Little did I know I would ever have such young customers!

My phone rang. It was Holly, who was on her way to meet Mary Beth at the pool.

"Good to hear from you!" I answered.

"I know I haven't called, but I've been so busy."

"Busy with Ken?" I bravely teased. "When do you see him again?" I pressed.

"I'm telling you, it's innocent," she insisted. "We did meet at the art museum yesterday for a short while, since you asked."

"Nothing wrong with that!"

"He's just so nice, and I think he might be lonely."

"As are you, my friend."

"Don't get any ideas. I'm too old for an affair. I have to say that it's nice for someone to listen to all my craziness."

"I know. That's great. Where did the monster think you were?"

She laughed. "He sent me on an errand to take back a bunch of things he'd ordered online. I just covered by telling him it took forever."

"How is he feeling?"

"Not well, which means he rarely leaves the house now. He sleeps a lot. When he's awake, he's always angry about something. Naturally, it's always my fault."

"If you can ever get away for an overnight, I'm ready. It would be cool to go to that quilt show in Kansas City coming up. They have a lot of antique quilt dealers, according to their brochure."

"That won't happen. I'm at his beck and call. What's new with you?"

"Can you get your hands on the latest *Spirit* magazine? My first column is in there."

"Goodness! Congratulations! I'll pick one up. I'd better take out a subscription. Okay, I'm at the pool now. I must go. Love you!"

"Love you, too!"

CHAPTER 110

Stitching my Christmas block the next day started quite awkwardly, but once I got started, I could almost see my design come to fruition. The morning was quiet and relaxing as I drank my coffee and caught up on emails. As I thought of Susan's offer to help me make a Feathered Star, I thought winter might be the perfect time to do so. My phone beeped with a text from Laurie.

Hate dating. This won't work!

I laughed.

It didn't go well?

Out of practice. Never again!

Okay, I hear you! Love you!

Love you!

Poor Laurie. She never did have a good attitude when it came to men. Her marriage when she was very young ended in a quick divorce, which didn't help her at all nowadays when it came to trusting men. She wasn't truly happy until she opened her shop. I give her credit for giving marriage a try.

The door opened, and two teenage girls came in to ask for a donation for their school's trivia night. This was a first for me, so I wasn't sure how to respond. Did all shops agree to contribute?

"I'm not sure everyone would like to win something that's an antique," I responded.

"Well, we were hoping you would donate a gift certificate," one girl suggested.

"Sure!" I answered. "Good idea. I can do that."

"Thanks, ma'am," the other one responded. "You sure have a lot of old stuff in here."

I nodded and smiled at the youths. In their minds, the old stuff probably included me!

I got back to my quilt block, like an old lady should. My phone rang, and I saw that it was Kitty.

"Hey, how's it going?" she asked.

"Great! Everything is safe and sound."

"That's good. We are in Charleston, South Carolina today and are having a wonderful time. Their antique prices sure are higher here."

"Well, it'll keep you from spending. I'm glad you're having an enjoyable time."

"Has your niece arrived yet?"

"Not yet. Thanks for getting the crib ready."

"Sure. Hope it works out. How has business been?"

"I have nothing to compare it with, but I'm surviving."

"That's the name of the game! Thanks again for keeping an eye out for us."

"No problem. Enjoy your trip."

After talking to her, I was reminded that I needed to check on their places today.

I went back to stitching and started to feel discouraged at the lack of business. I let my mind wander and began to think about ideas for Carrie Mae's birthday gift. The only thing I remembered that she admired was Rosie's jewelry. Surely she didn't need more jewelry, but if nothing else, it would work in a pinch.

"Hi, Ms. Lily!" Korine's voice said as she entered the shop.

"Well, hello! It's nice to see a live body today."

She laughed. "I know. I just came from seeing Carrie Mae and she was complaining, too."

"Did you know that she has a birthday coming up?"

She nodded. "I'm crocheting a shawl for her. I hope I'll have it done by then."

"Her friend is having a birthday lunch for her next week. Why don't you join us?"

"Really?"

"I'm inviting you, and Butler won't mind a bit. You can ride with me. In fact, we may all ride to the restaurant together."

"I'd be honored to be there if you don't think he'd mind."

"He'll be pleased that we thought to include you."

"Is there anything I can do for you today since I'm out and about?" Korine asked.

"Actually, there is."

"What?"

"I need to go check on Kitty's guest house and her antique shop. I just peek in the windows to make sure everything's okay. Would you mind watching the shop for a little bit while I check?"

Korine looked stunned. "I don't know. What if a customer comes in?"

"Well, ask if you can help them. If they ask questions that you can't answer, tell them I will be back shortly. Judging from today's activity, you won't get anyone."

"I don't know, Ms. Lily. I don't like being here alone."

"Well, okay, but you offered to help."

"Okay then, but be quick about it, okay?"

I smiled to reassure her. "Here's the cash drawer in case you have to put money away. You just open it up like this. See?"

She nodded.

I got my purse and coat and waved goodbye.

CHAPTER 111

As I approached Kitty's buildings, I saw a man looking in the window of the antique shop. He then went to the rear of the building. I parked my car and made sure he went on his way. Then, surprising us both, we nearly ran into each other as I came around the corner.

"Is this placed closed?" he asked.

"Yes. Can I help you?"

"Do you know when they'll be open again?"

"No, I don't. Sorry!"

"Okay, thanks," he said, walking away.

I watched him go down the street until I couldn't see him anymore. I double-checked the locks on the antique shop before I went across the street to check the guest house. I didn't go inside, but I looked in the windows and checked to make sure the lock was still secure. Around here, it didn't take long for folks to learn who was out of town and who wasn't.

I decided to stop at the cookie shop to buy Korine some cookies for helping me out. Of course, I had to include some cranberry oatmeal cookies for myself.

When I returned to the shop, I saw a car parked in front. The thought of a customer lifted my spirits.

"Are you Lily?" a woman asked as I entered.

"Yes," I answered as I looked around for Korine.

"Your friend who was here had an emergency and had to leave. She asked me to stay since you were coming right back."

"I'm so sorry. I was just gone about twenty minutes. Thank you so much for doing that."

"It was a bit strange, I'll have to admit, but she practically ran out the door, so I felt I needed to stay."

"I'm glad you did. What can I do to thank you?"

"Not a thing. You have a nice shop, by the way. I hope your friend is okay. She looked like she had seen a ghost."

I chuckled and didn't respond. As soon as the woman left, I got on the phone to call Korine. There was no answer. I was so angry and frustrated that I went outside to clear my head. It was then that I noticed the man from earlier walking several blocks up the hill. What could he be doing? My phone was ringing, so I went inside.

"I'm so sorry, Ms. Lily," Korine began.

"What happened? I hope you have a convincing explanation, Korine."

"I do, I do! Just listen. I was making small talk with the woman when she first came in. It was then that I noticed movement in the quilt room. I worried that someone else had come in. When I went to look closer, the floor lamp was flashing light and the lampshade was spinning. I couldn't believe my eyes. I felt someone in there. Has that ever happened before, Lily?"

It must have been Rosie playing with her, I thought to myself. "No, it hasn't," I sighed.

"Your place is crazy! I knew I shouldn't have agreed to stay."

"I'll check it out. I'm so sorry that I asked you to stay there alone, knowing how you feel."

"I won't ever do it again. I don't feel safe there."

"That's fine, Korine. You take care." I hung up feeling disappointed.

Just to make sure, I walked into the quilt room to check out the floor lamp. It wasn't even plugged in, so I didn't know what to think. In a way, it was like Doc's house that had no electricity but still flashed lights. What was I to do?

As the afternoon ended, I realized I hadn't made any sales and that the one customer I did have was essentially chased away. I went into the kitchen to pour a glass of wine. I opened the bottle Anthony had sent to me and smiled. I wondered if I would run into him again. He was so interesting and pleasant! I brought my rocking chair and quilt inside, feeling very down and discouraged.

I went upstairs and turned on the fireplace. I didn't think even Marc could cheer me up right now. As I often did when I felt alone, I turned on my laptop to see if there was any activity from my sisters.

A message from Loretta was first. She thanked Laurie for making a visit to Lucy and Sarah. She also commented about how much she and Bill were missing Lucy.

Laurie responded by saying that she, Sarah, and Lucy had gone to lunch and then done some shopping for Lucy. A cute photo of Lucy in her stroller was attached. Laurie made no mention of her disastrous date.

Lynn briefly commented on Lucy's photo and said that she wished Loretta would post pictures of their trip.

I didn't respond. Who wants to hear from an old maid who was unhappy in her old antique shop?

CHAPTER 112

The next day, I tried to convince myself that it was a new beginning and the day would be great. The Bible verse "This is the day which the Lord hath made; we will rejoice and be glad in it" never left my mind.

I paid some bills as I drank my coffee. I decided to call Carrie Mae and firm up the plans for the birthday lunch. She finally answered and admitted to sleeping in that morning. She certainly had every right after all the years she'd been in retail.

"Snowshoes will be checking on you, so you'd better look like you're open," I teased.

"I know. I'm getting slower and slower each day. Betty said I should open at noon, but I never could stand to turn away morning business."

"Well, not to mention that you are going to be another year older, so don't be so hard on yourself," I teased.

"Don't remind me."

"I took the liberty of inviting Korine to join us at your lunch. I hope it's okay, because she thinks the world of you."

"That's nice. I'm sure Butler won't mind. I'm glad she'll be coming along."

"I'll pick you up tomorrow around eleven thirty. How's that?"

"That'll be perfect. Betty will be here as well, and Korine can meet us here, too."

"This is a little embarrassing for me, Carrie Mae, but I am still at a loss as to what to give you."

"Not a thing, not a thing!" she insisted.

"That is not going to happen, so I want you to put your thinking cap on and remember something. When you were helping me with Rosie's things for the appraisal, you seemed to admire most of the jewelry."

"Well, yes."

"Was there a particular piece that you liked? Because if you could think of something specific, it would make you and me happy at the same time." I couldn't help but laugh out loud at my own awkwardness.

"Girl," she said, "I do remember a necklace of pearls and amethysts that happens to match a bracelet of mine that my husband got me many years ago. When I saw it, it took me back for a minute. I love the colors in it. I did think about buying it. The price was reasonable. I surely don't need it, but that is the piece I remember most. Do you still have it?"

"I do. Anything else?"

"It's too expensive, Lily," she argued.

"Let me worry about that," I said. "I sure wish your daughter could join us."

"Even if she were in the country, I'm not so sure she

would be comfortable coming along with us. I did hear from her, and she's having a wonderful time."

"That's good."

"How's that writing coming along? Be sure to save me a copy of the magazine."

"I will. Supposedly Alex and Lynn are going to bring me some copies. I'm working ahead and have lots of ideas."

"That sounds like you. I'd better cut a rug here, dear. Talk to you later."

I was looking forward to lunch and a pleasant day out. I loved talking to Butler about quilts and antiques. I had so many questions.

While it was on my mind, I got Carrie Mae's necklace out of the glass case and looked for a gift box to put it in. I was so glad this had a personal connection for her.

A knock at the door startled me. I opened the door quickly and apologized for not being open at this hour.

"Hi, I'm Tim Gilbert," the man at the door began. "I'm with *Spirit* magazine, and Robert told me to come out and get some additional photos around your shop and the area in general. I hope you don't mind."

"Oh, okay."

"From what I hear, there's a lot of interest in your column," he revealed.

"Yes, I'm getting some wonderful emails."

"I'll just wander around, if you don't mind."

"Sure," I said with some hesitation. "I'd like to approve any photo that you're going to use, if you don't mind."

"I don't think that will be a problem. Would you mind standing by this quilt rack for a photo?"

I took a quick look into a nearby mirror, pulled my

hair behind my ears, and agreed to the photo.

"The light is good here. Hold this red-and-white quilt in your hands, as if you really love it."

I chuckled. "I do love it," I said cheerfully.

"That's great. I like this one. Thanks," he said as he proceeded to the kitchen.

"What else do you do for *Spirit*?" I asked as I followed him around.

"Whatever needs to be done. Okay, I'll take the rest of the pictures outdoors."

I watched him from the window, and he took quite a few pictures of Doc's building. He then took a few of my sign, which made me think of Nick and his generosity. It was a cool sign that hadn't cost me anything, if I didn't count a frustrating date with Nick that went quite badly.

Three ladies drove up. They all looked about seventy or older. This could be great or not so great, I told myself.

"I understand that you have quilts for sale," one lady said before saying hello.

"I do. You've come to the right place. Please look around. If you need any help, just let me know."

In total silence they started pulling out, unfolding, and examining my merchandise. I stayed back to watch and listen.

CHAPTER 113

"These are so expensive," one said loudly as she looked at the tags. "Who would pay such a price?"

"They are really old, aren't they?" another said as she looked closer.

"The quilting on this one is terrible," a third complained. "You could catch your toenail on this one!"

"They don't quilt like you, Alice," the first woman commented. "Mom's Double Wedding Ring was so much nicer than this one. The quiltmaker even put the binding on by machine! I hate to see that."

"Well, if folks are paying these prices, maybe I should sell some of mine!" Alice threatened.

"You'd better not!" her friend scolded.

"Well, my kids don't want any of the quilts," the third woman added.

"Mine either," Alice noted. "I sure had hoped we'd see some new quilts in here."

"It's an antique shop, sister. Did you see the prices on these linens? I would have never had the nerve to sell mine if they were in this condition."

"Nobody seems to own an iron these days! Have you noticed?" the third woman said, shaking her head in disgust.

"I've just saved too many to use on special occasions, I guess," Alice admitted. "Mom did the same thing. Some pieces never made it out of the drawer."

"For the life of me, as I look at these other old things, I can't believe anyone would want these, much less pay these prices," her friend added. "I'm hungry. Are you all ready to go?"

It was obvious that none of them knew I was watching and listening from the other room. I didn't think they would have cared anyway. Their comments had some truth to them, but there was little to excuse their rudeness.

"Thanks for coming in, ladies," I said as they approached the door. "Enjoy your lunch."

One of the ladies nodded and smiled, but the others did not feel a response was necessary. Dealing with the public had its challenges. I knew enough to know this shop would not appeal to everyone, nor was I trying to accomplish that. I was a savvy shopper, but even in shops that I disliked, I always said "thank you" as I exited, or I would find something nice to compliment the owner on. I could not—would not—take this disrespectful visit personally. Perhaps one day Holly and I would be just like those women. I certainly hoped not!

The visit made me wonder if I could somehow use it in my column. "How to Manage Difficult Customers" might make for interesting conversation. If I made the column too humorous as I drew from my true-to-life experiences, it might look as if I was making fun of the customers. That would not be good for business at all. I might have to scrap the idea.

My phone rang, and seeing Marc's name brought a smile to my face.

"How's my baseball man?"

"He's ready for baseball season and misses his baseball lady very much."

"Ahh, that's nice."

"I'm calling on my way to the airport. My partner and I need to take some depositions in Dallas. It may take us a couple of days."

"I hope it's successful and gets you into warmer weather."

"Is everything okay out there?"

I paused, deciding not to tell him about my challenging retail experiences. "Yes. Tomorrow we have a birthday lunch for Carrie Mae," I announced.

"Please wish her a happy birthday for me."

"I will."

"I'll call you when I know my return schedule."

"Great. Be safe."

"You too, my love."

I hung up with a broad smile on my face. It felt wonderful to know I was his love. It was new and comforting, and I liked the sound of it.

The afternoon went better. There were a variety of miscellaneous sales, which brought my tally at the end of the day to over two hundred dollars.

I needed dinner and thought about my pleasant experience at Ashley Rose. It wasn't Thursday, so I wouldn't run into Anthony. I put my coat on and envisioned the French dip sandwich that Anthony had recommended.

Sally recognized me and said she was pleased to see me

again.

"On Anthony's recommendation, I'm going to try your French dip sandwich," I said.

"Fries or salad for your side?" she asked.

"A salad with French dressing to match my sandwich, right?" I joked.

"You want the Vintage Rose wine you had the other night?" Sally suggested.

"Sure, why not? What a good memory you have!" I smiled.

"You two sure hit it off the other night," Sally teased as she poured my wine.

"He was quite interesting."

"He usually sits there and eats his dinner without talking to anyone," she said. "I save the local morning paper for him because I know he likes to see it while he's eating. He's polite but is all business. I can't believe he stayed there to talk with you for so long."

I smiled. "Well, we both had the Italian neighborhood on The Hill in common."

"I see." She nodded. "He'll be in tomorrow. You should come back."

"No, I'm busy tomorrow. I'll catch him another time."

The place was busy, but I sat alone at the bar to eat my dinner. The sandwich was good, but I decided that it was heavy, juicy, and just perfect for a man. As I finished my wine, I thought about my crazy day and my next column.

CHAPTER 114

The next day was Carrie Mae's birthday lunch, so I didn't intend to open the shop. The sun was shining for a change and I looked forward to socializing with friends. I put the finishing touches on Carrie Mae's gift and wrote a personal birthday note for her instead of buying a card.

I checked my emails before I got dressed. There were several more short comments about my column, which boosted my ego for the day. It was just nice to know my column was being read at all.

An email from Sarah said she had already started packing for Augusta, so she could leave as soon as her parents got home from vacation. She attached another photo of Lucy, who was getting to be quite a fashion plate, thanks to her mother. I replied that I was looking forward to their visit and asked her to give Lucy hugs and kisses from me.

I decided to wear the new white top that I'd purchased in St. Charles. I wanted to look especially nice. I wondered if Korine would join us, since she'd had that unfortunate experience with me. What would she look like all dressed up?

I kept checking my watch because I wanted to be on time. There were a few cars driving by to see if I was open. Part of me hated to miss a possible sale, but today had to be devoted to Carrie Mae.

I parked in front of the Uptown Store and got out to knock on the door. Korine came to let me in. I pretended all was well and told her I was glad she was going with us.

"Well, Korine, you clean up real nice," I teased.

"You like my hair?" she asked as she turned to show me a scrunchie that was holding her hair back.

"I do, and I also like your earrings," I added.

"Good morning, Lily," Betty greeted me as she came down the stairs. "Carrie Mae forgot something. She'll be right down."

"We've got time," I assured her. "You really look nice, Betty."

"Thanks." She blushed. "I'm wearing lavender just for Carrie Mae, since it's her favorite color."

"Well, the gang's all here, it appears!" Carrie Mae said happily as she joined us.

"Happy birthday!" I started to sing. "Are you ready to party?"

Everyone laughed.

"I'm ready if you all are," Carrie Mae said, putting on her coat.

I apologized for having a dirty winter car, but no one was listening between their happy chatter.

I pulled in front of the Chandler Hill Vineyards' door to let the others out before I parked.

When I joined them, Butler was waiting in a small side room that had been reserved just for us. A beautiful flower arrangement with heavy touches of lavender was in the center of the table.

"Butler, this is too much," Carrie Mae said, overwhelmed.

Butler gave her a kiss on the cheek and a little hug.

"These flowers are so beautiful. Butler, this is my forever friend, Betty. You may have met her. And here's my dear sweet friend, Korine," she introduced. "Thank you for letting them share this day with me."

He nodded and gave us one of his classic smiles. "Nice to see you, ladies," Butler said graciously. "Betty, I think we have met before."

"I am just so honored to be here with all of you today," Betty replied.

"Have a seat; our waiter, Roger, will be at our disposal today," Butler announced. "We'll taste some interesting wines, unless you already know your favorite."

"Oh." Betty blushed. "I'd love to try any white wines that you might suggest."

"So would I," Korine agreed.

CHAPTER 115

"Do you have a merlot called Vintage Rose?" I asked Roger.

"We do," he replied.

Butler grinned. "I like a woman who knows what she likes. How about you, Carrie Mae?"

"Oh, I really shouldn't, but I like a red wine like Lily, so I'll try some of that Vintage Rose," she decided.

We engaged in light conversation until our wine was served. I rarely had wine with lunch, but this was a special occasion. I had to keep in mind that I was also the designated driver.

Butler tapped his wine glass to get our attention. "I'd like to make a toast to a special lady that I've had the pleasure of knowing for many years," he began. "Her knowledge and friendship have been a blessing to me."

I felt the same way.

"Happy birthday, sweet lady!" Butler toasted.

Carrie Mae's face glowed with happiness.

"Hear, hear!" we chanted and raised our glasses.

"I can't top that, Butler," Betty modestly said as she got choked up. "I love this lady. We have been through thick and thin together. Carrie Mae, Dorothy, and I were the original three musketeers in this town."

Carrie Mae chuckled and nodded.

Betty continued, "God bless Dorothy's soul, who is no longer with us. So here's a happy birthday to my best friend!"

We raised our glasses again.

"My," Korine said as she was about to break into tears. "All I can say to you, Carrie Mae, is thank you. I will forever be in debt to you, and I am so pleased to share this day with you."

We cheered.

"I've thought a lot about what I should say here today," I began. "There are no words to express what this lady means to me. She has changed my life forever, and I will forever be grateful. I love you! Happy birthday!"

We all took another sip of wine.

"Thank you, everyone," Carrie Mae said with tears in her eyes. "Each one of you has been a gift to me, and you have kept my life going. Butler, if I'd had a son, I'd want him to be just like you."

Butler blushed and blew her a kiss.

Carrie Mae continued, "Betty, you and I will go down together, so you'd better be up to the task!"

Everyone smiled and looked fondly at Carrie Mae and Betty.

"Korine, I will need your help more than ever as my senior years accumulate, so plan accordingly."

At that comment, everyone got quiet.

"Lily Girl has been a surprise in my life, and what a treat

it has been. I told her the other day that there's so much of her that was like me in my younger years. You have given me so much joy. I know you'll be successful in the yellow house down the hill." Everyone smiled while Carrie Mae continued, "I am so happy to be a part of your dream."

"Thank you," I said, feeling color rise to my cheeks.

"Ladies, I'd say we need to place our order before we all go to pieces," Butler teased, interrupting the moment while lightening the mood.

"That's what happens when you ask women to lunch, Butler," Carrie Mae retorted playfully. "Today isn't just about me. How are you doing?"

He paused. "I will never get over the loss of James, but some good things have come out of the tragedy."

At that moment, Roger came to take our orders. First, he carefully explained the menu to us as if we were children. Of course, everyone had questions about what was too spicy and what might be a good substitute. The experience was a good reminder as to why I never wanted to go into the food business. I ordered a salmon salad and a cup of baked potato soup.

When Roger completed the challenging task of taking our orders, Carrie Mae asked Butler if he had heard anything about any of his stolen merchandise. I was glad she'd asked instead of me.

"As a matter of fact, I've had some good fortune in regard to some of the items James took with him," he shared with a serious look on his face.

"That's wonderful!" Carrie Mae replied.

"It's all about having past relationships," Butler explained. "James got to know some of the antique dealers through me.

I had taken him to New York several times. When James approached the dealers about buying some of the items, they were nice enough to oblige him since they were my longtime trusted friends. I learned later that he sold the items at very reasonable prices, so they couldn't refuse."

"He was desperate for that money, I suppose," Carrie Mae guessed.

Butler nodded. "Well, I really wondered how those kinds of offers didn't give them cause for suspicion. However, they didn't have any reason to think that he didn't represent me. The quality of the goods was certainly obvious."

"Then what happened?" Carrie Mae asked.

"It didn't take long for them to learn about James's death," Butler explained. "News like that spreads fast in our industry. I had no reason to tell them. After all, James was not my son. To their credit, they contacted me immediately when they heard. That meant so much to me. No one wants to pick up the phone and tell people about their sad news, so I was glad I didn't have to."

"Don't I know it," Carrie Mae agreed.

CHAPTER 116

We were interrupted by Roger serving our lunch, which was presented beautifully on our plates. He refilled our wine glasses without hesitation.

"Bon appétit!" Butler said as we prepared to take our first bites. "Let's enjoy!"

I was starving, but as I ate, I wanted to know the rest of the story that Buter hadn't quite completed. He was engaged in asking Korine questions about herself so she would feel included. He then encouraged Betty to tell stories about Carrie Mae. The tales made Carrie Mae blush and threats about keeping their secrets arose, all in good-natured humor.

We were enjoying our lunch, and Butler was especially pleased about the special treatment we received from Roger.

"Before Carrie Mae opens her gifts, you have to indulge me. I have another surprise," Butler announced.

On cue, Roger and another waiter entered the room with a birthday cake that had many brightly lit candles. As we began to sing, Carrie Mae became overwhelmed.

"Goodness!" she said with both hands on her cheeks. "I don't think I remember a birthday when folks sang to me."

The two-tiered cake had lovely lavender touches with white roses. It was excessive, which I was sure Butler had done on purpose.

"Oh, I wish my daughter could be here to see this," Carrie Mae exclaimed as she shook her head in disbelief.

"Well, I'll start taking pictures right now," I volunteered. "Roger, would you mind taking a group picture?"

He gladly accepted, and Carrie Mae was delighted. As Roger cut the cake, the other waiter brought dishes of ice cream. Wine glasses were refilled, and cups of coffee were served. Korine seemed to enjoy the party immensely.

"So, Carrie Mae, do you think you could honor us by opening your presents?" Butler asked politely. She shook her head in disbelief at all the frills and attention.

"You all have done too much," Carrie Mae responded. "This gathering and lunch would have been enough."

"Lily, would you hand Carrie Mae her gifts?" Butler requested.

"Absolutely. They look wonderful!" I handed her the one that was most likely from Butler.

"Oh, look at this!" Carrie Mae bragged. "It's just too pretty to open!"

When I saw her expression as she opened the box, I knew it had to be special. It was a rare and collectible Steiff Moritz teddy bear, which was obviously coveted by Carrie Mae.

"How in the world did you find this?" she asked in disbelief. "I gave up trying."

The bear looked quite tattered and worn from its age,

but you would never think that mattered a bit, judging by its reception.

"I found it on a German website that I have purchased from in the past," Butler explained. "A collector like yourself was selling off some of his collection."

"It's perfect," she said, holding it close. "Thank you so very much."

"Why a German website?" Korine asked.

"They're made in Germany, although they have collectors all over the world," Butler explained.

"I've seen the new ones for sale, and they are quite expensive," I added. "Other than that, I'm clueless. It'll be hard to top Butler's gift, I'm afraid," I said as I handed Carrie Mae Korine's gift.

"Mine's not much," Korine apologized.

"Korine, Korine, you shouldn't have," Carrie Mae gushed as she held up a beautifully-crocheted lavender shawl. "You made this, didn't you?"

Korine blushed and nodded.

"I love this, and you know my favorite color! I could have used it downstairs on some of those chilly mornings. Thank you so much!"

"It is beautiful!" Betty added.

"Do you sell those?"

Korine shook her head. "Maybe I should."

"There's a big hint for you, Korine." Butler grinned. "I'll order one right now to give to my mother in the nursing home."

"Oh, my!" Korine answered, surprised. "Okay!"

CHAPTER 117

"Here's one more!" I announced. I knew this present was from Betty.

"This is like Christmas," Carrie Mae exclaimed.

"This one's from me," Betty said. "Carrie Mae and I give gifts to each other all year long, which makes occasions like this a little more of a challenge, don't you think?" She looked at Carrie Mae, who nodded in agreement.

"Look at this!" Carrie Mae said with delight as she opened the gift to see a box of handmade icebox rolls. "This is really why I love Betty. These rolls are scrumptious, and I am not going to share them with you all."

We laughed hard at Carrie Mae's candor.

"I'll give you the recipe," Betty offered.

"It won't happen," Carrie Mae joked.

"I would like it," I jumped in.

"It's my grandmother's recipe, which I know could be improved upon, but I want them to be like I remembered when I was growing up," Betty explained.

"They smell wonderful," Butler said.

"Thank you, sweetie," Carrie Mae said, blowing a kiss to Betty. "You know me so well."

"Where's your gift?" Korine teased me. "This one must be it!"

"My gift to her is not a surprise, because I checked with her ahead of time about my idea," I revealed. "I'm so glad I did, because she did have a memory of something I had that she admired. You all know how rare that is."

Carrie Mae was grinning from ear to ear as she opened my gift of the necklace.

"Oh, Lily, this is even prettier than I remembered. You all wouldn't know this, but I have the earrings and bracelet that goes with this."

"I remember," Betty said. "The colors of those stones are so you, and now you'll be all decked out."

"I don't know how to thank you, Lily. I remember when I saw it in Rosie's shop. It gave me such a pang of envy. I should have bought it then but decided against it."

"Now, Carrie Mae, that doesn't sound like you," Butler teased. "Let me help put this on you. It will be stunning with your dress."

We all agreed. I could tell that Carrie Mae was overcome with emotion when she tried to thank each of us.

"There's a big box under the table, Butler," Korine noted. "Is that for Carrie Mae?"

"No," Butler replied quickly. "I'll have to explain. I started to tell you about my friends contacting me after James's death. They were shocked and embarrassed that they hadn't contacted me to confirm my willingness to sell all the items he'd brought with him. I was quite disappointed when I learned they'd immediately sold the diamond-and-ruby ring that belonged to my mother," he said, his voice cracking as he tried to maintain his composure. "The other things that they sold did not have personal meaning to me. James had access to all my appraisals, so he chose the very best items so the dealers wouldn't turn him down."

"How sad," Betty said.

"So, back to our celebration today, we all have a lot to be thankful for, and even though it's Carrie Mae's birthday, I have something to pass on to Lily."

"What?" I questioned.

Butler handed me the large box. "Go ahead and open it," he said quietly.

Silence and curiosity filled the room. Why me? I opened the beautiful box and saw something wrapped in heavy white tissue.

"The Christmas quilt? You got it back?"

Butler laughed and nodded.

"Oh, good gracious!" Carrie Mae exclaimed.

I pulled it out of the box, and Korine helped me hold it open so everyone could see.

"I don't know what to say!"

"I was thrilled to have it returned to me, because I knew this quilt was appreciated by someone who loved it far beyond its monetary worth. We all know what it means to connect the right thing to the right person in this business. I knew no one loved this quilt more than you, and it now belongs to you, Lily Girl. Merry Christmas!"

More great novel series from Ann Hazelwood and AQS

Colebridge Series

#8853

#1256

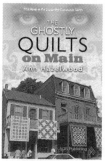

#1643

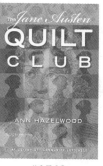

#1542

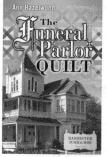

#1257

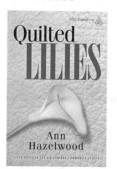

#1697

#7274

East Perry County Series

#10279

#12061

#12062

#12063

#12064

ANN HAZELWOOD

**Wine
Country
Quilt
Series**